ROBYNE OF SHERWOOD

PETER DAVID

CRAZY 8 PRESS

"Done?" asked the woman in green. She extracted the sword from his chest, picked up a cloth and proceeded to wipe the blade clean.

Amanda managed to nod.

"Good," she said, as casually as if they had been discussing the weather. "So...do you know anything about making weapons?"

"Everything. I helped him all the time. Learned it all."

"Want to work for me?"

The question surprised her. Then she decided to get down to business. She was being offered a job. The money earner in the house was dead, and she was going to need money to live. "How much does it pay?"

The green-clad woman actually chuckled. "Nothing."

Amanda considered that and then reminded herself that the woman had just saved her life. "Okay," she said with a sigh. "But... who are you?"

"Robyne of Sherwood," she said.

Amanda blinked in confusion. "Robin is a man. Was a man. And he's dead. Years dead."

Robyne slid her mask down to reveal her face. With a relaxed expression and a genuine smile on her lips, she looked rather sweet.

"I'm his daughter," she said.

PRELUDE

THE CLANGING OF THE SWORDS IN the distance merely served to drive Sir Henry further and further into the woods. He had been a leader of men long enough to discern what the clashing of weaponry told him. He could even distinguish the difference between the blades of his own men as opposed to the weapons being swung by his enemy's followers. He knew of a certainty that for every one of his men who was struck down, at least five of the others were meeting their ends courtesy of his men's broadswords. This day was going excellently. Finally, *finally,* this long and bloody battle would be over. Now he simply had to find their damnable leader and he could terminate this endless warfare.

The problem was that he had taken shelter in the woods, and the bastard knew this forest like the back of his hand. Tracking him down was going to be a problem unless he was stupid enough to reveal himself or something like th—

It was a damned good thing that Henry's reflexes were as rapid as they were, because it was the only thing that saved him. He caught the arrow's flight from the corner of his eye and swung his shield up at the last possible second. The arrow thudded into his shield with such power that it caused his entire arm to vibrate.

His lip twisted into a sneer and he called out, "So is this how the mighty Robin Hood ends his days? Firing from hiding at his greatest enemy instead of engaging him in combat, man to man?"

There was a long silence and he wondered if, hidden in the shadows of Sherwood, Robin was nocking another arrow and preparing to aim again, perhaps drilling an arrow directly into his head. That would certainly end the battle rather quickly.

Then he heard exactly the response he wanted to:

"No. It's not."

And there he was.

For years and years he had been battling Robin, but it always seemed as if the man didn't age a damned day. He was tall, powerfully built, and yes, a few gray hairs were intertwining their way into his golden locks, and into his facial hair as well, but he still seemed remarkably young. He had a longbow tucked over his shoulder, but he was unslinging it from its perch and dropping it onto the forest grounds. He likewise shrugged off his quiver of arrows so that the only weapon he was carrying was his sword. Robin appeared so confident of the situation that Henry was half expecting him to drop the sword as well and come at him barehanded, convinced that he could easily catch the Sheriff's blade and yank it from his hands. Who knew? Perhaps he could. The legends surrounding the man had grown so massively that some believed he could catch an arrow fired at him in midair.

"Ready to die, Sheriff?" he asked with a certainty that indicated that, to him, the climax of this battle was foretold.

Who knew? Perhaps it was.

"Always," the Sheriff replied.

They came at each other, their blades slamming together, and the final battle between Robin and the Sheriff was on.

⸺⸺

Little John was fighting furiously, and he was not getting a good feeling about this battle at all.

This entire thing had gotten badly out of hand. Why the hell had Robin allowed himself to be drawn into the Sheriff's challenge? Why had he left the security of the woods? How could he have been so foolishly confident that his own troops could take on the Sheriff's men? His men were trained soldiers while Robin's were men from villages who had bought into Robin's entire persona of the liberator who could vastly improve their lives and free them from endless taxation. Yes, it was flattering that they had so thoroughly accepted Robin's promise of dominance over the Sheriff's men, but honestly it sounded as if Robin had begun to buy into the stories that were told about him. Most of them had never happened, and the ones that did had blossomed in the retelling. People sang songs of how Robin single handedly defeated twenty men in combat. Well, John had been there, and it was five men, and Robin had his own people backing him up. Somewhere along the way, though, Robin himself had blurred fact and fiction, and now they were paying the price for it.

John was desperately trying to find a familiar face. Scarlet, Tuck, Alan, anyone. But he wasn't locating anybody. Furthermore, as he made his way around a hut, he was hearing the diminishment of swordplay. Someone was winning and he was getting the distinct impression that it wasn't his side. He and the men had deserted the field of combat, fleeing in full retreat, hiding within the village of Nottingham itself. For all he knew, the others had taken up residences in huts and such, but he suspected that they were not really doing that. The Merry Men were far too seasoned combatants to hide within the homes of civilians. If the enforced soldiers in their troop had run back home, that was fine, but Robin's core group was going to remain out there battling to the last man.

Except…what if John was the last man?

He came around the hut and skidded to a halt, because a guardsman was right there, turning just in time to see him.

John brought his sword up to block the man's slash, and suddenly pain ripped through his back. He staggered forward and heard a demented chortle behind him. He wasn't able to turn because he was already feeling paralyzed and sank to his knees. But he saw the shadow of his assailant cast against the hut wall.

That was when he saw something else: the shadow of a sizable blade being swept down and splitting his attacker's skull. He let out a startled cry and fell over, and the man in front of John reacted with the sheerest startlement. Then he brought his sword up and around to assail whoever the hell it was that had just come up behind John when suddenly a dagger hurtled through the air straight at him. He had leather armor covering his chest, but the base of his throat was exposed and that was precisely where the dagger thudded home. He let out a startled yelp that sounded more as if he were gurgling blood and then he stumbled backwards and hit the ground.

A lissome form came from behind him and he recognized her instantly. It was Marion.

Dressed in her forest greens, she seemed right at home with any of the Merry Men, but her mind was most definitely not on the rest of the band. Rather all of her attention was completely focused on Little John. "John, oh my God, we have to get you—"

He waved off her concerns. "I'll be fine. Don't worry about me."

"I can't find Mary or Basil! They ran off—!"

Her concern became his. The fates of everyone and everything else fell away as he shared her worries. "Then what're you wasting your time with me for? Go find them! Go!"

He slapped at her shoulder to drive her away. For a moment she looked reluctant to go, but finally she nodded, sprang to her feet, and dashed away from John. For his part, John allowed his head to slump back as he stared up at the heavens. It was remarkable what a beautiful day this was, with no clouds dancing across the perfect blue sky.

Then, much to his surprise, the sky blackened above him. He wondered if a storm was rolling in and had no idea that his vision was disappearing until a few seconds before his life fled him, at which point he was supremely irritated when he realized he wouldn't find out how the battle ended.

I hope Robin's okay, were the last words that flittered through his head.

———« »———

Sir Henry, the Sheriff of Nottingham, was becoming winded and he knew it.

He and Robin had been slamming together repeatedly for who-knew-how-long, and every passing second was making it harder and harder to maintain the battle. Robin, however, did not seem the least bit fatigued. If anything, he seemed to be getting stronger.

Robin came in close, their hilts locking together, and Robin used the proximity to lash out and slam Henry in the gut, doubling him over. He swung his sword down in a killing stroke and only Henry's own staggering caused the blow to miss. Henry bumped against a tree, bracing himself against it, endeavoring to find the strength to mount an assault. That was when Robin Hood charged him and at that moment Henry knew he was going to die.

And Robin stopped. And froze.

Henry's head snapped around and he saw what Robin was gaping at. It was a small girl, who couldn't have been more than five years old. She had shown up out of nowhere and was watching with her eyes wide and her jaw hanging down in amazement. She had a sheaf of blonde hair cascading around her shoulders and somehow seemed to be, not a girl wandering about, but a child who was as much a part of the forest as the trees or leaves or a deer. She was wearing a simple gold locket around her neck that momentarily attracted the Sheriff's eye.

"Mary!" called Robin, briefly distracted from the battle. "Get out of here, right n—"

Acting entirely on instinct, Sir Henry drove his sword forward. To his complete and utter shock, Robin failed to deflect the thrust, so diverted was he from the fight at hand. The point of the sword rammed into Robin's chest, and his eyes widened in shock. Even the Sheriff gasped in surprise, unable to believe that he had managed to drive his sword home.

The little girl who had been identified as "Mary" let out a horrified shriek. All the blood drained from her face, and when she howled "*Nooo!*" it didn't sound like a normal human scream but rather an outcry coming directly from a soul in torment.

The Sheriff yanked clear his sword and Robin tumbled backwards, blood swelling from the fatal wound and spreading all over his chest. There was life in his eyes but it was fading fast.

Mary ran to him, dropping to her knees, her tears dripping from her face and onto his.

"I'm sorry...I'm so sorry...I didn't mean..."

He stared up at her as darkness consumed his eyes. His voice gurgling as his lungs filled with blood, he managed to say, "You... you shouldn't have been here." Then his eyes closed.

Robin Hood was gone.

She refused to believe it. "No!" she cried out and began to shake him. "No, no!"

Henry likewise couldn't believe it. He had sought the man's death for years, and yet now that it had arrived, he literally could not conceive of having accomplished it. He decided to check Robin's pulse just to be sure.

He approached the body, reaching for the neck so that he could check for vital signs. The moment he drew near, though, Mary spun and snarled at him, "No! Get away from him! You bastard! Get aw—"

Henry wasn't inclined to waste time with her. He shoved her once and the child tumbled back and away. He removed his glove and placed two fingers against Robin's throat. Nothing. No pulse.

"Good," said the Sheriff. Then he paused and decided that one could not be too careful. He swung his sword down and around, through Robin's neck, and his head rolled away from his body. "Better," he nodded with approval.

He picked up the head. He wasn't looking forward to hauling a decapitated head back to his encampment. In point of fact, he found it somewhat disgusting. But he wanted a souvenir of his triumph, and this was obviously the only thing available.

That was when he heard a dangerous creaking behind him.

There is no other sound in the world like that of a bow being drawn. He spun and standing there, not ten feet away, was the child. She had picked up Robin's bow, had nocked an arrow, and was drawing it back as much as her tiny muscles were enabling her to. There was no anger in her face; nothing but pure determination. She was going to put an arrow into the Sheriff, and there was nothing that Henry could do to prevent her.

She released the arrow.

It flew three feet and thudded point first into the ground.

Of course it did. She was a child and the bow was supposed to be drawn by a full-grown man. As "noble" as her intentions were, as determined as she might have been, she lacked the strength to pull the bowstring back to its full extension and deliver its lethal load to its target. The quiver was lying on the ground next to the bow, and hurriedly she reached down to try and extract another arrow.

The Sheriff was not about to give her the opportunity. He dropped the head as he took two strides over to her, grabbed her by the front of her blouse and shook her fiercely. She dropped the bow and the Sheriff lifted her off her feet and slammed her up against a tree. He brought his sword around, ready to drive it into her throat.

She did not fight back. Instead, to his utter astonishment, she reached up and wiped the tears from her face. Then she sniffed deeply, closed her eyes, and waited for the lethal blow.

She's ready to die, he realized. *She probably blames herself for Robin's death...which may well be the case, considering she distracted him. In a way, I owe her a debt.*

Once more, the locket glittered at him.

He sheathed his sword.

Mary opened her eyes in surprise as she heard the blade slide back into its sheath. Then he reached up and wrapped his hand around the locket. With a quick pull he snapped it off the chain and released her. She slid to the ground, staring up at him in shock.

He smiled as he shoved the locket into his belt. "A less sanguinary souvenir of the day." He nodded toward the bleeding item he was now prepared to leave behind. "You can keep the head."

He walked from her the short distance to his horse, climbed

aboard the beast and rode away. As he did so, he kept his ears open to hear if she burst into the torrent of tears he knew welled within her.

He heard nothing.

⊷ ⊶

As the Sheriff rode into his encampment, one of his men, Dinidore, strode up to him, thumping his fist against his heart in greeting. "Sir, the day is ours," he said with obvious pride. "Only Robin Hood is—"

"Dead," said the Sheriff as he swung his left leg up and over, dismounting from the horse and landing lightly on the ground. "I saw to it myself. It's been many years coming, but finally, *finally*, we're rid of him and his Merry Men."

A wide grin split Dinidore's face. "Congratulations, Sir. And I have something to show you."

That pronouncement caught the Sheriff's attention. All their goals had been accomplished. What could he possibly be shown that would build upon the triumph? He followed Dinidore into the tent, quite curious as to what the soldier could reveal to him that would top the day's accomplished goals.

He stepped into the tent and immediately saw what the soldier was eager to show him.

It was a young boy. Five years old, with thick, matted black hair that was clearly tinged with blood. That was because he was bleeding from what appeared to be a vicious head wound. He had clearly been in the midst of a fight and had not gone down willingly or easily. A nurse was in the process of wiping them down, using a wet cloth to clean away the blood that seemed quite determined to continue. She glanced up at the Sheriff and said, "I'm getting it under control. It's bad; he'll have scars. But he'll recover."

Henry knew him immediately. He had spotted the boy at Robin's side on a couple of occasions, watching the man with reverence, clearly learning all he could.

"I'll be damned. Is that who I think it is?"

"Yes, sir. We wanted to wait for your decision. Should we dispatch him?"

The nurse looked alarmed. She was clearly not thrilled with that prospect. The notion of two men discussing whether or not to take the life of a helpless five-year-old was certainly not something that brought her any comfort.

"Absolutely not," he said firmly. "He could serve to be remarkably useful." He clapped the soldier on the back, which truthfully was more familiar than he tended to be, but he was feeling very much in the mood. "What a magnificent day this is. Robin Hood and his men dead, and we have his son."

"It's said the boy has a twin sister," the soldier reminded him.

Henry nodded. "I believe I met her."

"Should we seek her out as well?"

At that, the Sheriff threw his head back and laughed loudly. "Don't be ridiculous. A girl? What threat would she be?"

———« »———

Night had fallen like a shroud.

Mary was wandering through the forest. She felt terrible and looked even worse. She had been carrying Robin's head for a time because she believed she had to. It was her father's head, after all. He was dead, her mother had disappeared. Who else was going to care for it?

But then, as night had consumed her, she had tripped over a fallen branch and the head had tumbled out of her hands and rolled away. In the darkness she could not locate it, nor did she really have the drive to do so. So she strode away, leaving it behind, and although she was ashamed to admit it, felt as if a weight had been lifted from her shoulders. Now all she had to worry about was the fact (in her mind) that she had killed her father. She absolutely knew this to be true. Her presence had drawn his attention away from the Sheriff at a critical moment, and he had paid for it. She was sure her mother would kill her when she told her the truth, except with her mother gone, there was no great likelihood of that.

Her brother was gone as well. He had thrust himself into battle, using the skills that their father had taught him, and it had very likely not served him at all. Why had her father not trained her? Why—?

Don't think about that. Do not dare think about that. He was your father and if he had no desire to provide you experience in combat, then that was his choice and he had reasons for it.

She looked down at her hands, at her clothes. They were both thick with blood, thanks to her father's bleeding head that she had carried through the forest. She absently wiped them together as if that would somehow dispose of the blood, and naturally it had no effect at all. Mary sighed heavily and that somehow removed the stopper that she had placed upon her tears. They flowed down her face, dripping onto her dress, and she sank to the ground, her legs curled up under her. She bawled like a helpless infant, which was exactly what she felt like. Mary wanted to dig a hole into the ground, crawl into it and pull the dirt over her.

She had no idea for how long she cried, and then a rustle of leaves caught her attention. She looked up and there was a woman standing a short distance away. The woman was cloaked and the raised hood obscured her features.

"Wh-who are you?" she managed to get out, her voice quavering in her throat.

The woman drew back her hood and stared down at Mary. She was an old woman, with crow's feet at the corners of her eyes and a surprisingly gentle smile. Her eyes seemed to be glittering as if she had deep, inner knowledge of things that Mary could only guess at. Her hair was dark brown with streaks of gray in it. She nodded toward Mary and asked, "Whose blood is that on you?"

"My father's."

"Where is he?"

She wanted to lie but couldn't find the words. "Dead."

The woman cocked an eyebrow. "And your mother?"

"I don't know."

For what seemed an eternity, they simply stared at each other. Then the woman extended her hand to her. "Come with me."

Mary couldn't help the fact that she was still a bit suspicious. "Are you a nun?" she asked cautiously.

"No. I'm the Magistar. I'm part of a secret order called the Beguines."

Mary frowned. "I never heard of them."

The Magistar chuckled at that. "What part of 'secret' was unclear? Come. I'll keep you safe until your mother shows up."

Slowly Mary reached up and took her hand. It felt rough, but also surprisingly warm. "And if she doesn't?"

"Then I'll keep you safe until you're old enough to keep yourself safe."

That somehow seemed a reasonable offer to Mary, although she didn't have the slightest idea how long that would be.

The answer, as it happened, was fifteen years.

BOOK ONE

Robyne and Innis Rae

CHAPTER 1

He Lives or Dies. It's Up to You

AMANDA SCREAMED AS HER HUSBAND'S PALM slapped across her face. He did it with such force that it knocked her off her feet. She tumbled to the ground and tried to roll away from him, but her husband, Ralf, strode forward and drove a foot into her side. She cried out once again and screamed for help, but no one seemed the least interested in responding to her pleas.

She tried to sit up but pain lanced through her. She prayed he hadn't cracked a rib or done even more extensive damage to her.

Ralf stood over her, a thick layer of sweat dripping off his bald head, his thick black mustache looking as if it had developed a life of its own. His profession as a blacksmith had given him sizable arms that were laced with muscle. "You had him, didn't you?! You had Oswald!"

She felt liquid dribbling from her nose and reached up to wipe it away. It was blood, thick and dark. Her tongue ran over her lip and she could discern a cut there as well. Everyone who saw her the next day was going to ask what in God's name had happened to her. She knew what she would tell them: she had taken a spill. It was a lie and everyone would know that it was a lie, but they would nod and speak words of sympathy and tell her that in the future she should really have a care about where she stepped. She wasn't about to admit that her husband had done this to her. Not that she thought he would be disciplined for it; hell, plenty of men would likely congratulate him for showing his arrogant wife who was in charge. She just despised admitting her utter helplessness in the situation.

"I didn't," she said. "I swear I didn't!"

"Then why would he lie about it?!"

"He said it to your face?"

"He said it to other men at the pub! Again, why would he lie?"

She tried to stand, but her legs were wavering in weakness so much that she had no strength to do so. "To make himself sound better than he is! He's a farmer with no wife! So he wanted to sound like he'd had a woman! Plus he probably wanted to upset you," her mind was racing, coming up with additional options. "He's never liked you. Maybe he wants to get back at you!"

He reached down and yanked her to her feet. Her legs were still so weak that she was unable to stand on her own, and it was only his strength that was supporting her. "Or maybe *you* wanted to get back at me, eh?"

She shook her head so furiously that it looked as if it was about to tumble off her neck. "I never did!"

Ralf snarled down at her. "I give you good, woman! You're lucky to be married to the best blacksmith in town!"

"I know, I know!" she said desperately.

"*Then why did you lay with him!?*"

"I didn't, I swear!"

That was obviously not the answer that he had been seeking, although she had no idea what response she could have made that would have brought an end to this battering. The continued denials, however, were clearly not it, because he pivoted and threw her to the other end of the small cottage in which they resided. She crashed into the wall and cooking utensils from an overhead shelf clattered to the ground.

"I'm bloody sick of you!" he bellowed.

There was a sword lying on the table. He grabbed it up and pointed it at her. He didn't have to say anything. His intent was clear.

"No!" she cried out.

"I'll cut you apart and replace you with another while your blood's still warm!"

She knew he could do it, too. He could batter her to death, then haul her body out into the forest and leave it there. He wouldn't even have to bother burying it. Someone would stumble over it and when he was questioned, he could easily say that she had wandered off on her own and some highwayman had taken advantage of her, robbed her, and then beaten her until the life had fled her. No one would ever gainsay him because it would be impossible to prove otherwise.

Amanda wondered what it would be like to die. She wanted to think that she had led a worthwhile life, but the fact was that she hadn't actually accomplished a damned thing. She had wasted her life and now Ralf, damn him, was going to end it.

He advanced on her and suddenly the door was kicked in. A green clad woman was standing there, wearing leathers and a hood and a piece of green cloth wrapped around the lower half of her face that obscured her features. She had a bow slung over her shoulder, a quiver of arrows on her back, and an arming sword in her hand.

"What the bloody hell?!" said Ralf.

He was standing on the other side of the table, and he shoved it to one side so that he could get at her. He launched his assault and the blades clanged together, creating such a deafening ringing that Amanda feared she might go deaf from it.

Half a dozen times he swung the sword at her. He had no grace, no artistry in his assault. Instead he was slamming away at her, trying to overwhelm her through sheer brute strength. But the green-clad woman wasn't having any of it. Instead she easily deflected every blow. She didn't even seem to be working up a sweat. Her glittering blue eyes never shifted their focus from him.

Finally she lost patience with him. Abandoning his tactless slamming of his sword, he tried instead to thrust the blade at her, clearly intending to run her through. She easily sidestepped him and then drove her knee up into his ample gut. He gasped and doubled over, and that was all the opening she required. She swung her blade around and down and knocked the sword out of his hand, sending it clattering to the floor. He cried out and tried to reach for it. No go. She kicked him viciously in the head and knocked him back. Amanda gasped as Ralf crashed heavily to the floor with such force that the ceiling actually rattled.

The woman stood over him, one foot on his chest, keeping him pinned. She turned to Amanda and said in a rough, no-nonsense voice, "He lives or dies. It's up to you."

Slowly Amanda approached her fallen husband. She wiped away the continuing flow of blood from her nose, which had slowed to a trickle. She stared down at the man who would have, only moments before, been happy to slaughter her in cold blood.

Her mouth twisted into a snarl and she said, "Yes, I had Oswald, and he was better than you'll ever be." His jaw dropped, his face became flushed, and she turned to the woman and said with a voice that could have frozen a stream in its bed, "Kill him."

The green-clad woman didn't hesitate. She slammed the sword down into Ralf's chest. He only had time to cry out once in protest, and then his head slumped back.

He was dead. Stone dead.

"Go tell the authorities," said the green-clad woman, "that you were minding your own business and some masked thief broke in, argued with your husband, and killed him. Tell them that he did that to you as well," and she indicated the bruises on her face. "They will believe you."

Amanda didn't respond to the woman; instead she kicked his corpse. She didn't even know she was going to do it until she did, and once she did it the first time, she couldn't restrain herself. She delivered multiple kicks to him as his dead body simply shook from the repeated impacts. The woman who had slain him turned and closed the door she had burst through, but otherwise said and did nothing until Amanda had finally gotten all the anger and hostility out of her system. Once she had done so, she sagged into a chair and took several deep breaths to try and slow her breathing, regain her calm.

"Done?" asked the woman in green. She extracted the sword from his chest, picked up a cloth and proceeded to wipe the blade clean.

Amanda managed to nod.

"Good," she said, as casually as if they had been discussing the weather. "So...do you know anything about making weapons?"

"Everything. I helped him all the time. Learned it all."

"Want to work for me?"

The question surprised her. Then she decided to get down to business. She was being offered a job. The money earner in the house was dead, and she was going to need money to live. "How much does it pay?"

The green-clad woman actually chuckled. "Nothing."

Amanda considered that and then reminded herself that the woman had just saved her life. "Okay," she said with a sigh. "But...who are you?"

"Robyne of Sherwood," she said.

Amanda blinked in confusion. "Robin is a man. Was a man. And he's dead. Years dead."

Robyne slid her mask down to reveal her face. With a relaxed expression and a genuine smile on her lips, she looked rather sweet.

"I'm his daughter," she said.

CHAPTER II

Ye right bastard! I'll have yer balls for this!

SIR LEWIS DABBED THE CORNERS OF his mouth, removing the last of the crumbs from its edges and then placed his soiled napkin on the table. He was a powerfully built man who looked as if he'd be much more at ease pummeling an enemy to death with his bare hands rather than devouring a lovely meal, but one had to attend to one's duties. A servant promptly stepped in and removed the napkin. Lewis paid the servant no mind, because his attention was entirely focused on the gentleman sitting at the far end of the table. "I trust the dinner was to your satisfaction, Sir Henry?"

Sir Henry was likewise cleaning his face carefully with a cloth and he also dropped it to the table. A servant snatched up that one as well. "Absolutely splendid, Lewis."

Lewis gestured toward the closed door that led out to the corridor. "Are you sure you don't wish to feed your men…?"

Henry shook his head and leaned back in the chair. "No, they ate earlier. They are fine."

Lewis nodded. He was tempted to argue that they could at least be offered the option, but decided it wasn't worth it. Certainly Henry should know what his people did and did not require. Besides, there were more pressing needs concerning him, such as why in the world this entire social engagement had occurred in the first place. He leaned forward, interlacing his fingers on the table-top. "I have to admit, this dinner was rather unexpected. When you stopped by, I was actually concerned..."

Henry cocked a single curious eyebrow. "About what?"

"Well," said Lewis, "you serve Lord Collins and there is little love lost between us."

"You shouldn't dismiss him out of hand."

Lewis's face twisted in concern. "I don't dismiss him. I fear him. I fear he could drive the peasants into revolt with his merciless taxes and, in case you haven't noticed, there are far more peasants than us."

Henry shrugged as if he were indifferent to the conversation. "He is merely carrying out the King's orders."

"Richard!" Lewis sniffed dismissively.

Upon hearing Lewis's response, Henry suddenly looked both surprised and concerned. "You have no respect for the King as well?"

There was a hint of warning in his tone, but it went right past Lewis. He began to count off his concerns on his fingers. "He raises taxes endlessly to fund his crusades. He has no regard for his people. Honestly, there are times I think we were better off under John..."

Henry cleared his throat and when he spoke his tone had changed to one of straight up warning. "You realize you speak treason, Sir Lewis."

From nearby, a female voice spoke up: "Muh husband speaks treason? Surely the day must be ending in the letter Y."

Henry turned and saw that a remarkably well-built woman had entered the room. Her accent made her decidedly Scots, as did the plaid tartan that she was wearing. Her blazing red hair was tied back in a long braid. Her arms were exposed, revealing considerably formidable biceps. She walked with a confident swaying motion, as if she was certain that she could physically take down anyone she encountered...which was entirely possible. "Ye know muh husband is opinionated, Sir Henry."

Henry blinked owlishly. "I don't believe we've been introduced."

Lewis made a sweeping gesture, as if he were introducing an entire court of individuals. "This is Innis Rae. My wife."

"A Scotswoman?" Henry knew he shouldn't comment on it, but he couldn't help himself. There was a look of incredulity on his face that was most distinctive.

"An unlikely match, to be sure," said Lewis, who did not seem especially inclined to explain how the two of them had met. "Now, Sir Henry, as you must—"

Brought back to business by Lewis's obvious intention to return to the subject, Henry raised a finger and overlapped what Lewis was saying. "I must not anything, Lewis. Your words are treason and cannot be permitted." Then he softened his voice to sound less demanding. "But I will give you the chance to retract your vicious statements and apologize."

Lewis's eyes narrowed in suspicion. Henry couldn't quite believe it. Here he was being generous to his host, and Lewis seemed to be dismissing his generosity out of hand. "I'll do no such thing!" Lewis informed him.

Innis Rae's eyes darted from Lewis to Henry, and there was growing concern in them. She, at least, appeared to understand the impending gravity of the situation. "Lewis...do as he says."

His head snapped around as he glared at his wife, clearly annoyed that she was endeavoring to contradict and undercut him. "I'll not! How dare you—!"

She wasn't having any of it. "It's a trick. He is trying to trap you into an offense. Apologize. It means nothing."

That, as it happened, was exactly the wrong thing to say to him. He was on his feet and he thundered at her, "It means something to me! I'm not going about encouraging revolt! I'm just speaking my mind."

Henry had stood up and now he had come around the table, approaching Lewis slowly. "Last chance, Lewis."

Lewis looked astounded. He moved away from his seat and now stood there, gaping at Sir Henry as if the man had just revealed the presence of a third eye in the middle of his forehead.

"You're out of your mind. What do you think is going to happen here? Do you think we're going to fight?" He laughed at the very idea. "You are a guest in my home and I will take no action against you. And you left your sword at the door when you entered," he pointed out. Apparently that fact alone was sufficient to convince him that he was not in any danger.

"That is true," said Henry. "I did."

He was standing only a couple of feet away from Lewis, and suddenly he swung his hand up as if he was about to shake Lewis's. A dagger snapped forward out of his sleeve and then it was in his hand. It happened so quickly that Lewis had no time to react as Henry shoved the dagger forward into Lewis's chest. A stunned Lewis cried out in shock, and Innis Rae screamed so loudly it was nearly deafening. There was nothing to be done as Henry yanked the dagger free and blood spouted from Lewis's chest like lava from a spewing volcano. Lewis staggered back, astonishment on his face. He was dead and literally could not believe it. He tried to speak but all he managed to do was move his mouth and watch blood swell from it. He staggered, reached for the table to try and brace himself, and failed utterly. Lewis collapsed to the ground with a heavy thud and lay still.

Innis Rae howled in fury and there was death in her eyes.

⟶—« »—⟶

Basil and Drogo, having pretty much nothing else to do, were hanging about outside the dining hall.

Basil was a slender young man, with a square jaw and deep set blue eyes. His thick black hair would have hung down to his shoulders, but he had it tied back in a tail. He was seated in a rather nice chair.

There was another chair nearby and his companion could have sat, but he chose not to. His companion was a massively built man, so thick around the chest and arms that he seemed much older than his twenty years, the same age as Basil. Far more distinctive was the thick leather mask that he wore that covered the right half of his face. His dark eyes glittered from within as he continued to keep watch on the hallway as if expecting an enemy to come charging out at any point to attack them. Basil noticed his eternal vigilance and shook his head in amusement. "Drogo, you could relax for at least a few moments."

"One never knows," rumbled Drogo.

"One generally does. My father is having dinner with an old friend. That's all. What could possibly hap—?"

He wasn't able to complete the question because he abruptly her the horrified scream of a woman. He and Drogo exchanged looks and then headed straight for the dining room.

⚬

Innis Rae stopped screaming almost immediately. That startled Sir Henry, whose typical experience with women was that when they reacted with horror, it then required long moments for them to regain their composure and bring themselves back down to some manner of normal level.

That was not the case here. The Scotswoman managed to acquire control over herself almost immediately. Perhaps she had merely been startled and did not actually have any manner of deep affection for her husband.

That, however, turned out not to be the case. Instead she crossed quickly to a wall that had a halberd, a battle axe that was mounted on a five-foot pole. Unlike other such weapons that Henry had seen, however, the blade was massive: at least a third larger than such heads typically were. And the shaft itself appeared to be solid oak. No matter the woman's size, it was doubtful that she could even remove it from the wall, much less use it in battle.

"Don't bother, Madame," Henry said dismissively. "That's far too heavy for..."

She yanked it off the wall and swung it around as if it was the weight of an infant.

"...you?" he finished, his voice trailing off.

She did not bother with any words. Instead she came right at him with an inarticulate roar of rage, whipping the axe back and forth in the air as if she were warming up. The table separated them, but that proved no obstacle as she clambered over the table. He dodged barely in time as she slammed the axe down. The blade struck a chair that had been just behind him with such force that it split the piece of furniture in half.

"Ye right bastard!" she howled. "I'll have yer balls for this!"

He tried to lunge at her with his dagger, despite the fact that he despised the notion of attacking a woman. As it so happened it didn't matter, because she caught his hand and twisted it. The dagger tumbled out of it and clattered to the floor. She kicked it and it skidded away, sliding under a cabinet, out of reach.

He was beginning to wish that he had made more of a fuss about giving up his sword rather than surrendering it at the door, although he quickly came to realize that it likely would not have made any difference. Innis Rae did not seem as if she had the slightest intention of slowing down. Indeed, she'd probably have wrestled the sword from his grasp and used it to behead him.

She swung right and left. He kept dodging desperately, backing up, and then he spotted a short sword mounted on the far wall. He ran for it, grabbed it off its holders, and swung it around defensively.

Innis Rae broke it.

He was stunned. It was tempered steel. Yet the woman's axe had cut right through the blade as if it had been a large stick of butter. He was left with a small fragment of it that wasn't going to do him the least bit of good. She had already disposed of his knife easily enough; certainly an inch of a sword blade would be utterly useless.

It was at that moment that he knew he was dead. He was starting to think that maybe killing Sir Lewis had not been the best idea he'd ever had.

She swung the axe up and around and down, and Henry prepared himself to die.

It was at that moment that Drogo was suddenly standing there.

A head taller than Innis Rae, he managed to catch the handle. They wrestled against each other, Drogo grunting from the strain, Innis Rae snarling. "Let go, ye bampot!" she spat out.

Henry was concerned, because Innis Rae was putting up a hell of a fight, and if she overpowered Drogo, then Henry was done. That, as it turned out, was not what happened. Instead Drogo managed to overcome her, yanking the battle axe from her hand. She lunged for it, and Drogo never gave her the opportunity to grab it. Instead he brought the oak staff slamming down onto her face. It brought a satisfying crack, which Henry was reasonably sure was the sound of her nose breaking. That, however, was insufficient to bring her down. Instead she lurched about, shaking her head, trying to dispel the dizziness that was threatening to overwhelm her. Drogo didn't give her the opportunity. He swung a fist fiercely and drove it into Innis Rae's face. Her head snapped around and she *still* attempted to recover, but it was hopeless. Her legs collapsed under her and she fell.

But not all the way. She caught herself, landing on her hands and knees, and tried to pull herself to standing. Henry couldn't believe it. How much stamina did the damned woman have?

Drogo was not about to find out. As she desperately attempted to get to her feet, he laced his fingers together and brought his two intertwined fists down on the back of her head. Innis Rae went down again and this time she didn't move.

Sir Henry walked over and stood next to her, staring down at her insensate form. For a moment he waited for her to suddenly lunge back to life and continue the assault, but when she didn't budge, he let out a low sigh of relief. "Well done, Drogo."

Drogo shrugged. "Well, you don't keep me around for muh good looks."

Henry was tempted to drive a foot into the unconscious woman's midsection, just for some payback, but decided that it wasn't remotely gentlemanly. Whatever else, he had to maintain some decorum. "Basil, all of Sir Lewis's estate and holdings are forfeited to Lord Collins. See to the paperwork, would you?"

Basil nodded and then indicated her body. "What do you want done with the woman?"

Henry shrugged. "You're the sheriff, Basil. That's up to you."

Drogo tapped the short sword that was hanging from his belt. "I could just attend to her now. Won't give us any problems if she's sleeping."

Basil shook his head. "No. She doesn't need to lose her husband and her life in one day." He pursed his lips, gave it a moment's thought. "She's Scots, Drogo. Return her to Scotland."

Drogo bowed slightly. "As you wish, milord Sheriff."

CHAPTER III

I DON'T KNOW!

EVENING HAD FALLEN ON NOTTINGHAM, AND the darkness was absolute, as it typically was.

That did not deter Robyne, who confidently strode toward the convent despite the fact that there was no light to guide her. There was a saying about being so confident in one's ability to locate something that it could be done blindfolded. That was certainly the case with Robyne, who knew every step of the way to the convent with that much certainty.

She saw its shape in the shadows ahead of her. It was a relatively small building. There was a large garden in the back where the Magistar grew various vegetables, including tomatoes and such. The main useful feature of the building was a sizable oven, which was fired up every morning so that it could provide baked goods that were sold in the village each day. Consequently every morning the convent reeked with the satisfying aroma of freshly produced bread. Her nostrils vibrated just thinking about it. It was such a joyous way to start off each day.

It was just a shame that she couldn't take any actual joy from it.

She remembered when she had been capable of such feelings. Back when she had been a little girl.

Back when she had been Mary...

←—«   »—→

Mary has followed the Magistar to the convent. She has seen the building from time to time, although she cannot recall seeing any nuns hovering around it. She has always supposed that they were just incredibly shy and tried to say out of the sight of normal people. Honestly, she was not even entirely sure what a nun did. Something with God, she believed. What exactly, though, she did not know. She had once asked her father what nuns did, and he had laughed and said, "They get rescued." That did not seem like much of an answer, but when she asked her mother, Marian replied, "Ask your father," so that seemed more or less a dead end.

The Magistar enters the convent, the door creaking on its hinges. Mary follows her. She sees the Magistar kiss her fingers and touch a crucifix on the door frame, and Mary follows suit. Not because she necessarily believes in Christ; her father certainly was skeptical and her mother dismissive. But the Magistar does it, and so does she. It seems polite.

"What's a beguine?" she asks, curious about the woman's earlier declaration of what she was.

"Well, we try to emulate the teachings of Christ. We tend to disdain riches, living a life of simple poverty, and we take care of the poor and sick, and help with religious learning."

"Like priests and monks?"

"Yes, except we take no oath. It's purely voluntary. If I decided to be something else, do something else, I could go off and do it."

"Are you going to?"

"No."

"All right," Mary says with a shrug. Then she pauses and asks, "How did you know?"

The Magistar had been leading her through the narrow corridors, but now she stops, turns and stares down at Mary. "Know what?"

"How did you know to show up in the woods?"

The Magistar is intrigued by the question. "You don't believe in coincidence?"

"I don't believe in anything anymore."

It is such a flat, depressed statement that it utterly captures the

Magistar's attention. She is about to contest the child's worldview, but then she stares at the little girl with blood-soaked clothing and realizes this is not the time.

"Come, I'll show you," and she gestures for Mary to follow her. She does so.

She brings her to the study. It is slightly musty, but otherwise seems quite comforting. There is a small fire burning in a fireplace. The Magistar tosses a log onto it. It is not the fireplace, however, that catches Mary's attention. It is the large table in the middle. A detailed map of Nottingham and the surrounding area is etched into it. It is some of the most remarkable artwork she has ever seen. The Magistar points to the table and Mary walks over to the edge, staring down at it, her attention fully engaged. She runs a hand gently over it.

"This is how," says the Magistar.

Mary slowly circles the table. "I don't understand."

"I have a special pendant that I dangle over it, made for me by a…well, not a magus exactly, but a gentleman who trucked in some of the same occasional miracles that our lord indulged in. It points to wherever I may be needed, and I go there."

"Can I see it?"

The Magistar reaches down to her neck and pulls carefully at something Mary now sees is dangling there under the folds of her robes. She extracts the pendant and holds it up so that Mary can see it. Mary stares at it. She does not recognize its curved designs, although she is reasonably sure it's supposed to be two snakes intertwined. If that is the case, she can't say she is exactly enamored of it, but mentally she shrugs in indifference.

The Magistar extends it to her and Mary takes it carefully. As she studies it, the Magistar asks the question she has been dreading:

"Who are your parents, child?"

She briefly considers not answering it so that the Magistar doesn't learn information that could be damaging to her, but she lacks the inner strength or determination to carry out a charade. "Robin and Marion," she says.

"I see," says the Magistar. "Formidable parentage."

"They're gone. I don't know where Mother is, and Father..." Her voice trails off as she stares down at the blood on her clothing, and very softly she gives voice to the knowledge that has haunted her ever since it happened. "He's dead because of me."

"Did you slay him?"

Mary appears a bit surprised at the question since, on its surface, it is clearly ludicrous. Then she understands it. It's absurd, but it's a reasonable query. She shakes her head and then explains, "I shouldn't have been there. He was looking at me and a bad man killed him."

The Magistar shrugs. "Sounds as if your issue is with the bad man, not you."

Mary does not bother to answer. The Magistar clearly does not understand. That's fine; she doesn't have to. It's Mary's burden to carry, not the Magistar's. She shifts her attention to the pendant, which she is holding over the map. It continues to dangle there, unmoving. "Nothing is happening.'"

"That's because there is nowhere for you to go right now. Nowhere that you would make a difference. That will take time."

Mary lays the pendant down on the map. "How much time?"

As long as it takes.

She scowls at the Magistar. "You're annoying."

"Everybody tells me that."

⸺※ ※⸺

Robyne shook off her recollections as she strode into the study. There was the Magistar, as if no time had passed, dangling the pendant over the map. It seemed as disinclined to stir as it had been when the child Robyne had been had attempted to use it.

"See anything?"

The Magistar tilted her head from side to side in a broad attempt at a shrug. "Some things developing. Nothing definite."

There was a turkey leg sitting on a plate next to the Magistar. She slid it over to Robyne. "Eat."

"I'm not hungry."

"You're never hungry. Eat. *Now.*" She tapped the table insistently to indicate that it was not a request.

With an irritated sigh, Robyne dropped into the chair opposite the Magistar. She reached over, pulled the metal plate the rest of the way over to herself and picked up the turkey leg. She took a large bite out of it and began to chew slowly.

"How did it go with the woman?" asked the Magistar.

"Got there just before she was slain. Cut it somewhat thin for my tastes," she said.

"Take it up with a magus," said the Magistar.

Robyne put the leg town. "Have you ever actually seen a magus? Other than the one that gave you the pendant?"

"Who says I ever saw him? So...the woman," she prompted, trying to get the conversation back on track.

"She's going to make us weapons." She took another bite of the leg.

"Us?" The Magistar snorted at the word. "There is no 'us.' There is you and your obsessions."

"I'm not obsessed. Why do you always say I'm obsessed?"

"Because you always are. Because you've never moved past your father's death."

Robyne stared at her for a long moment. "We aren't having this discussion again."

"We've never had it in the first place."

And Robyne slammed her fists on the tabletop so violently that it knocked over a glass of wine that the Magistar had set down. It was mostly empty but a small bit of it spilled onto the table. The Magistar hurriedly grabbed up a cloth and wiped it clean as she glared at Robyne.

Robyne didn't feel contrite, exactly, but she regretted the show of violence. She closed her eyes, composing herself. "I'm sorry. I shouldn't have...I...I'm sorry."

The Magistar seemed as if she wanted to yell at her, but she likewise calmed herself down. Instead of anger, there was sympathy on her face. "Mary..." she began to say.

"I'm not Mary," Robyne cut her off. "I haven't been for a long time."

The Magistar rolled her eyes. "Right. You're Robyne. R-O-B-Y-N-E. You've corrected my spelling often enough, and considering I taught you to read and write..."

"I know what you did for me."

"Saved your bloody life," she said, slightly under her breath but loudly enough that Robyne could easily hear her.

"I *know* what you *did* for me," Robyne repeated with greater emphasis. "And I have to—" She paused, then drew in a breath and let it out slowly. "I have to help others the same way."

"No, you don't."

"Yes, I do. Because it's what *he* would have done. And it's how I can repay you."

"But it's all you talk about," the Magistar pointed out. "You never discuss anything else. It's as if all you do is look around you and see nothing but evil in the world. Especially for women."

"Always for women," Robyne retorted. "Men have all the power. They don't see women as anything but pieces of chattel. Fathers marry off their daughters and never think about love. If I hadn't gotten there to save that woman, her husband could have thrown her body into the forest, claimed she ran off, and if they found her body, say he knew nothing about it. And nobody would question him," she continued, unaware that Amanda had been thinking the exact same thing at the time she had prepared to dispense with her husband. "And that's just the poor! The titled, they're even worse..."

"And you want to do something about it."

"Yes."

"Like what?" she asked reasonably.

"Like stop it."

"How?"

Robyne hurled the remains of the turkey leg into the fireplace and roared, "*I DON'T KNOW!*"

The Magistar stared at her. She didn't say anything. She just stared.

Robyne sighed heavily and dropped her head into her hands. "I'm sorry. I get like this when..." Her voice trailed off.

A gentle hand reached over and wrapped itself around one of hers. "I know," said the Magistar softly.

"It's tomorrow."

"I know," the Magistar repeated. "Fifteen years."

Robyne's mind flew back to that day, that horrible moment when her father's life had ended and her world had crashed apart around her. A decade and a half, and despite all of the Magistar's urgings not to, she still carried that guilt around in her breast like some dark cancerous thing eating away at her.

A nurse. When she'd been a child, her dream had been to be a nurse. Not an outlaw like her father; she'd wanted to help people directly, to heal them when disease inflicted itself upon them. Now that seemed like what it was: a child's desire. The world had moved her beyond that, but not substituted anything of any worth. There were increasingly more days when depression would overwhelm her and she would wonder whether that cancer was eating away at her soul. Did she even have one anymore?

"Fifteen years and I've done nothing except study and train. It's time. It's time for me to start doing what I'm meant to do." She heard her own words and wasn't convinced by them. She tried to shake it off and shrugged. "I'm in a mood."

"You're always in a mood," countered the Magistar.

Robyne glared at her immediately, but then she actually managed to find some humor in the moment. "Thanks," she said drily.

"I made cake."

"That sounds glorious," said Robyne, and as the Magistar rose to get it, Robyne thumped her head back down on the table.

CHAPTER IV

Sign this, would you?

IT WAS A STILL NIGHT AROUND Nottingham castle. Animals of the forest would, from time to time, peer out at it from within the confines of the trees and brush that shielded them from human eyes. They could not remember a time when the towering building had not been there, but could easily imagine a time in the future when it would be gone. A time when moss or ivy would crawl back upon the wall and slowly but inevitably return it to the forest which would be there long after mankind had abandoned it and the world itself. As long as humanity was there, the animals' lives would be under constant threat, but sooner or later—sooner or later—this annoying travesty called mankind would shuffle itself off this mortal coil and the animals would reign supreme once more. All that was required was time, and the animals had nothing but time.

The castle had originally been constructed as a vast wooden residence on the orders of William the Conqueror, but had been redesigned as a stone fortress by Henry II, the father of Richard the Lionheart. It stood near a crossing of the River Trent, and was a quite popular place for nobles to visit and spend time in the King's hunting grounds. At this particular point in time it served as the residence of Lord Collins, who presided over the generalities of life in Nottingham.

Collins was, by the era's standards, positively ancient: He was in his early sixties. He had managed to live that long by keeping his head down and making sure that those around him fought battles while he gave orders and stayed out of the limelight. It had worked so far and he saw no reason to change the way of doing things.

He was of moderate height and a slender man, with a round-ish face and a thick thatch of blonde/red hair atop his head. He was seated in his study, with Sir Henry opposite him and Basil just behind him, and the look on his face was that of sheer incredulity. When he spoke, it was with a posh accent that many people felt was totally affected. "He said that about me? And there were witnesses?"

Henry nodded readily. "His own wife testified to it. Apparently he spoke about you and the king in such disrespectful terms quite routinely."

Collins leaned back in his chair, drumming his fingers on the armrest. "These are dangerous times, Henry. Sedition of any sort cannot be tolerated. The King simply won't stand for it."

At that comment, Henry could not help but chuckle. "Considering his own brother attempted it, I should say not."

"So Lewis is dead."

"Yes."

"And his wife?" The woman's state of being was of great interest to Collins. If she indeed backed up Henry's description of her husband's actions, that would be all the political cover that Collins required to prevent any recriminations down the line.

Henry turned to Basil expectantly. Basil took a step forward and said, "She's in the dungeon to await transportation in the morning."

"An attractive woman?" Collins asked with interest.

Basil half nodded. "I would say so, yes, but…"

That was all Collins needed to hear. "Have her brought here. I wish to confirm the story. Lewis was a man with powerful allies. I do not need them spreading lies to the King and causing problems."

Basil and Henry exchanged looks, and then Basil cleared his throat. "I wouldn't advise that, milord."

"I'm not looking for advice," said Collins with obvious irritation. "I want it done. Now."

Basil paused as if he wanted to say something else, but then nodded and bowed slightly. "Yes, your lordship." He pivoted on the spot and headed out of the room.

"Your successor seems overly concerned about a woman, Henry," said Collins disdainfully.

"Not...overly," said Henry, knowing what was going to come.

—«   »—

The door to the dungeon cell creaked open and Innis Rae stared up at it. Her hands were manacled to chains that were anchored to the wall, and she scrutinized the men—Drogo and two knights—who strode in.

"This can go easily or with difficulty, Missy. It's up to you," said Drogo as he held up the key to the chains.

She said nothing. She just sat there, glaring at him with such ferocity that it was as if she was trying to shove a dagger into his brain. Drogo ignored it as he moved over to her, knelt, and undid the locks on the manacles. Then he stood up and extended a hand to help her stand.

She took the aid as she stood, her knees creaking slightly since she'd been seated on the ground for so long.

"Thank ye," she said, and then slammed her head forward. It impacted with Drogo's face and he cried out as he staggered backwards.

The two knights quickly advanced and Innis Rae shoved Drogo into them. He slammed into the knights and they staggered, momentarily discombobulated.

That was all the opportunity she needed. She bolted past them and into the corridor.

Two more knights were waiting for her and grabbed her by either arm before she could react. She tried to yank clear of them, but they were holding her too firmly for her to break free.

The other two knights that she had temporarily managed to incapacitate had now emerged from the cell, and each one of them grabbed her by the legs, hauling her off the ground. She struggled furiously in their grasp, but she had no leverage and the knights were strong men. They hauled her down the hallway as Drogo followed, shaking his head and rubbing the place where she had head-butted him. He wondered if she'd broken his nose and then realized it didn't matter. Who could care about yet further damage to his face?

Meanwhile Innis Rae was not going peacefully. As she twisted and fought against the men hauling her, she bellowed, "I'll kill you all! Ye right bastards! Yuir dead! Yuir all dead! Put me down and fight me like men, damn ye!"

It took long minutes but they finally hauled her toward Lord Collins's study. Basil saw them heading his way and he turned and opened the doors so that Drogo and his men would have clear passage. Collins gaped as the struggling woman was carried toward him. "Good lord!"

"As I said," commented Henry, and then he raised his voice and called, as imperiously as he could, "Woman! Restrain yourself before Lord Collins!"

She showed not the slightest interest in restraining herself, and so Henry pointed toward a particular chair that Collins kept around just for situations such as this. It had thick wrist restraints bolted to the armrests. The knights brought the furiously battling Innis Rae over to the chair and slammed her down into it, holding her arms immobilized so they could fasten the thick straps onto her. She tried to yank her arms clear once she was strapped in and spat at Drogo for good measure.

"Control yourself!" Collins shouted at her. "I will not ask you again!"

That seemed to catch her attention. "Promise?" she said.

He did not appear amused by her mild jest as he approached her. She noticed he was carrying a rolled up document and wondered if he intended to rap her on the head with it if she misbehaved. "Can you read and write?" he asked.

It seemed a harmless enough question. Unfortunately the answer was no, but she didn't feel like admitting it. "Yes," she said.

"Good." He unrolled the document in front of her.

She stared at it. The smell of the ink scrawled upon it was still fresh. It had only been written a short time ago. She looked at it uncomprehendingly but kept her face impassive so that she wouldn't tip off the fact that she had lied about her literacy.

"Where did you meet your husband?" he asked.

The question startled her because it was so personal. She spat again, this time at his feet. "None of yuir damned business."

He slapped her. The blow was so loud that the noise resonated in the room, and a red flash spread on her cheek from where he had struck her. She gave no reaction to it. She had no intention of giving him the satisfaction of having hurt her.

He then held the document closer to her. She was having a good deal of difficulty hiding the fact that she had no clue what it said. It appeared that Collins had figured out that she didn't actually understand the words and chose not to comment on her lie. Instead he explained it.

"This is a confession of your husband's crimes. I would like you to sign it. For the record. A simple X will do if you feel your full signature is too much trouble."

"Why would I do that?" she asked.

"Because I am your lord and am asking you to. That and there will be a considerable reward for you if you do."

Innis Rae considered the offer. "Ye mean money."

"Just so," said Collins.

"Ye expect me to sell out muh husband's memory for money." It was not a question but rather a flat statement, assessing what he was saying to her. She seemed to consider it and then said, "Let me make ye a counter offer."

"As you wish," said Collins politely.

Drogo was standing directly behind her and was caught completely off guard as Innis Rae jumped the heavy chair back and landed the foot of the chair leg on Drogo's foot. Between the force with which she drove it and her own body weight, it brought a considerable impact down upon Drogo. He let out an agonized howl and with a thrust of her powerful legs she sent the entire chair crashing back onto him. He went down with Innis Rae and the chair atop him.

That was all the opportunity Innis Rae required. Despite her awkward position, lying flat atop a struggling man, she flexed her arms with her power and determination and the upper section of the chair burst apart. She scrambled to her feet. The armrests were still attached to her wrists, but she was free of the constraints the chair had placed upon her.

The two knights who had brought her up to the room had remained, and they came at her now. She didn't wait for them to reach her. Instead she charged into them with her full body, an action they were completely unprepared for. So it was that between her size and speed, she was able to knock them both aside, sending them tumbling to the ground. They tried to get up, but she didn't give them the opportunity. Instead she used the arm rests themselves as clubs, smashing them into their heads and causing them to slump back.

Now Basil was approaching her and he had a dagger in his hand. He thrust it at her and she sidestepped it, catching the blade in her hand. She tried to yank it from Basil's hand, but he held on tightly, with the result being that she hauled him to within an inch of herself, snarling into his face. Blood was trickling from the palm that was gripping the blade, but she ignored it. Basil seemed stunned that she was not remotely incapacitated by the agony she must have been feeling, and that was all the opportunity she required to shove him aside. With the dagger still in her grasp, she flipped it to her undamaged hand, gripped the hilt tightly, and advanced on Henry.

Henry did not appear the least bit concerned. His indifference sounded an alarm in Innis Rae's head. Why wasn't he worried? Considering she was about to gut him, it was strange that he didn't seem worried. *Probably overconfident,* she thought.

"That was a mistake," Henry said calmly, nodding toward the dagger.

She thought that that was some manner of threat, that he was trying to warn her she was making a blunder by preparing to stab him to death. She opened her mouth to respond, but to her bewilderment, nothing emerged.

Innis Rae staggered as the world around her suddenly turned sideways. She fought with supreme effort to right herself but she couldn't find her balance. Beginning to realize, she looked down at the blood that was still oozing over her palm.

Basil stepped back into her point of view. "A particularly useful toxin on the blade," he said coolly. "Good night, Madame."

"I'll...get ye...all," she managed to say, slurring every vowel, and then her legs went out from under her. She collapsed, unconscious.

Henry nodded approvingly. "Good use of the dagger, Basil."

"Thank you, father." Very carefully he picked up the blade and slid it delicately into its sheath. Then he turned to Drogo, who was shaking his right foot, trying to restore feeling to it.

"Get her back down to the dungeon, Drogo. I doubt she'll give you much trouble."

"Yes, sir," said Drogo. He gestured to the two knights, who had gotten up from being knocked to the floor, to pick up Innis Rae's unconscious form. They did so and hauled her out of the study.

"Henry," said Collins.

"Yes, milord?"

He held the document out to Henry. "Sign this, would you?"

"Yes, milord."

He extracted a pen from a nearby inkwell and scratched "Innis Rae" at the bottom of the document.

⊷⊷ ⊶⊷

Basil sat on the edge of his bed, removing his boots, as Drogo stood at attention near the door. That greatly amused Basil, who had given up telling Drogo that nothing bad would happen if he relaxed once in a while. Yes, Drogo was his friend, and had been for as long as he could remember. They had grown up together, after all. But Drogo was also responsible for Basil's safety, and it was a duty that he always took very seriously. It was in his nature to be wary of attacks from any quarter, and his oft-proclaimed sentiment was that the entire point of surprise attacks was to catch one off guard. So if one was always on guard, such an eventuality could never occur. It made sense to him and Basil had no hope of convincing him otherwise.

"How does a woman like that fall in love with a man?" asked Basil.

Drogo pondered it. It was really more of an offhand remark than an actual question, but Drogo truly seemed to be considering it. "He must have been quite the man."

"I suppose," said Basil. He looked up at Drogo and waved in a general manner toward Drogo's face. "You know, you don't have to wear that around the castle. No one cares."

"They care. The just keep it to themselves."

They exchanged long looks, and then Drogo sighed and reached up to the back of his mask. He undid the straps and removed it to reveal his actual face.

It was horrifically scarred from burns, as if someone had shoved a flaming torch into his face. He reached up and touched it experimentally, hoping against hope that he would actually feel some manner of sensation, but once again there was nothing. The scarred expanse of skin was as dead as it had been for years. "Happy?" he asked sourly.

"It's not a matter of happy. I just…" He paused. "I would be dead if you had not burst into that flaming cottage and dragged me out. You got that way because of me. You don't have to hide it."

"It's better that I do."

"How? How is it better?"

"Because if I wear it, I'm a creature of mystery. When I take it off, I'm just a monster.

Something to be feared or pitied."

"That's really not the case."

"It really is."

Basil wanted to argue the point, but he gave up. There was a more pressing subject on his mind. "It wasn't right, what father did, was it." It was not a question but rather a stated affirmation of the thoughts already going through his mind.

"The man was speaking treason against your lord and also the King."

"Then he should have been tried for it," Basil said insistently.

Drogo clearly did not agree. "Your father tried him, found him guilty, and executed him. Done by the book."

"There should have been a jury."

Drogo leaned back against the door. "To carry out the sentence that we all know would have been found? Basil, you're the sheriff. I'm not sure what world you're living in, but you might want to think about joining this one.

Basil wanted to counter the argument, but realized that Drogo had made a valid point. That was one of Basil's greatest weaknesses. He looked at the world around himself and saw it, not as it was, but as it could be. There were so many changes he wanted to make in it, changes that would improve the lot of the lower class and needy. He also strongly believed in equal justice for all classes: that the high born would be treated exactly as the low born, and all crimes should be subject to reviews by their peers. He had no idea why he felt that way—certainly his father did not share his opinions—and yet the beliefs were solidly part of his makeup. He wondered why, certainly not for the first time.

But there was no point in dwelling on it. He certainly wasn't going to change Drogo's mind. He stretched and yawned and said, "I suppose you're right. Well…time for bed."

Drogo nodded, and stared at him…

And he cannot stand it anymore. He charges at Basil, grabs him, falls down onto the bed atop him. Basil gasps in surprise and confusion, having no idea what is happening. Then Drogo brings his lips fiercely down upon Basil's, and at first Basil tries to push him away. But then sensations that he did not even know he had begun to flow over him, and he returns the passion, gasping into Drogo's mouth, returning the kisses with an unexpected ferocity. Drogo's hands start to move over his

"Drogo?"

Drogo, still leaning against the door, snapped back to reality. Basil was staring at him in confusion, having no idea to where his mind had wandered off. "Are you okay?"

"Yes. Yes, of course." Drogo shook his head, banishing the brief daydream back to the inner workings of his mind, ideally to remain hidden there forever. "Right, time for bed."

"Good night, Drogo."

Drogo nodded, opened the door, stepped out into the corridor and shut the door behind him.

And because, for once in his life, he let his guard down, he neglected to put the mask back on his face.

A serving girl was walking down the hall, carrying a bin of dishes. He turned to face her and she let out a startled shriek, losing her grip on the bin. It crashed to the floor and a number of plates tumbled out of it. "S-s-sorry, milord," she stammered as she crouched to gather them up and return them to the bin.

"I'm not your lord!" he snarled at her, causing terror in her eyes. "I'm not *anybody's lord*!"

She looked down, ashamed to meet his angry gaze, and started picking up plates. Drogo wanted to storm off down the corridor to properly convey his fury, but slowly he realized that that would in fact accomplish absolutely nothing. With a heavy sigh he crouched near her and began to help her get the dishes back into the bin.

And then, so his utter shock, she rested a hand on his arm. "I'm really sorry," she said with genuine, sincere regret.

He stared at her and then angrily yanked his arm away. The last thing he needed was the sympathy of a serving wench. To hell with her. To hell with all of them.

Drogo pulled back on his leather covering and stalked off down the hallway.

CHAPTER V

Stick to Weapons

THE KNIGHT COULD NOT RECALL A time when he had felt quite so weary.

He glanced up at the full moon in the sky, visible over the tops of the towering forest trees. He felt as if he had never been as tired as he was at that moment, although he knew that he was kidding himself. He had fought his way through the Crusades. He had been in the midst of glorious battles that left bodies stacked up like cordwood. He had been covered with blood on many an occasion—the blood of his enemies, of course. In those cases, not only had he been physically tired, but also emotionally. He had come to feel as if his very soul was relentlessly battered by the incessant killing of people. Innocent people, oftentimes. He had seen the corpses of women and children splayed upon ground thick with red. He had smelled the stench of stomachs and bowels ripped open and searched for hidden treasures. He had seen so much, in fact, that daily he had to convince himself not to throw himself upon his blade and put an end to it. But the bottom line was that the knight was a fighter, and as far as he was concerned, he wasn't about to give in to death quite that readily.

He could sense his horse was fatigued as well. He eased the tiring beast over to a spring and dismounted. His sword was still attached to the saddle since he didn't think he would have need of it. The knight knelt by the stream to refill his water skin, figuring that after that, he would bring the horse over to the spring and let it drink as well. He kept his helmet on, as he typically did. He had grown accustomed to the protection that it provided for him in any number of ways.

Just as he finished filling the water skin, he heard a familiar sound directly behind him. Despite the fact that he was armored in thick chain mail and helmeted, he still moved remarkably quickly as he clambered to his feet and spun to see what was happening. Was someone sneaking up behind him, prepared to attack?

Hardly that, as it turned out. It was a boy, scarcely into his teens, it appeared. Between the ragged style of his clothing and the dark hue of his skin, it was obvious that he was a gypsy. The sound of a blade being extracted from a scabbard wasn't the boy drawing on him; rather he had yanked the sword on his horse out of its holder and was clearly about to flee.

"Put that down," warned the knight. "Don't move."

Naturally the gypsy moved. He turned and sprinted away as fast as he could, considering he was hauling the knight's sword with him.

The knight gave a low, irritated growl as he clambered up onto his horse and snapped the reins. As tired as the beast might have been, it rose to the occasion and took off after the gypsy.

The boy was making no effort to hide his course. Had he attempted stealth, endeavored to hide, it was entirely possible that the knight would have been unable to follow him. But the boy had no interest in attempting to lose him, which set off bells of warning in the knight's mind. It was entirely possible that he was leading the knight into a trap, and if that were the case, who knew the odds the knight would find himself in? As it so happened, however, the knight did not really care. The worst possible outcome would be that he would die, and honestly, as far as the knight was concerned, that would hardly present a problem to him. Indeed, in many ways, it would be a blessing.

The horse was overtaking the teen and suddenly he skidded to a stop, turned and grinned at the knight. The reason that he ceased his fleeing was readily apparent. Half a dozen gypsies had materialized from the dark, as if the shadow was their homes. They faced the knight defiantly, clearly challenging him to attempt an assault. There were six of them, and he was unarmed. Despite his armor, they obviously thought it was going to be a very brief encounter.

As it so happened, they were correct.

The knight had brought his whinnying horse to a halt. Now, very slowly, he reached up and removed his helmet, giving the gypsies a clear view of his face.

The gypsies gasped in unison. Most of them were stunned into silence; a couple of them muttered in some language that the knight did not understand.

The teen who had stolen the sword immediately dropped it, staring down at it in horror, and then rapidly wiped his hands on his pants legs. The other gypsies slowly began to back up.

"Boo," said the knight.

That was all the impetus they required. As one, they turned and sprinted off into the darkness of the forest. The shadow swallowed them as easily as it had previously spat them out.

The knight descended from his horse, picked up the fallen sword, and slid it back into the scabbard. "Idiots," he muttered disdainfully, and then climbed back onto the horse so that he could return to the stream and provide his animal with some much-needed water.

The village market was thriving that particular morning. Typically anyone passing through Nottingham swung through to replenish their stocks, and Robyne was always happy to serve them.

She stood behind the counter of the bakery stall, calling out the various breads they had to offer in a light, sing-song voice. Doing so made her almost nostalgic for the young girl she used to be, that persona that she had long ago left behind her. She was determined to fight for the lives of those around her, but was all too conscious of the sacrifices she would have to make in order to accomplish her goals. Whatever it was, she was willing to go through with it; no matter what it cost her personally, she was determined to do it.

My God, think of something else. Focus on something pleasant. There. There is a mother, walking with her little girl in hand. The child is smiling up at her mother, beaming with love. Right there is purity and innocence, encapsulated in that one girl. Enjoy that. Bask in it. Don't even consider what would happen if her mother were cut down in front of her, and what that would do to...

DAMMIT.

Suddenly there was someone standing in front of her. It was Amanda. The bruises she had sustained were fading nicely. With any luck her full beauty would be restored and there would be no trace of the damage her brute of a husband had caused her. Amanda was smiling but then quickly tried to assume a distant attitude, as if she were afraid she might convey some genuine friendliness with her. Robyne felt as if she were being overcautious, but did nothing to indicate that. She simply stood there and tilted her head in greeting, as she would with any customer. "Morning, Miss. How may I be of service?

Amanda was holding a basket and she said, "Just some bread. That would be fine." She said it in a rather loud voice, as if she was worried that someone might be listening and desperately wanted to appear casual. The only result was that it attracted odd looks from some passersby who didn't quite understand why some woman was yelling about wanting bread.

Robyne rolled her eyes and Amanda immediately understood her error. She drew closer to Robyne and lifted the basket. She withdrew from it a very nasty looking dagger and held it up so Robyne could see it clearly. The blade was beautifully tapered. There was also what appeared to be a small disk at the base of the hilt, which she imagined to be a decoration. "Looks good," said Robyne in a low voice.

"Watch," said Amanda. She tapped the disk and a second blade slid out of the top of the hilt. It was slightly shorter than the main blade, but looked just as lethal.

Robyne's eyes widened and she let out a low whistle. "Nice. *Very* nice."

"Retracts easily too." She touched the disk two more times and the blade slid back into the hilt. A casual glance would never reveal the knife's secret contents.

"You're a genius," said Robyne, as Amanda handed the knife to her.

"I'm a widow with plenty of time on her hands. Thanks to you."

"You're welcome."

"How much for the bread...?"

"You're joking, correct?" Robyne slid the loaf of bread into Amanda's basket.

Amanda stared down at the bread and then looked at the dagger in Robyne's hand. She frowned thoughtfully. "Have you ever considered slicing it and selling it that way?" she asked.

Robyne looked at her as if she had lost her mind. "What, people can't slice it themselves? Isn't that insulting, implying they're that incompetent? 'We don't trust you to slice the bread properly so we've done it for you!' Seriously?"

"I guess..."

"Stick to weapons," Robyne said firmly.

Amanda nodded and walked away, and Robyne was suddenly startled by a low, crisp voice speaking to her from her immediate right. "Can I see it?"

Her head whipped around and she saw a helmeted knight standing there. He had no markings on him, no crests or anything that indicated allegiance.

"See what?" she asked, as if she didn't have the slightest idea what he was talking about. She had slid the dagger up her sleeve and it was nestled against her arm.

"The dagger that woman gave you in exchange for bread."

"What dagger?" This seemed to be the best plan. She was reasonably sure she could deny it all day.

The knight sighed deeply. It sounded odd, reverberating in his helmet. She wondered why he didn't take the damned thing off. "My child, I am not the youngest of individuals, but my eyesight remains quite sharp." He paused for a moment and then said, "I'm honestly not interested in giving you trouble. I'm a knight."

Robyne took no comfort in that. "Yes well...around here, being a knight isn't necessarily the best thing to be for people such as myself."

"That's a pity to hear," and he sounded quite sincere about it. "Knights should stand for something to aspire to."

That sounded like a genuine aspiration of something she had once dreamed knights could and should be: representatives of a higher purpose. Men who fought on behalf of God's justice rather than the whims of various lords and rulers. "Whom do you serve?" she asked.

"I served King Richard. Now I am...a free lance, I suppose. I pass through towns and such, help where I can. Tend to stay to myself otherwise."

She cocked her head inquisitively. She had never had an extended conversation—or really any kind of conservation—with a knight. She wondered if there were more out there like this one. "Why are you wearing a helmet on your head?"

"Where else would I wear it?" he said, sounding rather reasonable when he asked the question. "So...the dagger?"

It was clear that he was not going to let this go, and she began to be concerned. If she put up too much of a fight over this, who knew if he would report her for suspicious activity to the Sheriff and his minions? That was not remotely aggravation that she needed. So she reluctantly withdrew the dagger from her sleeve and held it up to him.

He took the dagger and studied it, turning it around as he held it up to the eye slit in his helmet. He was studying the hilt and then he spotted the flat disk on top and recognized it for what it was. "What does this button do?" He began to reach for it and instantly Robyne saw the danger. If he pushed the button, the second blade would snap out of the hilt and go right into his eye. It would probably be fatal.

"No!" she said. She managed to control herself sufficiently that the exclamation wasn't in the form of a shout as she snatched the dagger out of his hand.

He clearly had no idea why she had done it. She held the knife vertically so that the hilt was nowhere near either of them and then tripped the switch. The blade obediently snapped out.

The knight let out a low whistle. "You saved my life."

She shrugged as if it were no big deal. "I just stopped you from making a mistake."

"What is your name?"

Robyne hesitated and then said, "Mary."

The knight stared at her as if his gaze were burrowing into her brain; as if he were capable of scooping out her thoughts at will. "No, it's not," he said. "Far too plain a name for a girl like you."

Then he turned his attention to the baked goods in front of her. He picked up a roll. "How much?" he asked.

"Tuppence."

He reached into a small bag that was hanging from his belt, extracted a coin and tossed it to her. She stared at it in surprise. "This is a shilling."

He nodded as if it were no major thing that he had given her six times the amount she'd asked for. Then he walked away, leaving Robyne wondering what had just happened. She did not have time to ponder it, though, because at that moment the Magistar was running up to her. She was holding the pendant in front of her and she was all business. "I've got something," she said.

That was all Robyne needed to hear. She had never been more ready.

CHAPTER VI

Well, that did not work out for you

THE PRISON CART ROLLED DOWN THE forest path, rocking back and forth as Innis Rae endeavored not to sway within. Drogo was taking no chances with her. Both her hands and feet were securely tied, the ropes far too sturdy for her to be able to break through sheer strength.

Basically the cart was a large cage on four wheels, being drawn by two large, black horses. Half a dozen guards ringed them, riding along on their own mounts. Drogo was seated next to the driver and kept glancing back at Innis Rae as if concerned she might somehow vanish from the back of the cart. He would have liked to ignore her, but that was most definitely not possible. The woman was relentlessly slamming her tied feet into the locked back gate of the vehicle. It wasn't making the slightest bit of difference. The padlock was holding firm, as it was designed to do. She did not appear to care, and if she was going to be doing this all the way to their destination, it was going to drive him out of his mind.

He was leaning on her axe, studying the weapon. It was quite formidable in and of itself, and she had certainly displayed an ability to use it in a lethal capacity. He wondered how in the world she had learned such things. She was a woman, after all. Who taught women to employ weapons in such a devastating manner?

The constant banging was getting to the driver as well. He muttered, "She's been doing that ever since we left the castle."

"She's probably going to do it all the bloody way to Scotland," Drogo concurred. "Fortunately enough we'll be transferring her over once we get to London and then she's their problem."

The driver glanced at the weapon that Drogo was studying. "Nice axe."

"It's hers. It's the only thing she owns. Figured I'd pass it on to her next keepers."

The driver seemed genuinely startled by that bit of information. "Surprised you're not keeping it."

"I'm a warrior, not a thief," Drogo said with a disdainful sniff.

Meanwhile one of the guards also seemed to have become fed up with Innis Rae's relentless hammering with her feet. He drew closer to her and said, "Sooner or later, you're going to realize that you're wasting your time, little girl. Sooner or later, sooner or later, you're going to stop doing that."

All that taunt seemed to do was annoy the hell out of Innis Rae, and once more she banged her feet into the cell door, this time with even greater ferocity than ever.

The padlock remained firm; however the latch that it was locked into snapped off, and the door swung wide open.

"Sooner!" she cried out and, grabbing the bars, yanked herself to her feet. Before the guard could react, she leaped out of the cage and slammed into him. She didn't have enough leverage to land atop the horse, but she had sufficient force and weight to send him off balance and tumbling off his mount.

Their mistake had been not tying her hands behind her but instead in front of her. That had happened because when they had endeavored to tie them behind her, she had ferociously fought them. When they demanded to know why, her response had thrown them: "Ah won't be able to scratch muh privates if they itch." That explanation had struck straight at the men's insecurities, not to mention conjured images in their heads that they could never unsee. So they had relented and tied her hands together in the front. The knots had been sufficiently strong so that trying to undo them with her teeth had been a waste of time, but it meant that she was able to still grab something in front of her. When the guard hit the ground, she was on top of him in an instant, and she yanked his sword from its scabbard. She shoved the blade down and in a heartbeat had sliced through the ropes binding her feet.

The guards, still on their horses, came at her from all directions. Drogo, having a feeling that half a dozen men might not be enough, leaped down from the seat, carrying the battle axe firmly in his hands. "Whoa, whoa!" he shouted, hoping to halt this useless escape attempt before it got too far.

Innis Rae saw him coming and, without hesitation, threw the sword right at him. He slapped the sword aside, which was fairly easy since it wasn't exactly weighted to be used as a throwing weapon. It turned out, though, that the thrown sword was merely a distraction. Even as it tumbled away, Innis Rae slammed directly into Drogo. They went down in a heap.

The edge of the blade was inches away from Innis Rae. The opportunity was quite literally in her face, and she took immediate advantage of it. She swung her bound hands around and down and brought them squarely onto the blade. It cut through the ropes and Innis Rae was free.

She got to her feet and grabbed the weapon's handle. But she didn't reckon with Drogo's strength. Even though he was on his back and she was standing, she wasn't able to yank it out of his grasp. The problem daunted her for a couple of seconds and then she slammed her foot into Drogo's face. That was enough to jolt it out of his hands. With the weapon now firmly in her grasp, she leaped onto the seat that Drogo had been sitting in and clambered up and past the startled driver. She was now atop the wagon, giving her a height advantage over the rest of the guards, even though they were on horseback. She swung the axe right and left, spooking the horses enough that they skittered back so that none of the guards could get near her.

Suddenly an arrow thudded into her shoulder. She staggered, crying out, and saw one of the horsed guards with a bow in his hand. He was reaching back into a quiver slung on his back, preparing to nock another arrow.

Innis Rae was not about to give him an opportunity. With a pained grunt she yanked the arrow out of her shoulder, turned it around and threw it like a spear. Her aim was superior to the guard's: whereas he had merely wounded her, her own throw thudded squarely into his chest. He cried out and tumbled back, falling off the horse.

It was all the opportunity she required.

She leaped onto the momentarily riderless horse and snapped the reins, trying to take control of the beast. But there was no room for her to maneuver. Guards were on either side of her, close and hemming her in. One of them came in behind her and grabbed her, catching her off guard and throwing her balance off. She couldn't maintain her seat on the horse and she tumbled to the ground, the beast moving away from her as quickly as it could. Now other guards were swarming over her, preventing her from moving, keeping her arms and legs immobilized.

One of the guards was atop her now, like a perverse version of love making, and he had drawn a dagger back, about to bring it down into her chest. "To hell with Scotland!" he snarled. "Your trip ends here!"

That was when an arrow emerged from his chest.

He looked down in shock and started to pitch forward. Innis Rae managed to catch him, shove him to the side, and scramble to her feet. The guards were too startled to react immediately, and all heads turned as the sound of a horse's hooves galloped toward them.

A green-clad masked woman was galloping right at them. She was swinging a bow back onto her shoulder and she had a hand outstretched.

"Come on!" she shouted.

Innis Rae was hardly in a position to question where the woman had come from. She grabbed the woman's hand and leaped upward. Between the power of her legs and a considerable display of strength on the woman's part, she was now on the horse's rump, holding on desperately to the woman in the saddle. The woman did not have to caution Innis Rae to hang onto her; she was already doing it with all her strength.

"*Get them! Get them!*" bellowed Drogo. Even as the guards took off in pursuit, he grabbed the bow and arrows off the fallen guard, clambered up onto the horse, and took off behind them.

The driver was left alone on the cart.

"So I should just wait here, then?" he called after them, but did not receive a response.

—«　»—

"Who the hell are you?!" demanded Innis Rae as the horse galloped beneath them.

"Robyne of Sherwood!" came the reply.

"Never heard of you!"

"My father, then. Robin Hood."

"Doesn't ring a bell."

Robyne fired a quick glance at her. "Seriously?"

"Who is he?"

"The greatest thief who ever lived!"

That explanation was utterly useless to Innis Rae. "A famous criminal, then?"

"He robbed from the rich and gave to the poor!"

Innis Rae sounded skeptical. "That doesn't sound like a proper way to do business!"

Robyne rolled her eyes.

Suddenly an arrow whistled past them. Innis Rae risked a look behind her and saw the guards in pursuit. She was hardly surprised. What else were they going to do, really? "Faster!" she called.

"You want me to go faster? Get off!" said Robyne with great sarcasm.

As it happened, the sarcasm was insufficient for Innis Rae, who took her seriously. "Fine!" she said and leaped off the horse.

"*No!*" shouted Robyne.

She needn't have worried. Innis Rae charged the nearest guard, who had not yet drawn his sword because he hadn't expected to catch up with her so quickly. She swung her axe and, thanks to the lengthy handle, was able to bring the blade resoundingly into his midsection. The guard cried out and tumbled backwards, and that was all the opportunity Innis Rae needed as she leaped onto his horse with one smooth move.

Robyne, despite herself, nodded in approval as Innis Rae took firm control of the animal and snapped its reins. Seconds later both women were galloping through Sherwood Forest as rapidly as they could.

For long minutes the guards pursued them. Robyne and Innis Rae did everything they could to shake their pursuers, leaping over fallen trees, branches, and small rivers. But they were unable to do so, the guards maintaining the distance and even gaining slightly.

Drogo, meanwhile, brought his horse around and nocked an arrow. He took aim and fired.

It thudded into the backside of Innis Rae's horse. The poor creature let out a terrified screech and went down, dumping Innis Rae to the ground.

Robyne saw it and let out an angry *"Bugger!"* Even as she cursed, she whipped her horse around and galloped back toward Innis Rae. She was pinned under the horse, desperately trying to shove the wounded animal off herself.

Guards had dismounted and they were charging toward her on foot. Robyne moved directly toward them, yanking out the dagger that Amanda had given her. She stabbed it forward and drove it into the chest of one of the oncoming guards. He staggered and she suddenly became aware of another guard coming in behind her. She pressed the triggering disk and the hilt's blade snapped out. Without even turning around she drove the dagger backwards. The blade sank into the base of the man's throat and blood gurgled up and out of his mouth.

She reached down, gripped Innis Rae's hand and pulled with all her strength. It took long seconds, but she managed to haul the larger woman out from underneath the horse. She was grateful to see that Innis Rae's legs appeared intact; thank God the weight of the horse had not crushed them. It was becoming clear that this Scotswoman was incredibly tough, even if it was annoying as hell that she had no clue who Robin Hood was.

"Come on!" she cried out.

"No, by all means, stay."

The sardonic voice of Drogo floated to them. He was sitting on horseback a short distance away and had a nocked arrow ready to fly. "I insist," he said. Then he frowned. "Who the devil are you?"

"The name's Robyne."

"Not the dead one, I assume."

"His spirit lives on," she said defiantly.

He chuckled at that. "That's all that's going to be living on." And he drew back the arrow, prepared to launch it directly into her chest and put an end to her abortive career.

So he was very startled when a very posh voice said, "Here now. Can't have that."

His head snapped around and he saw a fully armored knight on horseback a short distance away. The man seemed to have come out of nowhere. The silence of his approach was positively eerie. "A troop of guardsmen against two women? That hardly seems fair to me." He sounded like he was a scolding school-teacher having caught some of his students endeavoring to cheat on an examination.

Drogo had no patience for it. This day had been shite enough. He had already lost several of his men during what should have been an utterly routine undertaking and he was not the slightest bit interested in prolonging it. "This is not your affair, sir knight."

The knight seemed to find amusement in Drogo's proclamation. "Well, actually the advantage of being a knight is that you tend to get to decide what is and is not your affair. Now put your bow and arrow away."

The conversation was wearing far too thin on Drogo. "This arrow is going to find its mark, and if you do not go on your way, sir knight, then that target is going to be you."

"Very well," said the knight, clearly not caring about Drogo's threat. To underscore his indifference, he guided his horse to the right and directly blocked Drogo's shot.

"No, he's right!" Robyne protested. "This isn't your affair! I can handle this!"

"I've no doubt that you can," said the knight. Then he paused and amended the statement. "All right, that's a lie. I believe that in other circumstances you could attend to it quite well, but in this case you could use some aid."

"I am not joking, sir!" Drogo warned him.

Drogo's caution did not seem to perturb the knight in the slightest. "I didn't think so, because if you were, you were doing a shite job of it. No one is laughing."

That comment was the last straw for Drogo as he released the arrow. It thudded into the knight's chain armor...and went no further. He glanced at it and then tossed it to the ground. "Tell you what," he said, sounding sympathetic, "I'll give you a target you can penetrate."

He reached up and removed his helmet.

Drogo and the guards gasped. So, for that matter, did Robyne and Innis Rae.

His face had pink, sore lesions upon it. A couple of them were covered with dried blood. Clumps of his hair had fallen off and his scalp looked extremely dry. The reason for his appearance was instantly evident to the onlookers.

"He's a leper!" one of the guards whispered harshly.

"I can see that!" Drogo had absolutely no idea how to react, but he certainly didn't require one of his guards to declare something that was plainly evident.

"The name is Clarence. Sir Clarence," said the knight as if he were introducing himself casually at a party. "Well? Going to take another shot?"

Drogo swung the bow and arrow up and released a second arrow. But his hands were shaking when he did it, and consequently he missed his target by a good two feet. It thudded impotently into a tree and quavered there.

"Oh, bad luck!" said Clarence as if he were genuinely upset that the arrow had not embedded itself in his skull. "Of course, it would have been worse luck if you'd struck me. See, if a leper starts to bleed, the condition automatically spreads to everyone in the area. So if you want to dispose of these two women," and he nodded toward Robyne and Innis Rae, "then by all means, fire away. They'll contract the disease and die. Could take weeks, maybe months, but you'll have done your duty. Of course, on the other hand, *you* will be dead as well. So I suppose it depends just how much you want to accomplish your job." Then he seemed to give the situation further consideration. "Or maybe I'm just too far away and you're a bad shot. Here. Let me make it easier for you."

Whereupon he did the one thing that none of them wanted him to do: he calmly started to ride toward them. They backed up, clearly petrified. Drogo tried to extract another arrow but instead dropped it, his hands shaking beyond his ability to control them.

Clarence was relentless in his taunting. "Come on! Who wants to splatter my blood? There's plenty for all." Then he reached down and pulled his sword out of its scabbard. "Step forward, sinners, and allow me to absolve you of all your crimes!"

"*Bugger this!*" shouted one of the guards, and he wheeled his horse around. Within seconds not only was he gone, but the rest of the guards were directly behind him. Just like that, the only remaining threat to Robyne, Clarence and Innis Rae was Drogo, who desperately looked like he wanted to be anywhere but where he was. An instant later he made that desire a reality, and the three of them were alone.

"Pity," said Clarence, who seemed genuinely disappointed that the battle had departed so abruptly and in the other direction. Then he glanced down at Innis Rae. "Are you well, woman? Is your leg injured?"

"It's all right," said Innis Rae.

He reached down to help her to her feet. "Let me—"

"*No!*"

Startled at the vehemence of her denial, he pulled his hand away and simply stared at her. But then Robyne reached up toward him and said, "I could use a hand, good sir."

He stared down at her, studying her. "The young lady from the bakery stall."

Robyne blinked in surprise. "You have a good eye."

"You have an identifiable dagger," and he pointed to the weapon that was lying on the ground. "So I suppose we saved each other today. The scales are even." He reached down with his gloved hand and helped her to her feet. She, in turn, helped Innis Rae to stand. "You're not afraid of me." There was genuine wonderment in his voice.

Robyne shrugged. "You're wearing gloves. As long as you don't kiss me, sneeze on me or bleed on me, I cannot acquire your illness."

"Very true. Many people don't know that."

"Many people are stupid," she replied. Then her gaze shifted to Innis Rae. "But not you. I didn't mean you," she added hurriedly, clearly afraid she had offended Innis Rae.

"Ye could have. Because ah didn't know who Robin Hood was," Innis Rae said sarcastically.

Sir Clarence looked astounded. "How could you not know who Robin Hood was?"

"It's not muh bloody country, all right?!"

Robyne was not interested in continuing the discussion. "We really need to get out of here before they screw up their courage and return."

"I'd best leave you," Clarence began.

But Robyne would not hear of it. "No, come. Please. I owe you my life. Let me at least repay you with some food."

"As you wish," said Clarence.

⸻ ⸻

Clarence had allowed the women to go on ahead of them, although tracking them had certainly not been a problem. He knew that the

Scotswoman—"Innis Rae," he believed her name was—remained a bit uncomfortable around him. Doubtless Robyne was endeavoring to educate her as to the realities of leprosy so as to ease her concern. So he was giving them their distance.

Now, though, he came upon Innis Rae who was standing at the base of a tree. There was no sign of Robyne anywhere.

He dismounted from his horse and tied the reins off to a tree. Then he walked over to Innis, making sure to keep a discrete distance between them. "Where did she go?"

"Dunno," said Innis Rae. "Scampered up into the tree."

He stared up and couldn't see anything. The branches were so thick, the leaves so concealing, that it was indiscernible from ground level. Robyne had effectively disappeared into them.

Suddenly a large noose dropped down from overhead, dangling directly in front of Clarence. Robyne's voice floated down to him from above: "Loop it around your chest!"

Clarence supposed it was better than wrapping it around his neck. He did as she requested and then said, "Now wh—?"

That was as far as he got as the noose suddenly tightened around his chest and yanked him skyward. He had a brief glimpse of Robyne descending directly across from him, holding firmly onto the rope. Clarence kept rising upwards, through the branches, and then suddenly he was dangling in front of a platform. He realized it was a series of wooden planks hammered into the trees, stretching in several directions over a space of about a hundred yards. Then he glanced up and saw that the rope was threaded through a large wheel that was firmly affixed to branches overhead.

"I'll be damned! How marvelous!"

He only needed to swing on the rope a couple of feet and was thus able to attain a perch on the platform. He then undid the lasso and tossed it back down. Moments later Robyne had clambered back up into the tree. "There's a metal pot over there and a small stone pit that I built in which we can safely light a fire," and she pointed a short distance away. "Think you can do it?"

"I have every confidence," said Clarence. He extracted several pieces of flint and moved over to where she had pointed. Lying near the pit were several partly cooked rabbit corpses. It only took him several minutes to get the fire up and roaring and a short time later, the three of them were grouped around it. Robyne took one of the finished rabbits and divided it and then began on the other one.

"So," said Clarence. "Robin Hood's daughter, eh. King Richard thought very highly of him."

Robyne slowly shook her head. "King Richard abandoned him. Acceded to the will of nobles who had their riches hurt by him."

"Yes," Clarence agreed. "He became Richard's enemy. That doesn't mean you can't think highly of an enemy. Means you show respect."

"To hell with his respect." She studied him thoughtfully. "How did you get...you know..."

"Leprosy?" She nodded. "My wife. A good woman, she was. One evening she found a man bleeding in an alley. She tried to help him. Discovered too late what he was."

Robyne cocked her head slightly. "And you didn't...?"

"Run from her? Keep away from her? Exile her?"

Once more she nodded.

"She was my wife," he said with a shrug. "'Til death do us part. Her fate was mine." His glance turned to Innis Rae. "Since we seem to be asking questions about each other...what's a Scotswoman doing in England?"

"My man came to Scotland, looking for treasures and such. He found me."

"Love at first sight?"

She half-smiled. "Not exactly."

—⸎ ⸎—

Innis Rae charges the officious interloper, this stranger seeking riches in the Scots highlands. She does not know nor care about his name. All she wants is to dispose of this intruder and return to her tribe. Granted, she is not exactly the most popular individual among the others whom she calls "family." They believe that it is the place of the woman to support her husband and cook the food; the men get to do everything else. This does not sit well with Innis Rae, who is not the least bit anxious to take a husband and abandon her preferred activities such as hunting and fighting. There have been times where she was convinced that she had been born the wrong gender. That her disposition far better suited that of a man than a woman. Oh, she liked men well enough, but she wasn't the slightest bit interested in abandoning her identity to one just to get married.

None of that matters at this point, however, because she is busy attempting to kill someone.

She is using her customary battle axe, and he is ably defending himself with a sword. She has to admit that he is doing a good job; he certainly knows what he is doing. Every time she swings her axe he seems to anticipate where it is going and manages to deflect it repeatedly. He is not, she quickly notices, genuinely attempting to dispatch her. He is all defense, no offense, and that alone annoys the hell out of her. Clearly he is reluctant to attack her because she is a woman, and she finds that astoundingly patronizing. That is enough to infuriate her all the more.

She attacks even more aggressively, swinging the axe with dwindling attention to her whereabouts. Her opponent continues to deflect it and suddenly she changes the angle of the axe, swinging down and around rather than back and forth. The move catches him off guard and she sends the sword flying. "Hah!" she shouts and swings the axe around for the kill.

Yet the damned man dodges it, and not only that, but her lack of attention to her surroundings costs her. The axe thuds squarely into a tree and becomes lodged there. She tries to yank it clear, but the man moves too quickly as he charges forward and tackles her. The impact knocks her off her feet and she goes down.

The bad news is that their battle has carried them to the top of a hill and the man's collision sends them over the edge. The two of them roll down, still grappling furiously, hand to hand. There is much grunting as they roll and when they finally reach the bottom, she is on top.

She draws her fist back to smash him in the face.

He's smiling.

The unexpected reaction stops her cold. Her fist remains frozen in the air, and she wears an expression of bewilderment.

He begins to chuckle.

"What is so damned funny?" she demands.

He doesn't reply. Instead his chuckle turns into outright laughter. She doesn't have the slightest idea what it is that he finds so hilarious.

But it doesn't matter, because laughter, like any good virus, is contagious. It transmits itself to Innis Rae like an uninvited intruder and now she is laughing as well. She has no clue what in the hell is going on, but she cannot help herself. Within seconds both of them are roaring with laughter. She is laughing so hard that she rolls off him and they are lying next to each other in building hysterics.

It is her most pleasant memory.

———— « » ————

"What in the world were you laughing about?" asked Robyne.

"You know, I don't have the slightest idea," said Innis Rae. "It was just…it was the moment, I suppose. The idea that we were beating on each other and didn't know why. It was…it was amusing. And we laughed and we stopped fighting and then we…" Her voice trailed off.

Robyne looked relieved that she had stopped talking. "Yes, I don't think we really need any further details."

"He was a good man," Innis Rae said wistfully. "Didn't want me to be anything else but what I was." She paused and then added, "Stupid ass. God, I miss him."

A silence dwelt upon them for a time. They continued to eat, but even the smacking of their lips became quieter.

Finally, Clarence broke the silence, indicating their surroundings and saying, "So what is this place?"

"The fortress," Robyne said.

"Fortress?" Clarence echoed skeptically. "It's a few planks of wood."

"It's going to get bigger. I have plans."

"So do I," Innis Rae agreed. She had had a piece of rabbit skewered on a dagger, but she finished the last bite and then drove the dagger point into the wood with an emphatic thud. "I'm going to kill the monster that took my Lewis. That bastard, Sir Henry."

"Really." That was something that Robyne did not know. "I have my own interest in Sir Henry."

"I can imagine," said Clarence. "He killed your father."

Her head snapped around as she stared in shock at Clarence. "He told you that?"

"He told *everybody* that."

"Yes, well…I'm going to take him on," she said grimly.

"*We* are going to take him on," Innis Rae corrected her.

Robyne clearly wasn't interested in disputing her on it. Instead she nodded and said, "And then me and my followers, we're going to improve the lives of women everywhere in Sherwood."

"So you won't help men, then?"

The question seemed to throw Robyne slightly. "I suppose if there is one who is in difficulty, and I was able to help, then I would do so. But…" She considered the question. "There are many alternatives for men who are in trouble to seek assistance from. Not to mention that many are physically able to seek justice for themselves. Women, however…they are oftentimes helpless. The justice system—what there is of it—turns a blind eye to them. They have no rights in a marriage. As citizens they are indisputably second-class to men. I've seen repeated instances of it while I was growing up. Helpless women would come to the convent, seeking shelter, and the Magistar would always provide it. But sooner or later they would end up returning to their lives, because they knew nothing else and had no one to whom they could resort. Many of them wound up dead, or disappeared, which meant they were as good as dead. Now that I am grown, I am no longer going to tolerate it. Women need their champion, and if that is to be me, so be it."

"A worthwhile goal," said Clarence. "Although you are

definitely going to need a lot more followers. What are you going to call them?"

Innis Rae looked puzzled. "Call them?"

"Her father's followers were the Merry Men...oh!" said Clarence, hit with inspiration. "That's it! You said your name was Mary. Were you telling the truth?"

"Yes, but—"

"So they can be the Mary Women."

"No," said Robyne firmly.

"Just a suggestion."

"No," she repeated, since apparently he hadn't heard her the first time.

"Or maybe the Mary Maids," Innis Rae suggested.

"Better!" said Clarence. "Alliterative!"

"No!" Mary didn't want to shout for fear of attracting attention from below, but she could not have been more firm.

All was silent for a time. Then:

"It would be spelled differently, you see. M-A-R-Y, not—"

"Oh, shut up."

CHAPTER VII

Not again! Creeping hell, not again!

SIR HENRY, DROGO AND BASIL WERE walking down a corridor in Nottingham castle, and Henry was most definitely not in a good mood. "You can't catch leprosy that way!" Henry told Drogo in frustration.

"That's what I heard," Drogo said defensively.

"Well, you heard wrong. Anyway, the leper isn't what concerns me. It's this Robyne that's the problem."

"You think she's truly related to Robin Hood?" asked Basil.

"That is my concern, yes." Henry stopped walking and Basil and Drogo took several steps before realizing that he had halted. They waited for him as he thought. "What do you remember of him?"

"Nothing. I was much too young to remember. I know the stories, but..." He shrugged.

Henry's mind flashed back to that day so many years ago. The day he had entered his tent and saw Basil lying there, covered with blood and a bandaged gash on his forehead...

"Do the stories concern you?" he asked Basil.

Basil sounded indifferent. "He was a thief. You caught him and killed him. And now it's my job to catch and kill this daughter of his. Not entirely sure what there is to be worried about."

"Of course not." Henry patted him on the shoulder. "You're a good son, Basil."

"Thank you, father." Basil beamed at the compliment.

"We'll come up with a plan of attack in the morning."

Basil nodded and then asked, "Should I tell Lord Collins?"

"I'll inform him. It won't be a problem," Henry said with confidence he didn't feel.

———— ⚔ ————

"*Not again! Creeping hell, not again!*" bellowed Lord Collins, thereby proving that Henry had been absolutely right to be concerned.

Collins was in Henry's study, and his rage seemed to be towering above the parapets of the castle.

Henry did the best he could to calm him. "It will be attended to," he assured him.

It didn't seem as if Collins had heard him. He was far too preoccupied with ranting. "You cut off his head! How can we be threatened by someone whose head was cut off!?"

"We're not. It's his daughter."

That piece of information stopped Collins dead in his tracks. His eyes widened in shock, he dropped down into a chair and shook his head slightly, as if certain he had somehow misheard Henry's statement. "A woman? We're being threatened by a woman?! What kind of woman becomes a warrior!"

Much that was negative could have been said about Henry, but there was one thing that was quite true: He was extremely well-read. He began to tick off names. "Artemisia I of Caria. Queen Boudicca the Celt. Zenobia of the Palmyrene Empire..."

"You're making those up!" Collins said.

"I'm really not."

Collins considered the matter a moment, and then he began tapping his finger on his chair's arm for emphasis. "I want this ended, Henry. I want it done. Finished. I don't need the daughter of a popular hero, whom the people still remember fondly, starting up a new following. One week, Henry."

"To catch her?"

"That's correct."

Henry shook his head. "Lord Collins, if there was one thing I learned in battling Robin Hood, it's that attaching time tables to how long it will take to dispose of him is never a useful tactic. So I further assume that the same will apply to his daughter."

That was not remotely satisfactory for Collins. "Get. It. Done," he said, thumping his fist with each word in order to add emphasis. Then he stood up, turned and walked out of the room. If he had been a child, Henry mused, he doubtless would have stomped his feet as he went.

Henry sat there for a time, and then he walked over to a small, carved box on a bureau. He opened it, reached in, and extracted a locket. He snapped it open and there were two tiny drawings within.

One was of a little girl. She was smiling incandescently. Hers was the face of a child that had the entirety of her life in front of her and could not wait to live it. Anything was possible.

The boy seemed a bit more serious. He wasn't really smiling all that much. There was deep gravity in his face as if he was considering the future and contemplating not only his place in it, but what he could do to change it more to his liking. In Henry's imaginings, there was something else there as well: a determination to live up to the example his father had set for how to live. Here was a young thief in the making.

"I should've just taken the damned head," said Henry to himself and he snapped the locket shut.

BOOK TWO

Khalida and Alys

←—«   »—→

CHAPTER VIII

All the best castles have dungeons

THE YOUNG FRENCH GIRL SPED THROUGH the nighttime forest. Her breath was pounding hard in her lungs, and she could feel her heart thudding against her chest as if it was trying to exit her ribcage and liberate itself from her body.

"Girl" might have been a misnomer since she was clearly out of her childhood, but she had not yet reached twenty summers of age. Her hair was braided: two plaints brought around from the nape of her neck and joined around her head. It was typically a nice, neat way in which to keep her hair, but the running was causing it to become disheveled. Strands kept falling into her face and she incessantly had to braid it. Her skin was pale as newly fallen snow, not from illness of any sort, but because she was not accustomed to being out in the day very much. Her previous life she had remained inside much of the time, and even now, when she had acquired her freedom, she tended to walk around mostly in the shadows that served to hide her from casual view. It wasn't that she disliked the sun all that much; she just wasn't especially familiar with it.

The clothes that she had once worn had been far more majestic than what she was attired in now. She had traded her previous garments with a serving woman because she felt that, if she was noticed wandering about, she would draw far less attention in something more appropriate to the lower class. All she wanted to do was elude notice and capture.

How the hell her damned pursuers had managed to locate her, she could not even begin to guess.

What she knew for certain was that she had been crouched in front of the small fire she had built where she was just finishing devouring the bird that she had plucked, cooked and eaten. It had certainly not been her favorite meal, but she had to subsist on whatever she could find. Suddenly she had heard the noises of someone approaching her. She heard one voice very distinctly say, "I'm pretty sure she's this way," and that was all the evidence she had required to know that pursuers had caught up with her. There had to have been a tracker among them, someone who was capable of locating her purely through her scent. Quickly she kicked dirt on the fire to snuff it out, and then she grabbed up the one possession she owned. It was a morning star, a vicious weapon several feet in length. It had a solid black, round metal head with spikes projecting from it that could be lethal if the blow was delivered correctly and maim its victim even with a sideways blow. It had a sheath on her back in which it was typically securely mounted, but at this point she was carrying it in her hand and she had no intention of putting it down until she was convinced of her safety.

She started to run.

Somehow her movement managed to alert her pursuers, because she was able to discern the sudden increase of their steps behind her.

She was tired of fighting, so very, very tired. Yet it seemed as if it was going to be unavoidable once again.

Suddenly an arrow thudded into a tree just to her right. It was obviously a warning shot, because she would be useless dead. She was most definitely wanted alive. The idea doubtlessly was that she would stop where she was, turn around and surrender to her pursuers.

She met two thirds of the expectations. Stop and turn she most definitely did, but her hand was pitching forward in a dead-on throw. She sent the morning star hurtling, spinning end over end. It headed straight toward the bowman who had fired the arrow and was already in the process of nocking a second one. He didn't have the opportunity to finish loading it, because the morning star slammed him squarely in the face. He didn't even have time to grunt in pain but instead fell over backwards.

But he was not alone. Two swordsmen were right behind him. They had not yet drawn their swords because it was easier for them to run with their blades tucked into their scabbards, plus once again the problem that striking her with a sword would present in keeping her alive. But they were both burly men and certainly quite convinced that they could take down the French girl provided they could get within range.

That was something that she was determined to make certain would not happen.

She charged toward them, snatching the morning star that was embedded in the unconscious (and maybe dead) soldier's face and came right at them. They were thoroughly startled by the attack; they had incorrectly assumed that she would continue to flee and they could overtake her. Realizing the error of their ways, they reached for the hilts of their swords to withdraw them from their scabbards.

It was the right move, but much too late.

She slammed her mace into the head of the nearer of them. He staggered, shrieking from the pain of the sharpened studs upon it, and the girl whirled and brought it around into his gut. It not only knocked all the air out of him and began to cause bleeding in several places in his stomach, but it also served to double him over. She then shoved him into his companion just as the man managed to draw his sword. The impact knocked the second fellow off-balance and they crumbled to the ground entangled in each other. Of even greater significance was that the man dropped his sword.

It was all the opening the young woman needed. Dropping the morning star, she snatched up the blade and slammed it point down into the back of the man on top, driving it through him and into the chest of the man he was upon. Both of them screamed, their death agonies rattling in their throats. She could not have cared less. Instead she regarded the calamity she had caused and smiled grimly at her handiwork. Then she turned around to go on her way, confident that no one else was following her.

In that regard, she was correct.

She had absolutely no time to react as a fist came out of nowhere and slammed her squarely in the face. The last thought that passed through her mind was *Merde* and then darkness claimed her.

⸻ ⸻

Bowles was an experienced soldier, and also a superb huntsman and tracker. He had been so ever since he was young and became the principle food gatherer for his oftentimes homeless family. He was big and bulky and yet typically managed to move with so much stealth that people he was tracking didn't know that he was there until he was right on top of them. He had managed to parlay that into a rather impressive career and had recently hired himself out into the services of Lord Wilford. Now Wilford, who had heard of the impressive bounty being offered for the capture of the damnable French girl, had dispatched Bowles to try and track her down. He had done so, but the cost had been two of his men's lives and a badly injured third one.

Now the little spitfire was lying unconscious on the forest floor, and he picked up her morning star and held it over her head. He was sorely tempted to crush her damned skull with it. It would be a merciful dispatch: She would die in her sleep, no doubt dreaming about her homeland before her grey matter was pummeled into a dripping mass. It was a very appealing idea to him.

Unfortunately the mandate was not "dead or alive." So, with a frustrated grunt, he picked up the French girl and slung her over his shoulder. "Stupid bitch," he muttered. Then he walked over to his man who was still conscious, but bleeding from wounds on his face. "Can you walk?"

"I...think so," said the soldier, except his speech was deeply slurred and so it came out, "Idinso."

Bowles nodded, understanding him despite the impediment,

and then said, "Good. Then try to keep up." Feeling no need to continue the conversation, especially considering that the soldier was mostly incomprehensible, he turned and started walking.

The trip back to Wilford Castle went quite smoothly, but it was nevertheless lengthy. Fortunately the girl remained insensate and so it was with no incident that—as the sun slowly rose over the treetops—they drew within sight of the castle. It was not an especially large place, certainly nothing on the scale of Nottingham Castle, but was nevertheless rather impressive. The drawbridge was down and Bowles walked across it, nodding to two guards who recognized him immediately. They had no idea who the girl was but didn't bother to question him. That pleased him since he wasn't feeling especially talkative nor liked answering questions.

He strode into the main dining hall where he was fairly certain that Lord Wilford would be having breakfast. He was correct. The servants were lined up attending to him, and one dark-skinned young woman—a Moor, apparently—had just laid down bread and eggs before him. She looked up and blinked in surprise as Bowles strode in with the girl over his shoulder, and as soon as he was close enough, dropped her unceremoniously on the lengthy dining table. Wilford gestured to the Moorish girl to step back and she immediately returned to a small line of servants who were standing against a wall. She stepped in next to another Moor who looked like an older version of her: her mother, perhaps.

"You found her!" said Wilford. His thick black mustache was quivering with such joy it looked as if it were going to leap off his lip. "You tracked her!"

Bowles wasn't the slightest bit interested in Wilford's joy. "The little bint killed two of my men."

Wilford seemed genuinely surprised at that announcement. "How did she do that?"

"With one of their swords."

Wilford "harrumphed" deep in his throat. "Sounds as if your men didn't deserve to live. *Guards!*"

Several guards immediately came running in response to

Wilford's shout. As they did so, Wilford said wistfully, "We need a dungeon. All the best castles have dungeons. We need to get one of those." Then he gestured toward the limp body on the table. "Take her to the lookout tower and lock her in. It's high enough that she won't think about leaping out."

They hauled her away with no effort. It wasn't difficult since the damned thing likely weighed next to nothing. As they did so, he summoned over his messenger and said, "Get word to the king. He'll want to pick up his bounty."

"What about my payment?" demanded Bowles.

"When the king pays me, I shall pay you."

Bowles was not thrilled by the response. On the other hand, Wilford was a renowned skinflint and so it was consistent that he wasn't going to provide the reward until he had it in hand... although there was no doubt that Wilford would keep a share of the king's rewards for himself.

Cheap bastard.

CHAPTER IX

Come out here! Show them!

ROBYNE, CLARENCE AND INNIS RAE HAD remained in the fortress for the rest of the night, giving any potentially wandering soldiers time enough to give up in their search for them. She couldn't believe his bluff about leprosy had so fooled the guards. Robyne couldn't get over the lack of education in some people. On the other hand, she supposed she shouldn't knock it. Playing on the idiocy of others was one of the things that enabled her to survive as long as she had.

With daylight having arrived, however, and no sign of any intruders in the area, she and the others descended from the fortress and headed back to the convent. There was little discussion during the walk. Despite the fact that they had all slept, it had not been the most comfortable of nights. She made a mental note to acquire some straw mats for those occasions when she needed to slumber up there.

She could have just used her key to open the door, but decided that just marching in with two strangers wouldn't be the wisest thing to do. So she knocked on the door and waited for the Magistar to answer. Moments later the door opened and the Magistar looked in confusion at the people standing behind Robyne.

"I've brought company," said Robyne.

The Magistar looked in bewilderment at Clarence. "Why is he wearing a helmet?"

In response, Clarence reached up and removed his helmet.

She studied him for a moment, her face betraying no reaction, and then she said, "Good choice." She stepped back and gestured for them to enter, which they did. Clarence reflexively started to put the helmet back on, but Robyne rested a hand on his forearm and shook her head slightly. He actually smiled at that. He had a nice smile.

Minutes later they were seated around the map table in the study. Clarence was sipping a cup of tea while Innis was downing her second stein of beer.

"They need somewhere to stay," said Robyne.

"I suspected as much. Well, we certainly have sufficient space here."

"This is a convent, yes?" said Clarence. "May I ask…where are the nuns who once worshipped here?"

"I killed them all," said the Magistar.

Innis Rae nodded approvingly. "That's efficient."

"She's joking," Robyne assured her. But then a bit of doubt filtered into her mind and her gaze shifted to the Magistar. "You… *are* joking…?"

The Magistar actually chuckled, which Robyne found unnerving for some reason. "They died of natural causes. Or traveled to Jerusalem. And two got pregnant."

"She's still jok—" Robyne began to reply, but then she saw the Magistar shake her head slightly and immediately fell silent.

"In any event, I have several cells that could accommodate you. They are rather plain, of course, but I'm sure they will suffice."

Clarence pondered that for a moment and then said, "If you have some sort of cellar, I would prefer to reside there. I think it's wiser if I stay out of sight."

"You *all* need to stay out of sight," Robyne said firmly.

This pronouncement immediately angered Innis Rae, who was already on a short fuse. "What, you mean I'm supposed to hide here?"

"Lord Collins's men are certainly looking for you," Robyne reminded her.

It was clear that Innis Rae required no reminders. Instead she thudded the table with her fist so violently that it almost caused Clarence's cup of tea to up end. He managed to catch it before it tipped over and spilled. "Let them find me! Let them bring me to him! Ah'll kill him with muh bare hands and dispatch his bastard lackey, Henry, as well!"

"Unless they kill you from ten feet away with an arrow."

Her voice softened slightly. "Then ah'll be with muh husband."

The Magistar shook her head. "No, you won't. You won't be cavorting in some fictional heaven. You'll be rotting in an unmarked grave somewhere and you'll never get your revenge."

"How do ye know ah seek vengeance?"

"You're a friend of hers," said the Magistar, nodding toward Robyne.

Robyne and Innis Rae exchanged looks, and then nodded in unison. Innis Rae's response of "That's fair" overlapped with Robyne's "Makes sense."

Then Innis Rae continued, "But ah still can't just sit here on my arse for days, weeks on end." She looked at Clarence. "What about ye?"

"Actually," said Clarence with a small smile, "it would be nice to have some peace for a time. Provide me with books and I shall keep myself amused."

Innis Rae found that statement funny and did nothing to hide her reaction. "He reads," she said to Robyne, snickering a bit. "Figures."

"*I* read," Robyne said.

That received a startled reaction from Innis Rae. "Seriously?"

"Seriously. If you want, I could teach you."

"Reading is for poets and ribbon clerks," Innis Rae said dismissively.

"Really? Do I strike you as either?"

Innis Rae had no response to that, and the Magistar wasn't inclined to sit around and wait for her to come up with one. "Come with me," she said authoritatively.

She took her into a back room and sat her in a chair. Then she went to work on Innis Rae's copious hair. She unbraided it until it was fully unleashed, cascading down the chair. "How attached are you to your hair?" she asked.

"Ah'm not attached t'anything anymore," she said with a slightly mournful air.

"Good," said the Magistar and, producing a pair of scissors, she went to work. She cut vigorously and rigorously until it was trimmed to just under over her shoulders. Then she left the room and moments later returned with a bottle filled with some black liquid.

Innis Rae regarded it suspiciously. "Am I supposed to drink that?"

"My God, you're an idiot," retorted the Magistar. "Just sit there and be quiet."

She proceeded to upend the black liquid into Innis Rae's hair. Innis Rae began to protest but was pre-empted by a brisk "Shut up" from the Magistar. Normally she would never tolerate being addressed in such a manner, but for some reason she sat there and took it from the Magistar.

Some time later Robyne, who had grown bored waiting outside, walked in just as the Magistar was finishing toweling dry Innis Rae's hair. It was now short and black, an excellent disguise for anyone looking for a long haired red-head. "Excellent," said Robyne.

Clarence was standing just behind her and was studying Innis Rae critically. "Her clothing remains rather distinctive, though."

"I have that covered," said the Magistar confidently.

She forced Robyne and Clarence to return to the study and there they remained, sitting in silent communion, until they heard an outraged yell from Innis Rae. They exchanged puzzled looks and then the Magistar entered the study. Innis Rae did not follow her out. "Come out here! Show them!" the Magistar shouted.

"No! Ah look ridiculous!"

Robyne had little patience for the back and forth. "Just get it over with! Get out here!"

There was silence for a long moment and then slowly Innis Rae walked into the room. She was dressed head to toe in a nun's habit. Furthermore she was wearing spectacles.

Robyne and Clarence managed to keep themselves together for several seconds and then they couldn't contain it any longer: they erupted in laughter.

Innis Rae rolled her eyes.

CHAPTER X

I should have taught you better

The Reconquista has come to Saragossa, the capital of Aragon in Spain.

The reason for the Reconquista is simple: Moors and Muslims have inhabited much of the Iberian peninsula for several centuries, and Christians have decided they want it back. Fortunately enough, in later centuries, hatred toward the Muslims would fade and rulers would cease to harass them. But this is not that age.

The local kings have formed alliances with some Englishmen who opted to aid them in their endeavors, rather than join Lionheart on yet another one of his endless crusades, and the wealth and treasure that's been accrued has made it worth their while. Now those troops are stampeding through Saragossa, sending the dwellers screaming and running for their lives.

Bahja peers out the door of her small house, urging her young daughter, Khalida, to stay back. Her husband calls to her, telling her to withdraw into the relative safety of the domicile, but she does not. She is transfixed, watching in horror. The soldiers are cutting down people, and yes, those people are attacking, but they are armed with shovels and farming implements, not weapons. They are neither soldiers nor battlers. They are simple people who are desperately fighting for their lives, and they are, to the man, losing.

Her husband comes forward, grabs her, and tries to slam the door. But a large, gloved hand prevents him from doing so. There is a sizable white man keeping the door open, and he is shouting at her husband in some language she cannot understand. Her husband has no intention of letting the man into the house and continues to shove the door as hard as he can. He is unsuccessful in doing so as the man violently throws the door open, knocking her husband to the ground.

Quickly he scrambles to his feet and grabs the only implement that he can possibly use as a weapon: a small trowel. It is a laughable mismatch. The intruder is wielding a broadsword; her husband has no chance.

But he is operating on behalf of his family, desperate to save them. He lunges forward with the trowel and the soldier knocks it aside with one hand and brings his sword whipping around with the other. It slams into his midsection and Bahja screams as she sees her husband pitch forward. He whispers something to her that she cannot hear and she watches in horror as the light vanishes from his eyes.

Khalida cries out and runs to her father. Unable to grasp that he is dead, she keeps shouting for him to stand, to get to his feet and make this very bad man go away. He does not respond, of course, his soul departed. The concerns of mortals are still prevailing for his widow and now fatherless child, though.

Bahja wants to attack the man, to assault him with her bare fingernails and try to inflict damage upon him. She knows, however, that is a useless undertaking. He will no doubt cut her down as ruthlessly as he did her husband, and then what of her child? Khalida would be an orphan with no means of defending herself. He would kill her, or enslave her, or worse.

And then she sees the way he is regarding her. There is clear, obvious lust in his eyes. So he is a man, like other men. The thoughts of how she and her daughter can survive immediately flitter through her mind, and even as she cringes, she realizes it is the only way.

Slowly, very slowly, she drops to her knees and bows her head. Khalida stands there, confused, unsure of just why her mother is being so subservient to the monster that just killed her father, and is even more bewildered when her mother tugs on her arm, indicating she should follow suit. The entire notion is anathema to the child, but she does as she is instructed and kneels at her mother's side.

Thus it was that they entered the service of Lord Wilford.

———«———»———

Bahja stood with her back against the wall, her customary place, as Wilford spoke with the man who had brought a woman to breakfast. At first Bahja thought that it was a corpse. She couldn't fathom why in Allah's name he would have been so delighted over the presentation of a corpse unless it was the body of an enemy. And this was just some slight girl. What possible threat should she have posed to Wilford? Then she saw a slow rise and fall of the girl's chest and realized that she was still alive, although the large purple bruise on her skull indicated she'd likely be suffering from a severe headache when she woke up.

Khalida was just moving away from the table to return to her mother's side, and that was when Bahja suddenly felt something in her belly.

It was a kick. From within.

Her eyes widened in horror and for a moment she considered the possibility that she was imagining it. She had remained barren for some years and had assumed that Khalida was the only child with which she was to be blessed. Considering who the man was that was screwing her, she had been grateful. Now, though, she felt a movement that she had not expected ever to feel again. When it had been the first kicks of Khalida, she had been filled with such joy, such wonderment. It was sixteen years after that memorable event, but the pure delight from that sensation remained with her to this very day. This latest sensation, however, filled her with the exact opposite sensations. She felt violently ill. If she could have vomited up the creature, the monster that was taking up residence in her belly, she would have done so.

———«———»———

Khalida glanced at her mother and saw the distress in her eyes. She noticed her hand hovering around her belly and whispered out of the side of her mouth, "Stomach ache?"

Her mother managed a brief nod and forced a smile. "Nothing. It will pass. Can you cover for me? I feel…unwell."

That was not a problem for Khalida. Normally Bahja was the one who would clean up after Lord Wilford, but Khalida was happy to step in. If her mother needed a bit of time to herself, Khalida would provide it for her. That was not an issue.

Her mother nodded, patted her on the shoulder, and then slipped away.

Khalida remained where she was as Wilford dictated to the messenger exactly what he wanted the message to say and he scribbled it quickly on a note. It managed, momentarily, to take her mind off her mother. Something was wrong. Bahja was never especially good at covering her emotions, that much Khalida knew all too well. So if she had hied herself up the stairs, there must have been something that was disturbing her. It was just a matter of determining what it was.

Once the messenger had departed, Wilford finished his breakfast and did not bother to sit and wait for anyone to come clear away the dishes. Khalida was grateful for that. He summoned his weapons bearer and had his sword strapped on. Clearly he was going to engage in his weekly ritual of hunting, and he always brought a sword with him in the event that some massive beast endeavored to engage him. He and his men exited the room and Khalida cleared up the leftovers, glad that he had departed. She brought them into the kitchen and left them to be cleaned. She glanced briefly at her place on the floor, the thin straw mat where she curled up at night and endeavored to sleep. She had lost track of the number of times that she had attempted to slumber and just lay there, staring up at the ceiling and dreaming of the life that had been lost to her years ago. Then she managed to shake it off and refocus on checking in on her mother.

She had no idea whence her mother had gone, and it took her long minutes to finally locate her upstairs. She was in, of all places, Lord Wilford's bed chambers. She was standing near a window, gazing out at the forest that ran to the edge of the property, and did not even turn to acknowledge Khalida's entrance.

Khalida shut the door behind her. Now she knew something was definitely wrong. Her mother was always very aware of the world around her and her lack of response to Khalida's arrival was very much out of character. "What's wrong?" she asked.

In a sad voice, she said, "I should have taught you better."

"Taught me?"

"Trained you better. To defend yourself."

"I've learned plenty," Khalida assured her.

And she had.

—« »—

She has resided in the castle for some months and not a day goes by that she does not despise it.

The one thing that she and her mother have managed to accomplish is to learn the language these bastards speak. It is called "English" and it is a massive tie of internal contradictions. She has managed to wade through it and can generally understand it when it is being spoken to her. Being able to engage in conversation is somewhat more challenging, but she is learning and will continue to learn. Because really, what other choice does she have?

She is hauling a bucket of water to the horse trough that is situated in the courtyard. It is quite heavy and consequently liquid is splashing up and over the sides, but she does her best to keep it under control. She ignores the squires who are training with the maestro in the courtyard. To call them "squires" might not be exactly correct. They are the sons of various soldiers who work for Lord Wilford and he has the maestro work with them to teach them fighting skills.

The maestro. That is the name that Khalida calls him in her head. She has no idea what his real name is. All she knows is what she sees with her own eyes: He is a Moor, just as she is. But he is tall, extremely well built, with a head bereft of hair and a cold, implacable manner about him that indicates it would be an extremely bad idea to fight him. Not that Khalida would ever do such a thing. She is determined to keep her head down and not be noticed.

Not like Wilford had noticed her mother.

She thinks briefly about the times that her mother has been pulled away, brought to Lord Wilford's chambers. About the things that happen there she cannot imagine, nor does she want to. She shakes the images out of her mind and finishes pouring in the water.

The two boys are battling with wooden swords as the maestro watches them, correcting their moves, describing different offensive and defensive moves. One of them is moving faster than the other, and he successfully manages to send his battle mate's sword flying. It angles through the air and lands at Khalida's feet.

She stares down at it and then picks it up. She whips it from side to side as she had seen the boys doing, deflecting imagined assaults.

The boy whose sword it is stomps toward her, clearly irritated that she is even touching it, much less swinging it around in imagined swordplay. "Give it here, you little shite!" he snarls.

And she snaps.

It is most unexpected. She has endured the loss of her home, her freedom, her mother's unthinkable humiliation with as much restraint as she possibly can. Something about this boy cursing her out, though, pushes her over an edge at which she did not even realize she was standing. Without even thinking about it, she swings the sword around with such force and fury that—when it strikes the boy in the skull—he goes down like the proverbial ton of bricks.

The boy who disarmed him roars in fury and charges straight at her with his sword. He whips it around, determined to disarm her as he had done the other boy.

She ducks, the blade passing right over her head, and she jabs her sword forward. It strikes the boy in the gut, knocking the air out of him, and he staggers backward, momentarily confused over what happened. He recovers quickly, though, and launches an assault.

Khalida doesn't budge an inch. She has observed combat any number of times, and all the moves, all the parrying and thrusting, have settled into her mind and provided her with guidance. She does not have the skill to stand up to a fully trained knight in battle, not to mention the lack of bodily power. But she resolutely doesn't give any leeway to the boy who is assaulting her now. She blocks him, deflects him, waits for an opening and bangs the blade into his chest. He staggers, howling in pain, rubbing his chest to ease it.

Then he attacks once more, but he is blinded by pure fury. He has forgotten one of the most frequent lessons his teacher has endeavored to drill into him: Never become angry during a battle. It makes you sloppy. It makes you vulnerable.

It immediately costs him. Khalida sidesteps and, as he charges past her, knocks the sword out of his hand. He cries out in alarm as it bounces away and before he can react, she drives her knee into his guts. Down goes the boy, his arms clutched around his stomach, and he vomits his lunch onto the ground. Khalida watches it and for the first time in an age, she smiles. It is a cold and frightening thing to see, and only one person does.

That is when Khalida's feet suddenly leave the ground.

She tries to bring the sword around, but it is slapped out of her hand as if she were not holding it with her firmest grip. She is then turned around and finds herself staring right into the maestro's face. There is cold fury in his eyes and he draws her close, bringing her left ear directly to his mouth.

And he whispers, "Be back here tonight after supper."

Then he drops her to the ground and roars, "And don't you forget it!"

She is unsure what has just happened, but she's not about to question it. She manages to nod and then scampers away, remembering at the last moment to grab the bucket that she brought the water in. The two boys are still on the ground, one rubbing his head, the other still moaning and holding his gut.

Later Khalida returns as instructed. The maestro is waiting for her. He stares down at her and says, "What experience do you have in combat?"

"None," she says.

"I thought as much. You are already formidable. With some training, you can be unbeatable."

"That would be nice." She gazes up at him and sees a bit of her father in him. *"My name is Khalida."*

"Good for you." He hands her a wooden sword. *"Now do precisely as I do."*

She does. Month after month, year after year, until she is wielding a metal sword as effortlessly as the wooden one.

He never does tell her his name.

———— «   »————

"I've learned plenty," Khalida repeats, to herself as much as to her mother.

Her mother, though, is not listening to her. Her full focus is on the outside. "Every time Lord Wilford takes me, I never fight back. He said if I did, he'd kill you. I had to protect you."

"I know," says Khalida. For a moment she is nostalgic for the days when she was a child and did not have a truly clear idea of what was happening when Wilford availed himself of her mother. Now she knew, of course, and could only wish that she did not. "Sometimes I...I heard you. If I was walking past here. Heard him. He wasn't...subtle."

"Subtle?" Bahja snorts. "He was proud of it. And I endured it all for you." She shook her head. "You think that there is only so much you can withstand, but it turns out you have so much more endurance than you know. But then you come to a point where you reach your limit." She turned and gazed at Khalida. "I'm with his child."

Khalida's jaw dropped. "Are...are you sure?"

Bahja nodded. "I felt it stirring in my belly this morning. That bastard's bastard is growing within me. And I can't...I just...I just can't..." Then her voice dropped to a whisper as she said, "I'm so sorry."

She stepped up onto the window ledge.

Khalida screamed, *"No! Wait!"*

"I love you," her mother said so softly it was barely audible, and then she stepped through.

Khalida howled her name, but she was already gone. She didn't even scream during her descent, as if she welcomed it. Khalida heard a distant thud and the outcry of people from below, but she couldn't bring herself to look as she sank to the floor. Tears poured from her eyes, running down her face, an endless flow of them.

She cried until she stopped.

And she never cried again.

———«　»———

The funeral had been very quick and very minimal.

Since she was an impoverished servant, her mother didn't rate a resting place. Instead a pyre was constructed for her and she was tossed onto it.

The smell triggered memories for Khalida. She remembered as a child when the soldiers had stormed through her city, and they had clutched torches in their hands. They set buildings and people aflame, uncaring, laughing. The stench of burning meat seared itself into her memory, no matter how far down she had endeavored to bury it. Standing there, watching her mother burn, had brought it all back to her. No tears, however, appeared. She had cried all the tears she needed to in her life. She had nothing left to sob over.

Now she had retired to her mat in the kitchen and curled up in a ball, her arms wrapped around her knees that were drawn up nearly to her chin. The other servants steered clear of her since she was obviously not interested in the slightest bit in interacting with anyone. They could understand why. The girl was now an orphan, her mother having killed herself for no reason that anyone could discern. No point in speaking to the girl about it.

A pair of legs strode up to her. She didn't bother to glance up, figuring that whoever it was would know enough to leave her the hell alone. As it turned out, she was wrong.

"Why did she do it?"

She glanced up and of course, of course it was Lord Wilford. He was standing there with his hand resting on the pommel of his sword. "Why?" he insisted.

Khalida shook her head and shrugged. She wasn't the slightest bit interested in speaking to anyone, least of all him.

"There must have been a reason."

Once more she shook her head. She hoped that eventually he would tire of asking and just leave her alone.

He tilted his head, studied her, appraised her. "You know, you look so much like she did when I first took her. Perhaps you'll do. I'll see how I like you."

She had absolutely no idea what he was talking about, but she found out very quickly. He reached down, grabbed her by the wrist, and hauled her to her feet. Then he drew her to him and kissed her roughly.

His breath stank of beer and rot that originated from his teeth. The contents of her stomach roiled in revulsion as he shoved his tongue against hers.

Her eyes darted and she saw a skillet sitting on a counter near her. Her hand speared out and she grabbed it. It felt heavy. *Good.*

Wilford never saw it coming as she whipped it around and brought it crushingly into the side of his head. Its sonorous *clang* echoed through the kitchen and he staggered from the impact. She brought it around a second time, and whereas the first blow had been glancing because their faces were in such close contact, the second one took him squarely. He went down, thudding heavily to the kitchen floor.

Khalida screamed in an absolute rage and she kept bringing the skillet down, again and again. The first two shots had been enough to scramble his brain, but she didn't care. The image of her mother standing there, looking lost, stepping out the window to her death, echoed in her mind and she kept hitting Wilford even though he stopped moving.

She stared down at him. He wasn't dead. His eyes were gazing listlessly up at her, trying to focus, and his eyes were the only part of his head that weren't soaked in blood. His breath was rasping in his throat.

She reached down and yanked his sword from its scabbard. She liked the heft of it. It was very well balanced. "You wanted to see how you like me? How do you like this? She killed herself because she was pregnant with your child! *Take that to the grave!*"

She drove the sword directly into his chest. His eyes went wide, he gurgled loudly as blood seeped out of his mouth, and then his soul left his body and made a swift departure for the bowels of hell.

I killed him, mother. I killed the bastard. Rest in peace.

The back door to the kitchen banged and the maestro strode in. "What's..." His voice trailed off as the answer was splayed in front of him.

Khalida made no move. The sword was still quivering in Wilford's chest. There was no point in denying what she had done, and why should she? She was proud of it. They were doubtless going to execute her; there wouldn't even be a trial. Fine. Her mother's soul was only recently gone; she would be able to catch up to her in no time.

For a long moment, the maestro said nothing. And then he spoke three words and only three words:

"Get out. Now."

Part of her couldn't believe it, but the rest of her could. Obviously the maestro's loyalty was far more to her than it was to the former master of the castle.

She yanked the sword clear of Wilford's chest and her expression hardened. "Not alone," she said.

—«　»—

The French girl lay on the floor, stared up at the ceiling, and contemplated just ending it all.

The notion certainly made a degree of sense. The fall out the window would be terminal, that much was definite, but perhaps that would be worth it. Her life of endless pursuit, of eternal mourning, would finally be ended, and she could rest in peace in the arms of the Lord.

And her child...

Her child would never know his mother.

She shook her head, despising the notion. If she ended it all, then the bastards would win, and she simply could not tolerate that eventuality. She had to do something more. She just couldn't determine what yet.

That was when she heard a loud "ka-chunk" noise coming from the door. It was being unlocked from the outside.

She scrambled to her feet, ready to launch an assault. She knew that it would likely be useless. They weren't stupid enough to open the door, unprepared for her to undertake an escape attempt. There would likely be a dozen guards with swords and spears bristling, ready to dispatch her if she made even the slightest endeavor to attack them. Nevertheless, she had one advantage over them. She knew that they wanted her alive, while she would not hesitate to kill any of them that she could get her hands on.

The door swung open and she froze in utter astonishment.

A Moorish young woman was standing there, all by herself. She had a sword in one hand, and the French girl saw that it was still tinged with blood. In the other hand, she was holding the girl's morning star.

"We're leaving," she said. "I thought you might need this." Despite the weapon's weight, she tossed it effortlessly to the French girl, who snatched it out of the air and grinned lopsidedly.

"We're leaving...with their lack of approval, I assume?"

"Very much so," said the Moor. "Let's go."

—« »—

Khalida had no idea who the young French girl was beyond the fact that the late Lord Wilford had been exceedingly pleased to have captured her. That was all the incentive she required to spring her from her captivity. The girl seemed rather slight and not threatening, but Bowles had said she killed two of his men, so there was obviously more to her than there appeared to be.

They were heading down the long, winding steps that led to the bottom floor and escape, and that was when Khalida heard the sounds of feet stomping up the stairs, and shouted voices cautioning the approaching men to be careful. It was obvious what had happened. Wilford's body had been discovered, and they were going in pursuit of his killer.

She'd killed a man.

That truth echoed within her mind. She had killed the lord and master of the castle. Certainly she deserved to be punished for that. Her mother had always taught her that life was sacred...

Her mother, who had so despised the life growing within her that she had ended her own rather than allow it to develop and be born.

To hell with that. Wilford had deserved to die, and she would not spend one moment more regretting it.

She braced herself for the onslaught of men who were going to be in the way between her and freedom, but as it turned out, she didn't have the opportunity.

The guards came around the bend, one of the largest in the lead. But before Khalida could do anything, the French girl let out a horrific battle cry and charged directly into the fray. Just as a lion's roar momentarily paralyzes its prey, so do did the girl's howl bring the charging guards to a halt, and that was all the opportunity she required. She viciously swung her morning star and the mace crunched the lead guard's face. He staggered backwards and slammed into the guard directly behind him, and the second guard into the third. Like living dominos the row of half a dozen attackers collapsed one onto the other.

That was all the opportunity the girl needed as she leaped forward and landed on the prostrate form of the lead guard and slid down their bodies as if she were riding a slide. Khalida followed right behind her, and all the men could do was grunt as the young women's bodies passed right over them.

That was all that was required for them to attain the bottom of the stairs. A corridor stretched in front of them, and Khalida—who knew every foot of the castle all too well—gestured for the French girl to follow her.

Then their way was blocked.

It was Bowles, the man who Khalida had last seen delivering the unconscious French girl to Wilford in the first place. He had his sword out and a sneer on his face.

"Richard is on his way, you French slut," he said. "You can't get away."

"*Va te faire foutre,*" the girl snarled in response. Khalida had no idea what it meant, but she suspected it wasn't complimentary.

Once more, the fact that Bowles was trying not to kill her served in her favor. Her assault was non-stop as she came straight at him, swinging the morning star with rising fury. Bowles kept blocking the attacks with his sword, but he couldn't genuinely put together an offense. Perhaps he was hoping that she would tire herself out and he would be able to knock her unconscious again.

That wasn't what happened. Instead when she struck his sword for the tenth time, to his utter shock, the blade snapped off. He was left only with a very short blade and a hilt, and that was useless in a battle.

She swung the mace around, aiming it at his head, and for half a second it seemed as if his life was at its end. At the last second, however, the head of the mace stopped scant inches from his skull. She stood there, the morning star quivering in her grasp.

"When you see Richard," she warned him, "tell him I'm coming for him next."

Then she let the morning star drop to her side and she swung her right fist around. It impacted with his head and he collapsed unconscious to the floor.

Khalida heard the sounds of the guards behind them clambering to their feet. She grabbed the French girl by the arm and said, "Time to go." She nodded in response and the two of them sprinted toward the castle's exit.

There were two sentinels posted outside and they were stunned when they saw Khalida and the French girl sprint out through the gate. Immediately they endeavored to go in pursuit, but they had no chance. They were wearing heavy leather armor and were weighted down by broadswords hanging on their hips. The girls were unencumbered and light of foot. So it was that the men's attempts to overtake the girls utterly failed and within minutes the girls had vanished into the forest.

—« »—

Bowles was not happy when he came around.

"*You let them get away!*" he bellowed at the apologetic sentinels.

"They were moving too quickly," one of the guards began to explain.

Bowles didn't want to hear it. He swung his hand around and struck the guard in the side of the head, knocking him to the floor. "We have to find her! Richard is coming to get her and we're not about to greet him with a castle devoid of that girl's presence! I found her once, I can find her again!"

It was at that moment that the deep rumble of thunder sounded from overhead and lightning crackled across the sky.

"Shite," said Bowles with a groan.

And rain began to cascade. It poured for some hours, obliterating any tracks the women might have left behind them and cleansing their scents as well.

They were gone.

CHAPTER XI

Bless you, my child, for time and eternity

HENRY WAS SEATED AT HIS DESK when Basil burst into the room. There was huge excitement on his face. If he had witnessed Christ descending from on high in a chariot being drawn by unicorns, he could not have appeared more thrilled.

"What in the world is—?"

"The king is coming!" said Basil, his voice throbbing with anticipation.

"Which king? *The* king?"

"Lionheart himself. A messenger just arrived." He dropped into the chair that sat opposite Henry. "He's going to be stopping at Sir Wilford's castle and then coming here to see Lord Collins. Father, it's so exciting..."

"Yes. Yes, it is," said Henry. But there was a serious lack of enthusiasm in his voice.

That did not go unnoticed by Basil. "You don't sound excited." He sounded disappointed.

Henry shrugged. "I'm older. I remain reserved."

His reserve did not remotely rub off on Basil. "I'm going to go tell Drogo," he said with obvious enthusiasm.

"Yes, you do that," said Henry, and Basil was immediately out the door.

Although Henry appreciated Basil's attitude, he knew exactly why he didn't share it and it had nothing to do with his seniority.

The fact of the matter was that Richard was notoriously unpredictable. He could be singing your praises one moment and cutting you to pieces with his long sword the next. The fact that he was nicknamed "Lionheart" was very apt, because he really did have the heart and attitude of a lion. But it had nothing to do with bravery and everything to do with the fact that he saw the world in a predator/prey manner. Richard had no friends, no loyalty, save to his own causes. Nor did he have the slightest regard for human life. Granted, it might have seemed that, as a killer himself, Henry had no moral grounds upon which to stand in judgment on another person's priorities. Richard, though, lived in his own environment and it was a deadly place in which to reside. At the slightest whim, he could decide that someone didn't deserve to live and would dispose of them immediately.

And that could very well include Henry, Basil and even Lord Collins if he was in the mood.

"This will not end well," he muttered.

⸺«　»⸺

Innis Rae had to admit, she found it interesting.

Her life in Scotland had been far more makeshift than what she was seeing in Nottingham. She'd never resided in a city, growing up in the highlands where she had lived a very nomadic life. It seemed that enemies were constantly nipping at the heels of her extended family, and they tended to move around a good deal. Here, though, was a town where everyone was sedentary. People lived here, had their businesses here, interacted with each other. Business was as likely to be done through bartering rather than exchanging money. Passersby were browsing at various shops, buying everything from foodstuffs to articles of clothing. It all seemed very charming.

And everyone greeted her.

It's because they think you're a nun, you idiot, she thought, and she knew she was right. She had to admit, the Magistar had been absolutely right about disguising her in clerical fashion. People nodded to her, greeted her. The best moment, though, came when she was startled to see two of the guards whom she had escaped striding toward her. She was sure that she was going to find herself in a battle, right in the middle of the village. But instead they walked right past her. One of them glanced at her, nodded in acknowledgement of her, and kept going. They hadn't seen her face; they had just seen her vestments and assumed she was what she was pretending to be. It had been a truly inspired idea.

Not that Innis Rae would ever admit it.

Still, she felt detached. That was a problem, because Innis Rae was typically a very sociable woman. Everyone else was living in the world around her, but she was living inside the habit. She seemed cut off from everyone else. They didn't see her, just a holy sister. Which, she supposed, was useful considering the way the soldiers had just walked past her. Still, every upside had a downside, and she figured she was just going to have to get past herself and accept her new status. *It's just temporary. Once I put paid to Henry, I can return home...*

...to what?

She had, after all, deserted her people. She had joined with Lewis and left her family and few friends behind. They had not taken it at all well. If she came back to them, she'd likely have to grovel just to gain acceptance, and if there was one thing Innis Rae was not especially accomplished at, it was groveling.

So if she did avenge Lewis's death...then what?

She honestly did not have the slightest idea, and decided not to dwell on it lest she get a headache as a result.

She sauntered over to the bakery stand where Robyne was just finishing up with a customer. Innis Rae had trouble understanding how it was that Robyne could engage in such a pointless job during the day. Robyne was an adventurer, a fighter, a warrior. Why waste time pretending she was like everyone else? It just made no sense. Still, she figured that it wasn't her place to question it.

Robyne glanced up at her as the customer wandered away. "So

what do you think of our village?"

Innis Rae shrugged. "It's adequate, but ah still feel out of place here."

Then something caught her attention.

There were two young teens and they were laughing and sneering and jeering. The object of their derision was readily apparent. It was a small boy, and the poor child was deformed. His upper lip was cleft, a sizable opening exposing his gum and teeth. He had long brown hair that was partly covering his eyes, but she could see how hurt he was by the boys' words.

"Freak!" shouted the taller one. His friend declared, "You should've been put down at birth." The boy tried to back up, to get away from them, but the taller boy reached forward and shoved him. The boy cried out as he fell backwards, hitting the ground so hard that Innis Rae could feel it. He tried to get up, but the taller boy then kicked him, knocking him back.

Then the taller boy drew back his fist to strike the boy, and suddenly discovered that he couldn't. An iron grip had wrapped itself around his wrist, immobilizing it.

Innis Rae thrust her head forward into the boy's line of vision and when she spoke, her Scots accent was gone. Instead she had an immaculate British accent. "Apologize," she said.

If the boy was intimidated by a threatening nun, he didn't show it. "I'm not gonna apologize t—"

She didn't bother to wait for him to complete the sentence. She twisted his arm back and around, and she was pleased to hear an anguished shriek of pain. All his resistance melted away as he cried out, "I'm sorry! *I'm sorry!*"

Her glare shifted to the other boy, who was standing there paralyzed in shock. She didn't even have to give him an order. He immediately reached out and helped the boy to his feet. "Sorry, yes! Me too! So sorry!"

The boy retaliated by kicking him in the shin. He didn't have much strength in his leg and it probably didn't hurt very much, but the point was made.

It was at that point that the boy's mother came running toward them. Seeing what was happening, it was clear that she had figured out what the teens had been up to. Furthermore it was clear from her expression that she blamed herself for letting her son get out from under her personal supervision.

"Thank you! Thank you, sister!" she cried out, dropping to her knees and embracing the child. By that point the teens had fled the scene, one of them rubbing the arm that Innis Rae had twisted back.

"It was not a problem," said Innis Rae.

She started to turn away and then the mother said, "I…I don't know why God made my son like this, but…could you bless him?"

That stopped Innis Rae in her tracks. Slowly she turned around, stared at the child, and then sank down to one knee to put herself at eye level. She reached over to him, placed a hand on the top of his head, and intoned, "May almighty God, Father, Son, and Holy Spirit, bless you my child for time and eternity, and may this blessing remain forever with you." Then, to punctuate it, she kissed him on the forehead.

"Thank you," said the boy's mother. "Thank you."

Innis Rae made the sign of the cross over the child's breast. "*Pax vobiscum,*" she intoned.

The mother and her boy then hastened away, even as she scolded her son—albeit gently—about going off by himself and getting into trouble. Innis Rae then strolled back over to Robyne, who was staring at her with wide eyes. "Maybe ah do have a place here," she said, returning to her Scots brogue.

"You can affect a British accent?" said a clearly surprised Robyne.

"Ah figured it was better than for word t'get around that a Scots nun just showed up outta nowhere."

"And how did you know that blessing?"

"What, did ye think I was just some brainless, know-nothing Scots warrior?"

Robyne considered the question and then had to admit, "Well…yes, to be honest."

"Well, now ye know something different."

Robyne laughed.

⸺ « » ⸺

She was surprised that she had laughed. Robyne realized that it had been quite some time since she had done so. She wondered if she should be concerned about that.

Indeed, she was beginning to wonder about a lot of things.

With the day of business having come to an end, Robyne and Innis Rae were walking back to the convent. They were speaking idly about random things, but Robyne's mind wasn't really on any of it. Instead she was dwelling upon the broader aspects of what was happening.

The little girl that she had been the day her father died and mother disappeared…she was long gone. That child's hopes, dreams and desires had been killed along with her father. To this day she still carried copious amounts of guilt with her, and nary a night's sleep went by where her thoughts did not take her back to that moment. In each dream, the same thing happened. She was there, watching the battle, but she had managed to hide herself so that her father didn't spot her. Undistracted by his daughter, Robin had managed to dispatch the Sheriff. Because that was how his long enmity with the Sheriff was supposed to end: with the hero winning. Not being interfered with by his daughter.

In her early days, she would wake up sobbing and the Magistar would comfort her, would repeatedly tell her that she was being too hard on herself. Robyne could never accept that, but rather than coming around to the Magistar's point of view, she trained herself to keep it all in. The Magistar had, over the years, come to believe her when she said that she had slumbered soundly and the dreams had stopped haunting her.

Or perhaps not. Perhaps she knew Robyne was lying to her and she just allowed it. It was hard to predict what the Magistar knew or did not know. Even after all her years with her, she knew so very little about her. She never spoke about her past. Hell, she didn't even know the Magistar's real name. "I forget," was the only response she had ever gotten.

Her mind was wandering. She'd been thinking about how she had changed, and instead her thoughts had drifted to the Magistar. That was annoying. She should be able to stay focused.

"What's on yuir mind?" asked Innis Rae.

"Hmm?"

"Ah've been talking and ye aren't responding. Ye're obviously thinking about something else. What?"

"Nothing important." She immediately switched gears to the first thing she noticed as she pointed at Innis Rae's glasses. "How do you see out of those things?"

"It's clear glass."

That wasn't what she had expected. "Why does the Magistar have clear glasses?"

"Oh, *that's* the only question ye have about her?"

They had reached the convent and Robyne pushed open the door.

A huge guardsman within whirled to face her. He had an insignia of a lion upon his tunic that Robyne didn't recognize. His hand rested upon the pommel of his sword as if he was anticipating an attack.

"The hell—?!" Immediately Robyne's hand went for her sword, and then she realized she wasn't wearing it. She was in her ordinary civilian clothes, not the outfit of Robyne of Sherwood.

My God, they've figured out who I am. They've captured the Magistar. We're all going to wind up on the gallows.

"Let them through," a voice boomed loudly from within. The authority of it was unmistakable and the guard immediately got out of their path.

They entered, passing more guards along the way. They didn't make eye contact with them, even though the guards were clearly studying them suspiciously as if concerned they were going to produce daggers out of nowhere and launch an assault. Which, in fairness, Robyne would have done if she'd been armed.

They moved past them and entered the Magistar's study. There was a bearded man sitting there, his chin thick with a blondish/gray beard and a look of insufferable smugness on his face. But his eyes glittered cold and cruel.

He was wearing a crown.

Robyne couldn't believe it. She had been expecting Sir Henry, not...

"Lionheart?" Her voice was scarcely above a whisper.

"It is customary to kneel. One knee will suffice," said Richard the Lionheart.

Despite the severity of the situation, Robyne remained standing for a moment. Then she saw the face of the Magistar, who was seated across from him. There was a decided warning in her eyes. *Do it. Now.*

Robyne dropped to one knee. Then she noticed that Innis Rae was still standing. The Scotswoman looked more curious than anything else. Robyne quickly tugged on her wrist to urge her to follow her lead, and it seemed as if Innis Rae was briefly considering holding her upright position. Apparently, though, she thought better of it, and she sank to the floor next to Robyne.

"Much better," said Richard approvingly. "You may rise."

Slowly they did so. Robyne was about to speak and was astounded to discover that no words were coming out. Her throat had constricted. She cleared it and then managed to say, "May... may I ask why you are here, your Majesty?"

He gestured toward the Magistar. "I am simply visiting with my old friend, Theresa.

We've known each other for quite a while, and since I was in the vicinity, I thought I would stop by and reminisce about old times."

The Magistar smiled gamely. "It has been wonderful, Majesty, but I'm sure you have much to do."

"Yes. Yes, indeed. I have a package that is being kept for me and it is time that I recovered it."

He stood then and reached out for her hand. She obediently presented it and he suavely—or at least he likely imagined it to be—kissed it on the knuckles. "Farewell, my dear."

Robyne and Innis Rae remained where they were as the King and his soldiers filed out. For a long moment, nothing was said. Then:

"Ye fucked him, didn't ye?" said Innis Rae.

Robyne couldn't believe it, and made no effort to hide her shock at both Innis Rae's coarse language, and the insinuation that there had been anything physical between the King and the utterly chaste Magistar. "Innis! Are you insane?! She didn't—"

As she spoke her gaze shifted to the Magistar, and she was stunned to see the woman look down and away from her, and some color rose in her typically pale cheeks.

"Oh, sweet Jesu..." she breathed.

The Magistar sighed and when she spoke, she sounded annoyed. "I was young, I was pretty, and he was the damned king."

"Oh my God," said Robyne.

"You thought I was virginal?"

"*Yes!*"

Innis Rae chortled, which irritated Robyne. "Ye just know everything today, don't ye."

"And 'Theresa?' Your name is Theresa? I've known you fifteen years, you never told me that!"

"Names have power. Has it not occurred to you that I lied to Lionheart so he would not have power over me?"

"Fine." Robyne crossed her arms and said sternly, "So what's your name? Really?"

The Magistar opened her mouth and then her body sort of sank. "Theresa," she admitted.

"Fantastic." She paused and then, unable to help herself, asked, "Is there anyone else you've slept with?"

"Oh, yes," said the Magistar. She started to tick them off on her fingers. "Prince John. Charlemagne. Robert the Bruce."

"All right, all right," said Robyne.

"And my night with Julius Caesar..." She whistled at the "recollection."

"Shut up!" said Robyne.

Clarence chose that moment to enter, coming up from the basement. "I was downstairs and it was hard to hear. Was that Richard?"

"Yes," said the Magistar.

"What did he want?"

Innis Rae gestured toward the Magistar. "Visiting his old lover."

"Really?" He cocked an eyebrow. "I don't know whether to think more of you or less."

The Magistar moaned.

CHAPTER XII

Kill them all

THE FRENCH GIRL SAT IN FRONT of a campfire, allowing the warmth of it to wash over her. For the first time in quite a while, she could actually feel her body relaxing. She couldn't recall the last time that had happened.

Suddenly a branch broke in the darkness and that was all that was required to dispel her sense of ease. Instantly she reached toward her morning star, prepared to leap into battle yet again. Fighting was becoming second nature to her. Indeed, she was beginning to believe it was actually her first nature. She had come to love the action of combat. Of using her morning star against her enemies, of proving her power by laying waste to all those who would try to bring her down. It was the only satisfaction she seemed to derive these days.

A dark form emerged from the woods and the girl's breathing returned to normal when she saw it was Khalida. Her hand moved away from her morning star and she dropped back to the ground.

Khalida had been out searching for some animal to kill so they could eat. Considering her hands were empty, it was obvious she had likewise come up empty. "Sorry. Nothing," she said apologetically. "I guess the animals are hiding from us. They don't want to be eaten. Imagine that."

The girl nodded and returned her gaze to the fire. Khalida sat opposite her and studied her with open curiosity. "I heard them speaking about you in the castle. Who are you?"

"Alys," said the French girl. She pronounced it "ah-LEES."

"Yes, but…who *are* you?"

"No one of consequence."

Khalida clearly found that very hard to believe. "Then why is King Richard interested in you?"

Alys shrugged.

"Alys," and she reached out to take Alys's hand. "I'm on your side."

To her surprise, Alys yanked her hand away. "No one is on my side," she said firmly. "Everyone serves themselves."

"That's not true."

"Name me someone who actually cares."

"Robin of Sherwood," she said without hesitation.

Alys looked at her curiously. Obviously to her it had been a rhetorical question; she had not actually expected an answer. "Who?"

"A hero from a decade ago. And now word is there's another one. A woman this time."

"A woman hero?" said Alys in surprise. "There are such things?"

"Apparently so."

"Well, that's good, I suppose. That's good. How did you hear about her?"

"One of the guards in the castle has a brother who was escorting a Scotswoman prisoner to London. He said some green-clad woman came riding up out of nowhere and rescued her." Khalida started warming to the story. "There were about twenty of the guards, and the woman just cut through them all."

"By herself?"

"No, she had a band of women behind her, like half a dozen or so. And they came swooping in with swords and shields and sent the guards running. It must have been glorious," she said with a sigh. "I wish I'd been there."

"As do I."

"Anyway, I'm thinking maybe we can find her. Maybe she can help."

Alys didn't respond. She had withdrawn into herself because the thought of making some serious change to her life was so overwhelming for her that she was having difficulty processing it. She had become so accustomed to the hopelessness of her situation that it was difficult for her to try and move beyond that.

Khalida finally grew impatient waiting for her to reply. "Who *are* you?" she demanded. Something in her voice had changed. She was no longer asking out of curiosity. Instead she was asking so forcefully that Alys drew an inference from it: If she didn't get a response she was satisfied with, she was just going to get up and leave Alys to fend for herself. She had no idea if she was correct in the assessment or not, but she realized that even the prospect of being left alone wasn't appealing to her. She had come to like Khalida. Or perhaps she was just pleased that she had finally encountered someone who was actually willing to help her without desiring anything in return.

She let out a low, haggard breath, and then she spoke. "I'm a young woman whose parents sent her off to be married to a man who didn't want her. He married someone else and now I'm running rather than be sent back to my parents who got me into this situation in the first place. Satisfied?"

Khalida considered it a moment and then said, "Not really."

"I don't care," replied Alys. She was no longer giving any thought to Khalida. She picked up her morning star, clambered to her feet, and threw it as hard and fast as she could. The result was a loud impact as it struck something in the darkness, and a body fell.

Khalida, confused, yanked out her sword and ran toward the place from which the sound had originated. She skidded to a halt when she saw what was splayed on the ground.

It was the corpse of a deer. It lay on the ground, its head shattered, the mace lying next to it on the ground.

Alys picked up her morning star, then reached down to her boot. She produced a dagger from the top of it. The blade glittered in the moonlight as she handed it to Khalida. Khalida stared at it questioningly.

"*I'm* not skinning it," said Alys, and she turned and headed back to the campfire.

Khalida sighed and crouched to get to work.

———— «   »————

King Richard expected to be greeted by Lord Wilford when he and his men strode into the castle. He anticipated that Wilford would come to the gate, and was quite surprised when the lord of the manor failed to do so. He strode forward into the main hall, fully assuming that Wilford would be there with some sort of explanation as to why he had failed to present himself.

Instead, to his surprise, all the servants and guards were there, having dropped to one knee with their heads lowered. One guard in particular seemed to be dominating the scene, having positioned himself so that he was at the front of the group. Richard strode up to him and gazed down upon him.

"Where is Wilford?" he said. He did not give everyone leave to stand, as he customarily did.

The soldier closest to him, keeping his head lowered, said, "He is dead, your Majesty."

"Dead? Who are you?"

"I'm Bowles. I served him."

"How did he die, Bowles?"

"A female servant killed him."

Richard liked to think that he managed to face the world with a certain degree of aplomb. That he took bad news in stride and never allowed others to discern what was going through his mind. Nevertheless, this was an instance where that was simply not an option for him. The news rocked him so thoroughly that his jaw dropped open upon hearing it. "A female?" He could scarcely conceive it. Women existed to keep house affairs in order and provide and care for children. That was the extent of their involvement with the world. The notion that one would be able to dispose of a warrior such as Wilford...

"How did she do it? Did she poison him? That's it, isn't it. Did something to his food or drink."

Bowles shook his head. "No, Majesty. As near as we can determine, she bashed his head in with a skillet and then stabbed him to death with his own sword."

Lionheart sank into the nearest chair. "She beat him *in combat?*"

"I would not describe it in quite that way, but in a sense, yes, that is accurate."

He couldn't fathom it. What in God's name was the world coming to, that such an aberration could happen? He cleared his throat and said, "I assume she has been executed for her crime."

Bowles didn't respond immediately. That alone alerted Richard to the fact that the situation was even more dire than he had originally thought.

Then Bowles muttered something that Richard wasn't quite able to hear. "What was that?" he said. "Repeat it."

"She escaped."

"Escaped!" Now Richard was back on his feet, and his hands were shaking with a fury that he knew all too well. It was anger that normally could only be dissipated by killing someone. In this case, the target was clearly Bowles.

Don't kill the messenger. Do NOT kill the messenger.

His damnable better angels were doing everything they could to try and pull him away from such a destructive course of action. He breathed in and out deeply, trying to will his pounding heart to slow down to a more peaceful rate. He closed his eyes and forced himself to calm down before he did something he might regret.

"You know what?" he said finally. "This is not my problem. If Wilford allowed himself to be killed by a woman, we were better off without him." He nodded, approving of his own words. "Where is Alys?"

"She—"

He hesitated.

Richard did not like that hesitation. "She *what?*"

"She escaped with the servant," said Bowles. "I tried to stop her, your majesty, but—"

That was it.

Richard yanked his sword out of its scabbard, whipped it around, and sliced it right through Bowles's neck. His head thudded to the floor amidst terrified shrieks from the female servants. The rest of Bowles's body paused there for a moment, as if contemplating some additional thought to offer, and then it flopped forward like a dead mackerel

His breathing was fast and ragged, as if he were in the midst of a great battle. All around him the women were still crying out, gasping, sobbing. "Shut up," he ordered and instantly they fell silent.

He stared at them, studying them, his slow gaze taking them in and assessing them. How many of them had helped the woman kill Wilford? How many of them had aided in Alys's escape? How many of them secretly despised him and longed for nothing but his demise?

Richard turned to the captain of his guard. "Kill them," he said. "Kill them all and burn the place to the ground."

The man's face remained impassive. He did not react in the slightest other than to nod.

Richard stalked out of the castle. The chopping noises of people being cut apart, the screams of the dying echoing all around him, they resounded in his ears but he paid it no mind. His thoughts were on to other things.

Or on one thing.

Where the hell was Alys?

⟵—« »—⟶

It was an age since Lord Collins had seen King Richard. Yet now here he was, seated in a chair opposite Collins's desk, looking as imperious as if he were upon his throne.

Richard seemed utterly detached from the world around him.

Although his eyes were nominally on Collins, it seemed as if he were staring inward, contemplating demons that were raging about inside him. The reality of the world around him seemed to hold little to no relevance, and Collins were quite disturbed about that.

This was, however, the King of England. It was far outside of his purview to second guess him or attempt to render judgment upon him. Richard had, as the saying went, far bigger fish to fry.

Still...

"You dispatched...*all* of them?"

Richard nodded. "When there is betrayal by one servant, the gate is wide open for additional conspirators. They were all compromised and so could not be trusted. Do you not agree?"

There was a world of danger in that question and Collins was instantly able to discern it. "Oh, absolutely," he said immediately. "You did the right thing, Majesty."

"Of course I did," Richard replied. "I am the King. Whatever the King does, by definition, is always right."

It was hard for Collins to find a basis upon which to object to that sentiment.

Richard then sat there, his mind clearly preoccupied. Since he didn't seem to be inclined to keep talking, Collins felt the need to prompt him. "How can we help you, Majesty?"

Richard looked up at him. He seemed surprised to realize that Collins was still sitting there, which was odd considering that he was in Collins's home. "It should be obvious," he said. "Find Alys. Her only ally is some servant girl. Dispatch the servant and bring Alys to me."

Collins felt his heart sink. Richard had already disposed of a soldier who had failed to hold on to her, and slaughtered and incinerated an entire castle of servants for no other reason than they had been associated with the girl who helped her. Now he was foisting the responsibility of finding her again onto Collins. Which meant that if he failed to do so, he would likely share the fate of the soldier whom Richard had smited with a blow of his sword.

It was the exact sort of situation that Collins had managed to avoid and was, indeed, the reason that he was still alive. Speaking with a sense of confidence he did not remotely feel, Collins said, "We can do that easily, can we not, Sir Henry?"

Henry was standing a short distance away, leaning against the door. He was a perceptive man, was Sir Henry, and he was easily able to determine what was going through Collins's mind. His expression told it all: He knew that Collins despised the responsibility that Richard was placing upon him, and he was doing everything he could to shift it over to Henry to share it. That meant that if Collins was executed, Henry would likely be right alongside him.

"Absolutely," Henry said without hesitation. "With little to no effort."

"You see?" Collins leaned back and smiled as if that pronouncement solved the entire difficulty. "Not a problem, Majesty."

Collins was worried that Richard would start asking him how, but apparently the King was willing to take his word for it. "That is good to hear. Now…tell me about this 'Robin Hood' whom I've been hearing tell about." He shifted his gaze to Henry. "I thought you dispatched him."

"I beheaded him myself," said Henry.

"Did it grow back?"

"It's a woman, pretending to be him," Henry told him. "I believe it may be his daughter."

"Perfect. Just perfect. What the hell is happening with women these days? It seems as if they are uniting to try and make my life more difficult." He shook his head. "He was such a valiant warrior, Robin was. A shame that he chose to ally himself with the wrong side." Then Richard considered the matter and his mind shifted back to his priority. "So how are you going to find Alys? Send out search parties? Trackers? She will likely try to hide in the woods for as long as she can."

Henry now moved forward and he was shaking his head slightly as he did so. "No, she won't. It is a woman's tendency to seek allies. I expect that she will follow in the same course. Why should we go to extreme efforts when others can do it for us?" Then he turned and shouted, "Basil! I know you're out there listening in! Get in here!"

The door swung open and Basil and Drogo entered. They marched smartly forward and then each dropped to one knee.

"Oh, get up, get up," Richard said impatiently. He was obviously not in the mood for the demands that accompanied his office. "This entire royalty business can be so tedious sometimes."

Basil and Drogo got to their feet and Basil couldn't prevent himself from bowing. "It is an honor to meet you, your Majesty."

"Yes, it is," Richard readily agreed. "And who are you again?"

"Basil is my son and our Sheriff."

"Ah. And I assume I can count on him to get the job done?"

"Absolutely. Basil...here is what I need you to do..."

And he laid out the plan to capture Alys.

CHAPTER XIII

Oh. Well, he likely had it coming.

THE MAGISTAR DANGLED THE PENDULUM OVER the map, feeling frustrated...and not for the first time.

She could tell that Mary, or Robyne, or whatever she was calling herself his week, was itching for action. The need to avenge her father's death, to try and make substantive changes in the world, burned fiercely in her breast. She wasn't designed to spend her days selling baked good at a booth. And the Magistar was worried that if she couldn't provide missions upon which to send her, she would start going off on her own and likely get herself killed in the process.

She had no solution for her problem, and suddenly the pendulum presented her with one. It began to spin, angling to the side. She shifted her hand to follow it and seconds later it was pointing straight down at the church.

The Magistar knew it all too well. She had never particularly liked the priest who officiated over it. His priorities seemed much more about personal existence than they did about the teachings of Jesu. There was a monk who lived alone in a monastery that seemed much more devout to her, but that wasn't anything she needed to care about just then. Instead all that mattered was that it appeared Robyne's presence was required there, and it was up to her to make sure that happened.

←—« »—→

The church seemed rather run down to Khalida, but she didn't especially care. To her, it was exactly what she and Alys required: a place of shelter.

They had managed to take refuge in the forest, to find a haven there. But she disliked being at the mercy of the elements, plus they were always exposed and out in the open. She felt as if an attack could come at any time and from any direction. Khalida was starting to feel as if her head was swimming, having to remain perpetually alert every moment of every hour. Even during the times when she was supposed to be sleeping while Alys kept watch, she slept so lightly that a single cough would waken her.

But a church was for those who were in deep trouble. At least, that was what she understood them to be for. Her family had never been terribly religious. For that matter, the events that transpired in her village which resulted in her father dying and she and her mother being marched off into slavery had gone a long way to convince her that there was no God looking down upon them. If there were, then clearly He was such a heartless, indifferent bastard that the thought of praying to Him was anathema to her. However, her antipathy toward the prospect of a deity didn't prevent her from deciding to take advantage of His house of worship.

She knocked on the door but no one came to answer it. Cautiously she pushed it open, paranoid that there might be some sort of trap waiting for her. Perhaps a phalanx of guards who somehow intuited that she would be there and were lying in wait for her.

There was no one attempting an ambush. The only individual in the place was a single priest. He was preoccupied lighting an array of candles at the front of the church, and when he turned and spotted them he jumped slightly, clearly surprised to see them there.

"We knocked," said Khalida, indicating the door that she was closing behind her and Alys.

"Sorry, my dear," said the priest. A few strands of white hair were clinging with determination to his head, and his jaw was a bit jowly, as if he had lost weight but the skin had not snapped back.

"My old ears are going, I fear. I didn't hear you. Come in, my children, please. You are...unfamiliar to me. Who are you?"

"My name is Khalida, and this is Alys," she said.

"Have you come to pray?"

"I'm...not especially religious."

"I'm not at all," said Alys. She spoke with a flatness that indicated more than indifference, but rather hostility. It seemed that she had no more admiration or faith in the Lord than did Khalida.

That didn't seem to bother the priest. All he did was smile gently. "It does not matter if you believe in God or not, my children. He believes in you. Can I be of service to you?"

"You're poor, right?" asked Khalida.

He shrugged. "It is my vow to remain so. Monies that come in go to maintaining the church and helping others. I keep enough to maintain myself, but that is all."

"There's someone who robs from the rich and gives to the poor, and I was wondering if you knew of a way to find them?"

He stared at her cautiously, and she realized she had to be discreet. She lowered her voice and said, in a whisper, "Robin Hood."

The priest regarded the two of them thoughtfully. "I believe that I can," he said finally. "Have a seat."

They did as he instructed, dropping into the nearest pew. Khalida let out a sigh of relief. It seemed such a blessing to be sitting in an actual seat, rather than being perched on a log or squatting in the dirt.

"I will be back shortly," he promised them. "I will bring you some refreshments."

"That would be great," said Khalida.

"I'm not hungry," said Alys.

"Shut up," said Khalida without even looking at her. Alys frowned in annoyance but didn't say anything in response.

The priest nodded to them both, rose and walked into the church's back room where he kept his various books and writings. The vicar was there, polishing the candlesticks that were arranged on the table. Once he was in the privacy of his office, the priest's entire demeanor changed. He went straight to his desk and rummaged around on it before he found what he was looking for. He held it up and displayed it to the vicar.

It was a wanted poster. It read, "*Wanted: Alys of France, Countess of Vixen. One hundred pound reward. Contact: Sheriff of Nottingham.*"

"How's this for timing?" he said in an excited whisper. "This was dropped off half an hour ago, and she's sitting right outside! Get to the castle immediately!"

The vicar paused.

"What? What's wrong?" asked the priest.

"You're...selling out a girl in need?"

"She's not a girl," said the priest. "She's something that the Sheriff wants. She's likely some sort of criminal. Perhaps even a murderess."

"And the one hundred pounds reward has nothing to do with this?"

"Do you have the slightest idea how much good we can do with one hundred pounds?" said the priest. "I'm sure you do, because I know it as well. Now get going!"

Once more the vicar hesitated, but then he nodded and slipped out the back door of the room.

The priest then hurried to gather some food for the girls.

———«   »———

Amanda glanced up from the forge as Innis Rae strode in. She couldn't help but notice the sizable axe that Innis Rae had strapped to her back, which she now removed and offered to Amanda. Amanda knew perfectly well who she was, because Robyne had informed her of the addition to her band. She hadn't been prepared for the size of her, though. Innis Rae was definitely the largest woman she had ever seen. She looked perfectly capable of going toe to toe with the heftiest of the guards that the Sheriff had to offer.

Still...

"A nun, eh?" she said. "Carrying an axe?"

"Nuns can't be too careful," said Innis Rae in a dry voice. "Hoping you could sharpen it for me."

"Not a problem."

She brought the axe over to a grinding wheel and started it spinning, pressing her foot down on a large pedal. Then Amanda brought the blade up to the wheel and held it up. Sparks flew as the grinding wheel proceeded to do its job. "So how did you meet Robyne?" she asked. She knew of Innis Rae's existence, but Robyne hadn't been especially forthcoming about the actual details of their first encounter.

"She aided me in getting away from the Sheriff's men."

"And now you're helping her?"

"She's helping me to get revenge on the bastard who killed my husband."

"Hunh," said Amanda. "My husband was killed, too."

Innis Rae cocked an interested eyebrow. "You want us to dispatch the piece of shite what did it?"

"Robyne did it."

"Oh." She considered that and then shrugged. "Well, he likely had it coming."

"Most definitely."

She ground it for a few more minutes, and then handed it back to Innis Rae. The Scotswoman swung it around tentatively, and then turned and slammed it through a thick piece of wood that was perched upright nearby. The axe sliced it in two with no effort. She nodded approvingly. "Excellent," she said.

Then her gaze shifted over toward a pile of assorted things lying in the corner: random pieces of armor, a broken sword, other objects. Something very specific caught her eye, though. She walked over and lifted a helmet off the pile. It was silver, with plating running down either side of it. "This is nice. Did you build this?"

"No. My husband took it in trade for shoeing the horse of some warrior passing through."

"It's beautiful," and she whistled in appreciation.

"You want it? Take it. I've no use for it."

At that moment the door to the shop banged open. Robyne was standing there. She was wearing her civilian clothing, but there was an unmistakable look in her eyes.

"We have a situation," she said.

CHAPTER XIV

Someone wants to see you.

KHALIDA COULD NOT RECALL WHEN WINE had ever tasted quite as good as it did at that moment.

She still remembered the first time she had tasted wine. Her mother had slipped her a half glass of some unfinished liquor during a time when the lord of the manor had had a gathering to celebrate some damned affair or another. Khalida had been ten years old at the time and the fluid had burned her throat as she had thrown it back far too quickly. "Sip it!" her mother told her, too late. She'd gasped and choked, but she did not spit any of it out. After that, though, she was very careful to heed her mother's advice and sipped it as delicately as possible.

And she was following the exact same procedure now. She sipped it gingerly, let it rest on her taste buds and then swallowed it. It tasted glorious.

In her other hand, she was holding a biscuit. It was slightly stale but still edible, and considering how her stomach was growling, it was much appreciated. Alys was doing the same, although Khalida couldn't help but notice that Alys was not exactly drinking slowly. Instead she guzzled down the entire cup, plus a second, and was pouring herself a third. Then again, she was French, so Khalida supposed that that was pretty much par for the course.

The priest was chatting with them convivially, telling them how pleased he was that they had come by. That he truthfully did not get a lot of people to the church lately. "Perhaps there is a downward spiral of faith these days," he observed.

Or maybe people have just begun to realize that all their prayers for divine intervention aren't going to do a thing to improve their lives and they've given up. But Khalida decided to keep that part of her thoughts to herself. No reason to try and stir up problems. Plus it would be rude. This was, after all, the alleged house of God. How impolite would it be to accuse the lord above all of being insensitive or uncaring or even nonexistent in His own home?

Instead she decided to shift the discussion back to her main concern. "So has Robin helped you in some way?" she asked.

"Oh, Robin helps everyone. The fact of the matter is," he continued, "I have had extensive dealings with Robin Hood. A true hero of our time."

Hero.

The word ticked a warning in Khalida's mind. *Shouldn't he have said "heroine?" But maybe not. You shouldn't be paranoid. He's a priest. He works for God. Then again, God didn't care when your mother got pregnant and killed herself over it.*

Cautiously, not giving the slightest hint of the thoughts in her mind, she said, "And you've sent for Robin?"

"Oh yes, absolutely. He should be here directly."

That was when she knew.

Her eyes narrowed. "*He* should?"

"Yes, any minute now," he said, unaware of the fact that Khalida's mood had shifted.

Slowly she got to her feet, staring down at him with unbridled suspicion. Alys had likewise caught the change in pronouns, but she apparently hadn't realized the priest was lying to them. Instead she was staring at Khalida questioningly.

"Alys, let's go," she said.

"What? Why?" said Alys.

"He doesn't know Robin. Which means there's only one reason he's keeping us here."

The priest began to get to his feet. "My child, I assure you that—"

She yanked out her sword and brought the point of it to his throat. She kept it leveled at him. He gulped audibly and sank back into his chair.

"Who did you summon?" she asked. "The Sheriff? The king? Who? Whoever it is, they're not going to like what they find if they show up here."

Alys was now standing and she tugged urgently at Khalida's arm. "Let's get out of here," she said.

The priest wasn't going to be doing a thing to stop them. He was trying to speak, but his mouth was moving and no words were emerging. He was clearly paralyzed with fear, perhaps certain that his meaningless life was about to come to an end.

It was at that moment that the doors at the far end of the church burst open. A black haired, bearded man was standing there, and there was another, much larger man behind him wearing some sort of leather mask covering one side of his face. There were also half a dozen guards accompanying them. Horses were whinnying outside; they had obviously served to transport the men here and were tied off at a hitching post outside.

"Greetings," said the man who was at the forefront of the group. Khalida noticed he had a bow slung over his shoulder and a quiver of arrows on his back, in addition to the sword he was holding in an almost leisurely grasp. "I am the Sheriff. There is someone who wants to see you."

"I bet there is," snarled Khalida. She kept her sword pointed at the priest. "Back out of here slowly, or the priest dies."

The Sheriff shrugged. "Kill him. He's served his purpose. He's of no use to us now."

The priest gasped, his face going deathly white. "No…please…" he managed to whisper.

Khalida growled in frustration. She had thought that the threat would cause them to at least back off temporarily, grant them a few seconds for her to come up with another plan. That, apparently, was not going to fly. This Sheriff really didn't give a damn about the priest. Why should he? He was focused on one goal and one only: apprehending Alys, and herself to a lesser degree. If Khalida died within the next few minutes, the Sheriff certainly would not be upset. He'd probably take her head as proof of her demise and be satisfied with it.

All this went through her mind in a second as she whipped the sword around and struck a defensive pose. She fully expected Alys to follow suit.

Alys did not. Instead she emitted a hellacious roar, swung her morning star around and charged straight at the newcomers.

Several soldiers stepped in front of the Sheriff and the attacking Alys, obviously seeking to protect him from her charge. Alys didn't care. They had swords out but no shields, and that was all the opportunity that Alys required. She came in hard and fast, whipping the morning star around, and it struck the nearest guard in the head. He was wearing armor, which protected his skull to some degree from the spikes on the mace's head, but it did little to shield him from the impact. His head and helmet rang and he went down as she kept swinging the mace, looking to take down anyone who was in range.

Khalida held back, afraid to draw anywhere near, because Alys's attack was literally out of control. She was wielding the mace so fast and furiously that she posed a danger to anyone who made the mistake of getting within range. Fortunately enough she was managing to dispatch anyone who was within range.

Then she saw the big, masked man advancing and she decided that she needed to get engaged.

She charged forward with her sword, momentarily distracting him from Alys. She brought it around, low and fast, but to her astonishment he caught the flat of the blade in his large hands. Gripping it tightly, he then drove the sword backwards, directly at Khalida. The hilt slammed her in the chin and staggered her, her mind swimming as she tried to focus her scrambled thoughts. It didn't work and instead she stumbled and fell backwards, thudding to the ground.

Alys didn't notice. She was too thoroughly engaged in combat, and she was succeeding in driving her attackers back. But then the Sheriff stepped forward, his sword firmly in his hands. She whipped the morning star around, but he deflected it with his sword. She came in again and this time he stepped back and the mace missed him clean; then he drove his sword upward and sent the morning star flying from her hand.

"Surrender," he said.

She did no such thing. She had one advantage: She knew that he had no intention of killing her. The point was to capture her alive.

Alys was not about to make it easy.

Khalida had never heard of *savate*. Neither had the Sheriff. But Alys was a master of the French fighting technique that had originated with French sailors, and she utilized it now. She leaped forward, spinning in the air, and her right foot slammed into the Sheriff's chest, knocking him back. He staggered and she kept coming at him, driving a series of furious kicks at him. The Sheriff did everything he could to block them, deflecting them with his forearms even as the bruises piled up on his arms.

Quickly he became fed up, and then for an instant she left an opening. It was all he required as he drove a furious punch forward, sending her flying backwards. She landed on the aisle, her eyes glazing momentarily.

"Take her! Take them both!" shouted the Sheriff.

⸺⸺

The church had only one nice decoration within it. It was a lovely stained glass window of the virgin cradling her infant son.

It shattered.

Robyne of Sherwood came crashing through it, an arrow already nocked in her bow. She landed squarely on one of the pews, steadying herself so that she didn't tumble off. She leveled the bow and fired off the arrow. It thudded into the chest of the nearest soldier and he collapsed with a single gurgled growl of protest.

By the time his body hit the ground, she had already reloaded.

The Sheriff and the others fell back, ducking behind the other pews. Her next arrow thudded into one and she had again nocked another arrow. "We are leaving!" she shouted at the two women on the ground.

They immediately scrambled to their feet as Robyne strode in front of them, firing another arrow directly at the Sheriff. Once again he avoided it, keeping his refuge behind the bench. That was fine as far as Robyne was concerned; as long as she kept him from attacking, that was perfect.

Robyne charged toward the front of the church, the women following her.

The moment they had passed him, the Sheriff stood, nocking his own arrow. He trained it on Robyne's back and was about to fire when a hand clad in a metal glove swept in and slapped it aside. The arrow thudded into the seat next to him. The Sheriff whirled and found himself face to face with a leper.

"Now, now," scolded Clarence, waggling a finger. "Can't have that."

He swung his fist and struck the Sheriff in the side of the head. The Sheriff went down like a bag of rocks.

The remaining guards immediately backed off as Clarence strode forward, passing through them with no difficulties.

―――«   »―――

"Are you Robin?!" shouted one of the girls.

"Yes!"

"Khalida!" she said, tapping her chest. "Alys!"

"*Later!*"

The three of them sprinted out of the church and found that Innis Rae, back in her Scots garb, was in the midst of combat. Several guards had remained outside to tend to the horses and Innis Rae was in full battle with them. One of the guards managed to get a blow in to her head, but the helmet that she was wearing—newly acquired from Amanda—deflected it easily. Meanwhile she was using her battle axe with devastating force, slicing into the guards, sending them staggering back with huge rips across their chests and blood welling from them.

"Ach, good. Ah was wondering what was keeping ye!" she shouted.

The guards had arrived on horseback, and now the confused steeds were winnowing to each other, unsure of what to do upon having seen their masters being cut down in front of them. Robyne didn't hesitate as she leaped up onto the back of the nearest one. "*Let's go!*" she shouted.

The rest of them followed her lead, each of them clambering up onto horseback, quickly bringing their mounts under control. "*Yahhh!*" shouted Robyne and galloped her horse forward. It did as instructed, charging away from the church, and the others fell in behind her.

They ate up ground as quickly as they could as the Sheriff and the others charged after them, but quickly fell behind.

The horses carried them speedily in the direction of Sherwood, but the town of Nottingham rested between them and their destination. Robyne knew they didn't have a choice. They were going to have to go straight through the heart of the town if they had any prayer of making their escape.

They pounded down the road, and the further their pursuers fell, the more Robyne's spirits lifted. This had gone more easily than she could possibly have expected.

The Sheriff had given her momentary pause, and she didn't know why. It was the first time that she had ever seen him, but she hadn't been able to get a measure of how formidable he was. She hoped that she would be able to face off against him at some point in the future. She envisioned driving her blade into his heart and took quiet joy in the notion. It was not the same Sheriff who had slain her father, but it would be close.

They galloped into the outskirts of the village and people pointed and shouted, recognizing her as their hero. Word about

her existence had spread, but this was the first time that the towns-
folk were actually seeing the green-clad heroine in person, and they
could not have been more overjoyed.

She caught a brief glimpse of a familiar face: the Magistar
was in the crowd. She looked concerned, though, and she shouted
something that Robyne couldn't make out. A warning, perhaps?
But a warning of what?

"*Shite!*" yelled Innis Rae.

Robyne snapped her gaze around and she saw what Innis Rae
was reacting to.

An array of soldiers was blocking them. They weren't guards
from Nottingham castle; the fronts of their uniforms had an insignia that Robyne recognized: the roaring head of a lion.

They had their swords out and they were clearly ready to do
whatever they needed to in order to prevent Robyne and her crew
from getting past.

Robyne saw only one option.

She vaulted off her horse and charged the brigade on foot.

They were clearly not expecting it, but didn't seem particularly
intimidated by the notion of battling a single woman on foot. They
had the higher ground, the elevation of being on horseback while
Robyne was on ground level.

Except she didn't attack the men. She went after the horses.

She came in fast, swinging her sword, and sliced through the
throat of the closest animal. The horse let out an alarmed gurgle
and staggered back as blood began to pour from its throat. It staggered and Robyne didn't hesitate as she swung around quickly and
rammed her sword through the throat of the next horse over.

Her actions did not go unnoticed by the rest of the horses. As
two of their numbers fell, the rest did not simply stand around and
wait to die. Instead they reared up on their hind legs, sending their
riders tumbling off their backs and falling heavily to the ground
below. Several of the men were stepped on by their own mounts
as the terrified beasts scrambled over them to get out of the killing
zone.

The women behind her cheered as Robyne backpedaled, her sword at the ready. The soldiers had managed to recover from their falls and now they were charging forward with their blades. Immediately the other women dismounted with their weapons at the ready.

The battle raged in the narrow, dirt streets of Nottingham. The air was filled with clanging as their weapons came together in a pitched fight. There were more soldiers on horseback, but they held back as the primary troops engaged the enemy.

Robyne's heart was pounding furiously against her chest. This was it. After all these years of living in solitude, in mourning, grieving over her long-lost father and missing mother, she was finally experiencing the life she had dreamt of. She was a warrior, battling the representatives of the evil bastards who had sway over the lives of the poor in general and women in specific.

Perhaps the female villagers would learn from what they were witnessing now. They were seeing a group of talented, powerful women going head to head with soldiers and beating them at their own game. Perhaps they would rise up in protest, acknowledge how shabbily the world was treating them and find a way to seize their own place in it.

They were cheering her on, that was for sure. They were shouting encouragement, pumping their fists in the air. The tidal wave of support that was pouring over her elevated her spirit, raised her up to a point of feeling invincible. *Throw all the soldiers at me that you want. I will rise up, I will destroy them all. I cannot be beaten.*

She heard an angry roar behind her and spun just in time to see the Sheriff of Nottingham charging right at her.

Innis Rae intercepted the charge.

He came at her furiously, but she deflected every thrust with her axe. He brought his sword up and around and Innis Rae slapped it out of his hands as if she were a parent disarming an angry child. He turned to grab up the fallen sword and Innis Rae picked him up in her powerful arms and threw him as far and fast as she could.

Another soldier came at Robyne. She brought her blade up and deflected the downward thrust of his sword. He advanced on her, his face twisted in fury, but she was quickly able to discern and preempt the thrust of his attack. He tried a feint but she saw it for what it was

That was when the cheering abruptly halted.

The abrupt cessation of sound confused Robyne. Not only that, but her opponents abruptly backed off. Her head snapped around and to her utter confusion, every person in the town had dropped to their knees.

What the hell—?

"Hello."

It was a familiar voice. She spun and saw what she knew she was going to see.

Standing there not ten feet away from her, Richard the Lionheart was studying her. He had out his sword, the point into the ground, his hands resting on the hilt.

"Nice day, is it not?" he said.

CHAPTER XV

I like taking chances

ROBYNE WAS MOMENTARILY STUNNED, NOT HAVING the slightest idea of how to react.

Alys, however, did not hesitate. Wielding her morning star as if she were prepared to stave in his head, she howled from the depths of her soul, *"Where is my child?! I want my child!!"*

She was set to charge straight at him, but Clarence held her back. "Calm, calm!" he pleaded. She struggled furiously in his grasp, shouting at him to let her go, that this was none of his business, but Clarence never wavered in restraining her.

King Richard stared at Clarence, clearly surprised. "Sir Clarence, as I recall. Time has not been kind to you, I see."

Alys had ceased struggling, but Clarence continued to hold her firmly just in case she decided to charge him again. "You're shorter than I remember," said Clarence.

Richard smiled slightly at that. "In the past, I was standing on my charisma." He gestured toward the women who were behind him. "So…apparently you have fallen in with brigands. This is, I assume, Robin Hood?"

"'Robyne' will do," she said.

"And what is your interest in all this? Why are you protecting Alys?" and he gestured towards the angry French girl.

"I protect all scorned women."

Richard chuckled at that. "You must be very busy. So…we seem to have a predicament here. You cannot succeed in sustained battle, you know," and he gestured toward the coterie of soldiers who were backing him up.

The truth was, he was correct. They were severely outnumbered, plus a number of the soldiers had bows. They could sit upon their horses and unleashed quarrels into them from a safe distance.

But surrendering was not in her makeup.

"I like taking chances," she said defiantly.

"Ah!" Richard's interest seemed to perk up upon hearing that. "You're a gambling woman, I see! I admit, I also have a bit of a fondness for making wagers. Tell you what," he said, sounding excessively cheerful. "You and I battle. I win, and you're all my prisoners. You win, you and your friends can go free."

There was some confused muttering from Richard's soldiers, who were clearly not enamored of the idea.

Khalida, though, knew exactly what to say. "Including Alys!"

Richard, to Robyne's surprise, actually appeared sympathetic. "All I want to do is return you to your parents, Alys."

She pulled away from Clarence at that point, although she made no attempt to charge Richard once more. "I want my son," she said intensely.

"I have other plans for him," said Richard.

Her mouth twisted into a snarl. "Then to hell with my parents. I'm not going anywhere."

He nodded, seeming to process her statement. "Very well," he said finally. "Her, too."

Beneath her mask, Robyne smiled as she stepped forward, but suddenly Clarence was blocking her path. He was facing Richard and declared, "No. I will fight you in her stead."

She pulled at his shoulder and whispered in annoyance, "Get out of the way, Clarence."

"Robyne," he said intently, "You can't beat him. He's Richard the bloody Lionheart."

"And I'm Robyne of bloody Sherwood. Now move or I'll knock you over."

Clarence was clearly about to continue his protest, but then he shrugged and stepped aside. Robyne advanced on Richard, her sword ready for battle.

Richard did not look especially concerned.

She came at him hard and fast. Their blades clanged together, the sounds ringing through the small village.

"Come on, Richard!" shouted one villager. "Kick her ass!" That was all he managed to say before a woman next to him spun and drove her fist into his chin. He went down.

That was all the impetus that was required as the villagers began cheering for Robyne, shouting for her to take down the King. And why not? He represented taxation, oppression, and everything else that made their lives such a hardship.

Richard kept backing up, which Robyne took quiet pride in. Clearly he had underestimated her skills and assumed that she would be an easy target. The fact that she was on the attack and that he was incapable of even beginning to mount a defense caused her spirit to soar.

Yet he was smiling. Indeed, he seemed amused.

Suddenly he stopped backing up.

"My turn," he said.

For the first time, he began to battle back. His moves were sure, unhurried, confident, as if the outcome of the duel was never in doubt. As if she had posed no threat at all.

That was when Robyne realized that she had miscalculated. His "retreat" had been methodical and calculated. He had been taking the measure of her skill and now had apparently come to a conclusion of how best to deal with her.

And Robyne began to back up. She had no choice. His attack was too aggressive for her to defend against.

"You're mostly self-taught, I suspect," said Richard as he continued to advance. "You have an admirable offense, and a sufficient defense." He was speaking pedantically, as if addressing a class of eager pupils. "But the problem is that these swords are damned heavy, and the longer you fight, the more tired you'll become."

The blade suddenly sliced across Robyne's left arm. She cried out in surprise and shock.

"That's why you can pretend to be a warrior all you want," Richard went on. "But in the end, this is a man's game. I assume Robin was your father; he was good at the game. I, however, am the best." Even as he spoke, he kept on attacking, and at the end of the sentence he sliced across her right arm as if adding punctuation and emphasis. She cried out yet again, and he stepped forward and punched her in the solar plexus. It knocked the air out of her and she gasped as she went down.

—« »—

Basil, lying on the ground next to the building, came back to his senses, shaking off the numbing effect of Innis Rae's powerful attack. What brought him back to full consciousness was the sound of swords clanging together. There was no cacophony of sounds; he wasn't hearing a pitched battle. What he was hearing was one-on-one combat, and he didn't have the slightest idea who exactly it would be.

He clambered to his feet and even as he did so, he unslung his bow from his shoulder in anticipation of requiring it. He peered around the building and he couldn't believe what he was seeing.

It was the outlaw, Robin Hood. It had to be her. He had glimpsed her only briefly when he saw her bursting into the church, and he had spent most of that time getting out of her way. But here she was now, big as life, and she was battling none other than Lionheart himself. Immediately Basil was able to deduce what had happened. She must have challenged the King to single combat, winner takes the day, and as near as Basil could determine, the fight wasn't going as she had anticipated. She was backing up and Basil saw a fresh wound on her left arm. Lionheart had obviously scored first blood, and it was probably only a matter of time before he was able to dispose of her.

Probably.

But Basil didn't like the odds. He had read a good deal about Robin Hood in his years, and there had been many a time when the man had miraculously managed to snatch victory from defeat's slathering jaws. If this was indeed his daughter, it was not impossible that she might share the same proclivities. That was not a chance that Basil was willing to take. There was simply no way he was going to risk the King of England being cut down by some street level cut-purse on his watch. If nothing else, his father might well have him executed for dereliction of duty.

Even as he readied an arrow, he saw Richard slash Robyne's arm again and then knock her to the ground. Matters were taking a positive spin, but no harm would be done if he prepared himself to end it before the tide could turn.

—«   »—

"You are finished, girl. Yield!"

The breath was heaving in Robyne's chest, but the fight was still in her limbs. "Death first," she snarled.

Richard shrugged. "I am more than happy to oblige."

Then two things happened at once.

There was a loud, alarmed female cry from directly behind Robyne, and the unmistakable sound of an arrow thudding home.

Robyne spun and her jaw dropped in shock.

The Magistar was directly behind her. There was an arrow quivering in her upper chest.

"Had to...protect you," the Magistar managed to say, and then her legs went out from under her.

"*No!*" screamed Robyne at the exact same moment that Richard cried out, "Theresa!" in a startled voice. Richard could have cut her down at that moment at his whim because she had completely forgotten about defending herself. Her full attention was on the Magistar as she tumbled to the ground. Robyne caught her before she could hit it and lowered her gently. The Magistar was breathing hard and fast, and her eyes were glazing over.

That was when Robyne heard another unmistakable noise: the creak of a longbow being drawn.

She looked up, straight into the face of the Magistar's assailant. The man who was targeting her for death.

———« »———

Basil had no idea where the woman who had intercepted the arrow had come from. One moment he had had a clear shot at Robyne's back, and the next the woman had literally thrown herself between him and his target. How the hell had she even spotted him? It was as if she was psychic or had some other manner of mental abilities that had aided her.

It wasn't going to make any difference, though. The woman was down and the green-clad outlaw was a perfect target. She wasn't even mounting any manner of defense since she was clearly stunned by what had just transpired. Basil was going to put an end to his false Robin Hood.

He drew the arrow back, ready to let fly.

Apparently alerted by the creak of the bow, she turned and stared right at him.

And Basil froze.

For no reason that he could discern, images suddenly began to slam through his head. A woman, gazing down at him with those same eyes that had looked upon him now. But it was not a face he recognized.

She was smiling down at him tenderly. She whispered, *"How is my little boy? You're going to be such a great man. As great as your father."* The words echoed between his ears, and the voice speaking them was both unfamiliar and as readily identifiable a tone as he had ever heard.

"Mother?" he said softly.

But that was absurd. This Robin woman couldn't possibly be his mother. First, she had died in childbirth. Second, her movements and what he could see of her face…this was a young woman, maybe around his age. It was simply impossible that she could be the woman who had given birth to him.

But the eyes...

Basil had no idea why, but slowly he lowered the bow. He couldn't fire at her, couldn't end her life without having some further idea of who she was and what she was to him.

Who is she?!

⸺⸻

Robyne had been sure that she was dead. Then, for no reason she could discern, a change had come over the Sheriff. His face had gone deathly white, and he had lowered his nocked arrow without even attempting to fire it. She had no idea why he had abruptly changed his mind, but she didn't care. All of her attention was on the fallen body of the Magistar.

She cradled the woman, softly moaning her name. The Magistar gazed up at her and when she spoke, her voice was gurgling within her throat.

"Don't...kill him," she managed to whisper. "Stop...killing..."

It was not remotely anything she expected the Magistar to say. The Magistar had never said anything to her before about taking the lives of others...

And then her mind flew back to the evening when she had first dispatched of Amanda's slug of a husband. She had told the Magistar what she had done, with her exhilarated heart pounding fervently against her chest, and she had waited for the Magistar to congratulate her on a job well done.

But the Magistar had not done so. All she had done was shrug slightly and say, "If it was necessary." Which had been a nonsensical thing for her to say. Of course it was necessary. The man was a brute. Robyne had given it no further thought, and the Magistar had spoken no more about it.

Yet now she had brought it up. Why?

"Why?" she asked, but the Magistar didn't answer. Instead her eyes rolled up and her head flopped back. She stopped breathing.

And Robyne went berserk.

She leaped to her feet, whipped her sword around so quickly that if Richard had not backed up out of reflex, she would have sent his head flying.

Robyne went into full attack mode, and this time when Richard backed up, it was not out of any sense of strategy or trying to assess her tactics. He was just trying to stay out of her way, blocking her attacks to the best of his ability. Robyne did not appear to care that he was thwarting her assault. She kept coming, kept hammering away. Her covered mouth was twisted in a sneer, but the truly terrifying thing was the glare from her eyes that seemed to threaten to tear Richard apart with just that look.

Several times Richard endeavored to switch to an offense, to bring the fight to Robyne. He had no chance. She didn't so much as flinch in the face of his renewed attempts at attack. Instead she kept coming and coming, and now it was Richard who was tiring in the face of her unremitting onslaught. His breath was coming raggedly from his chest. His efforts were slowing.

Then he made a mistake. He blocked a thrust of hers and she twisted quickly, brought her hand up and around, shoved his blade out of the way and then drove her own sword straight forward. It slammed into his shoulder and drove in and Richard howled in agony.

As one, the villagers gasped in unison. Richard's soldiers were likewise stunned. One of them started to charge forward but his captain clamped a hand on his shoulder and immobilized him.

Richard sank to his knees and Robyne yanked her sword out of his body. He cried out and covered the wound with one hand, attempting to stanch the bleeding. His sword slid out of his free hand; he was helpless. Robyne now stood over him with her sword pointed directly at his throat.

And she threw his words back at him: "Yield or die."

Despite the seriousness of the situation, Richard actually half smiled. Some part of him seemed amused by the situation. "You'd kill your king?" he said with mild incredulity.

"I never liked royalty much," said Robyne.

Richard took a deep breath and then let it out slowly. When he spoke again, it was not to Robyne, but to the men who had accompanied him. "We are leaving," he said.

"But your majesty!" one of his soldiers exclaimed.

Richard did not want to hear it. He was barely keeping his temper in check as it was, and when he heard the startled challenge of his soldier, his response was swift and with no hesitation. "I may be bleeding, but it is still king's blood! I said we are leaving! Now one of you idiots help me to my feet!"

Three soldiers promptly almost stumbled over each other in their attempt to do as they were bidden. One came in on either side and the third behind him and slowly they aided him in getting to his feet. His knees wobbled slightly but he managed to keep himself upright.

"This day is yours," he growled at Robyne. "But trust me: There will be plenty more days."

"I am counting on it," said Robyne.

He nodded slightly and then turned and walked away. For Robyne, it was as if he had already disappeared. She forgot about him completely and instead ran to the fallen Magistar's side. The sounds of horses' hooves told her that Richard and his men had departed, but she didn't care. She crouched next to the Magistar's body and tears began to roll down her face.

"Is he gone?" whispered the Magistar.

Robyne jumped back, startled. "What the hell—?!" she cried out.

If the crowd had reacted as one in voicing their shock when Robyne had stabbed Richard, that was nothing compared to their collective astonishment as the Magistar sat up. The arrow was still sticking out of her upper chest.

"How—?" Robyne gasped.

The Magistar pulled aside the top of her clothing and Robyne could now see that the arrow was lodged, not in her body, but solidly in a thick leather vest that had served to protect the Magistar from fatal penetration.

"I don't know if you noticed, but there are a lot of arrows flying around these days," said the Magistar matter-of-factly. "Can't be too careful."

She then yanked the arrow out of the leather vest. She did not notice what Robyne immediately spotted: There was now blood trickling out of the hole.

"You didn't kill him," said the Magistar. "Good. I'm glad that—"

"Uhm," Robyne interrupted, pointing at the now bleeding wound.

Puzzled, the Magistar looked down at where Robyne was indicating. Her eyes widened and she touched it gingerly. "Well, *that's* not good," she said. Then her eyes rolled up and she slumped back, unconscious.

CHAPTER XVI

I'm going to just stop talking forever

Robyne eased the Magistar onto her bed, checking to make sure that the bandages were remaining tight and in place on her shoulder. "There you go. You'll be fine," she said softly.

"Need more leather next time," said the Magistar in a soft whisper.

"There isn't going to be a next time. Don't you dare throw yourself in the way of an arrow to save me ever again."

"No promises."

Robyne sat up and was about to stand, but the Magistar gripped her by the wrist to keep her there. "Thank you for not killing him."

"Why would you care?" asked Robyne. "He's a murdering bastard with no regard for human life. Why should I spare him? More to the point, why would it matter if I spared him?"

"Because you can't be like them," said the Magistar. "Men as a whole do not give a damn about human life. People are no different to them than chess pieces, to be sacrificed and tossed aside when they no longer have any need for them. You have to show them a better way."

"You want me to teach them?"

The Magistar nodded.

"That's not my job," Robyne said. "I need to stop them, stop their abuses…"

"Then nothing will change," said the Magistar. "Mary…

Robyne...whatever you call yourself, you will not live forever. That is simply a fact. Whether you are killed in action or you die of old age on your bed, you cannot go on endlessly. If you truly wish to make changes, then you have to show men that there is a better way to live one's life. They have to learn from you."

Robyne stared at her. "You really think I can do that?"

She raised a hand and ran a finger along Robyne's chin. "I think you can do anything to which you put your mind." Then she yawned widely and her eyes began to close. "Go to your friends. I need to rest," and she waved Robyne off, dismissing her.

Robyne waited a moment more to make sure that the Magistar was sound asleep and then she moved to the adjoining study. Innis Rae and Clarence were already there, and the two new women—Khalida and Alys—were seated in chairs facing them. All eyes were on Alys, though, who was just sitting there, not saying a word. Khalida was gently rubbing her shoulder, assuring her that she could speak her mind and tell them the truth. Alys was not responding, though, but then she glanced up when Robyne entered. Robyne didn't sit down but instead just stood there, her arms crossed across her torso.

Alys's gaze met hers and then the French girl dropped her stare and suddenly seemed quite fascinated with the floor. She let out a low breath and began to speak.

"I am Alys, countess of Vexin," she said. "My mother died in childbirth. She was Constance of Castile. My father is Louis VII of France."

It was obvious that her companion was completely unaware of this. Her jaw dropped and she said, "Oh my God...sorry. *Mon Dieu.*"

Alys smiled very briefly at Khalida's turn of French.

"A bit far away from home, aren't you?" said Robyne.

Alys shrugged. "I've been here since I was eight years old. My parents arranged for me to be married to Richard Lionheart as soon as I was old enough. Until that day, I became a ward to Richard's father, Henry the Second. Years went by and..." Her voice trailed off.

"Ye fucked him, didn't ye?" said Innis Rae.

Robyne stared at Innis Rae incredulously "*Innis, for God's sake, she didn't...*"

Then Alys looked at Robyne and the answer was in her face.

At which point Robyne rolled her eyes. "All right, I'm going to just stop talking forever."

"Henry was a good man, believe it or not," said Alys.

"I'll opt for 'not'," Innis Rae said sourly.

"And he got you pregnant," said Clarence, now fully understanding all that he had witnessed when Alys had confronted Richard.

She nodded and when she spoke next, her voice sounded as if she was talking from very far away. "I labored for so long...all of me was covered with sweat. The bottoms of my feet were sweaty; how is that even possible? And when the baby finally emerged, the nurse congratulated me. Said it was a little boy. I put my arms out, asked to hold him. And the nurse bolted from the room. I heard my baby's cries as he vanished down the hallway. I tried..." Her voice choked a moment. "I tried to go after him but fell to the ground. I had no strength. I screamed after her, 'Where are you going? Where are you taking him?!' But I got no response. I let him go...let him take him..."

"You didn't 'let' anyone do anything," said Khalida. "They robbed you of your son."

"I don't know what happened to him. I never saw him. Until Richard just confirmed he was alive, I didn't know if they had just left him out to die." She hesitated, steadying her voice, and then continued. "I remained confined to Henry's castle while they tried to arrange a marriage to Prince John. My stepmother managed to kill that match. Finally I escaped. They've been searching for me ever since."

"Well, now they're going to leave you alone," said Khalida confidently.

It was not confidence that Robyne shared. "I don't believe that for a moment. As long as Richard lives, this will never be over."

Clarence stared at her impassively, his face not revealing the slightest hint of what he was thinking. "Are you suggesting we kill the King?" he asked as casually as if inquiring whether she wanted to go out for a walk.

All eyes went to Robyne, waiting for her to respond. And she realized that at that moment, she could reply in the affirmative and they would likely agree to follow her. Why not? Most of them weren't English citizens anyway and felt no loyalty to Richard, and even Clarence, the former knight, was obviously not a fan. They would line up behind her and try to determine the best means of killing the king.

Killing the king.

And the Magistar's words came floating back. About how important it was to show men that there was a better way to live than through murder.

"No," she said so quickly that it appeared as if she had not given the matter any thought at all. It seemed instinctive. "But we can make his life miserable. And Alys...we *will* find your son." She stretched out her hand and draped it on top of Alys's. "I swear to it. I swear on my father's memory."

To Robyne's surprise, Innis Rae reached forward and placed her hand on top of Robyne's. "As do I," she said.

Khalida did likewise. "You will hold your son again."

And Clarence placed his gloved hand atop the pile. "So swear all of us."

For the first time since she had met them, Alys smiled widely.

⸺ « » ⸻

Basil sat in his room, staring thoughtfully at nothing. The door was hanging partly open and Henry glanced in as he walked past. He saw Basil sitting there, seemingly detached from the world around him, and stuck his head in. "Is something wrong, son?"

At first Basil didn't respond, but then he shifted his gaze to Henry. "Father...you told me my mother died at birth, correct?"

Henry walked slowly into the room. "It was the single greatest loss I have ever known in my life."

"Except this afternoon I thought I...I had this brief flash of..."

"Of what?" He cocked his head curiously.

"I thought I saw her. I had this...this image of her in my head, talking to me."

Henry sat down in the chair that was opposite the bed and rested a hand on Basil's knee. "I know men who have lost limbs in battle. Arms, legs chopped off. And oftentimes they swear they can still feel the missing limb. It itches them, it aches them. The human mind makes up for things we've lost by convincing us we still have them. You lost your mother; your mind is trying to convince you otherwise. You can still feel her," and with his other hand he patted Basil on the chest, "...right here. And that's a very, very good thing."

Slowly Basil nodded and he smiled wanly. "That...that makes sense. Good night, father."

"Good night," said Henry, as he got up and walked out of the room.

It made sense, what Basil's father had said. His mind was just fabricating recollections of a mother's love that he had never known.

Except...why now?

Basil had not given his mother any thought in years. Why in the world had staring into the thief's eyes suddenly triggered memories that he could not possibly have had?

Without even being aware of it, his fingers drifted up to the faded scar that ran the length of his forehead.

The longer he thought about it, the more futile were his efforts to come up with an explanation. He decided to try and stop pondering it and get some sleep.

———— « » ————

Henry's face twisted in annoyance the moment he was clear of Basil's room.

"Shite," he muttered.

It had been the bitch female. That had to be it. Basil had seen her face and her damnable eyes had triggered some sort of recollection.

It had been so many years since he had adopted the boy, that he had become convinced any memories of his true past were long lost. The fact that his recollections were beginning to stir set Henry's hackles on edge.

He was going to have to do something. The problem was that he was unsure what.

BOOK THREE

Robyne and the Monk

CHAPTER XVII

"Do me less favors"

ELIZABETH HAD HAD A LONG DAY.

She did not resent her father for this. The situation was what it was, and even if she went the rest of her life with never smelling a chicken again, she still couldn't find it within herself to be angry over her lot in life. After all, there were others who had far less than she did and would likely have sold their souls to have even a fragment of what she possessed.

She moved slowly through the chicken coop, extracting newly laid eggs, speaking softly to the array of feathered beasts as they went about their business. Her forehead was dripping sweat and she would occasionally take a moment to wipe it dry.

The truth was that Elizabeth was not remotely interested in the daily obligations of her chores. She would much rather have spent her time studying. After all, she had the ability to read, courtesy of her mother who had deliberately made a point of teaching her. She didn't have the faintest idea how her mother had learned the ability to be literate; she had asked her on several occasions and her mother had always been obscure about it. "I will tell you when you are older," she said, and kept saying, and then one day Elizabeth was older and her mother was no longer there. Instead she was buried, having succumbed to something called the rot that Elizabeth couldn't even begin to understand. The disease had just devoured her mother from the inside out. One day she had been there, and then she had begun to get very thin and slowly wasted away until the only thing that seemed still alive were her eyes, blazing with life in a face that more closely resembled the human skull than an actual person. When she succumbed, her father said it was a blessing. As far as Elizabeth was concerned, it was a definition of "blessing" with which she was not familiar.

Her mother's passing also signaled a change in her father's personality, or at least so it seemed to Elizabeth. Typically he was a rather taciturn man, happy to allow Elizabeth's mother to do all the talking for the both of them. Left on his own to communicate with his daughter, her father—Thomas Carpenter, for such was his name and also his skill—withdrew into himself. He scarcely communicated with Elizabeth at all, content to toss her cursory greetings or inquire whether she had attended to some chore. She didn't think he blamed her for the loss of her mother, but it was evident to her that if he had a choice between mother and daughter, he would gladly have saved the former at the cost of the latter. At least that was what she imagined. He had never said or done anything to provide proof for that theory, but she couldn't help but think it nonetheless.

Perhaps she had too much of an overactive imagination. That's what she told herself as she gathered up the eggs, preparing to take them and sell them at the market. It wasn't a day job that especially thrilled her, but it got her out of the house and gave her some distance from her father, so she had no real reason to have any complaints about it.

Having finished gathering the eggs, she piled them carefully into a basket and headed for the center of the village. She had no table or booth set up; she simply had a regular corner at which she stood with her basket, selling eggs as briskly as she could. Fortunately she had a reliable enough clientele that they always knew where to look for her.

"Well, well."

It was a rough voice, one that she knew all too well. She glanced around and saw exactly what she knew she was going to see: a burly man with wide shoulders and an ill-fitting tunic that seemed to be the only garment he owned since it was the only one she ever saw him sporting. This name was Bartholomew, and he came to town once a week to garner supplies for his farm. He always made a point of swinging by to say hello to her. That alone was enough for her to find disconcerting. What was more problematic was that he clearly intended for her to be especially friendly with him, rather than business like as she was with all her other customers.

This was an attitude that her father openly encouraged. When she complained of Bart's attentions to her, her father would shrug and note that she wasn't getting any younger. The fact that she was barely sixteen never seemed to matter in the slightest. "There are sixteen-year-olds starting families!" her father retorted, which was certainly true enough. But she didn't see that as any basis upon which to live the rest of her life. At the age of sixteen, she didn't have the slightest interest in starting a family or even getting married. She wasn't sure what she wanted to do yet with her life. She had only brought that point up once to her father, though, because his retort to her had been short, memorable, and not allowing for a good deal of debate: "You will do what I tell you to do," he had said so firmly that she had seen no point in debating him in that score. She had nodded and said nothing in response since there really didn't seem to be anything else to say.

"Ten eggs this day, Elizabeth," growled Bartholomew. He wasn't especially angry; he certainly had no reason to be. That was just how his voice sounded, as if he were in a perpetual state of irritation. Elizabeth quickly counted out the requested number of eggs and he handed her the money for it. As he did so, he allowed his beefy fingers to rest momentarily on the back of her hand. Quickly, reflexively, she pulled free of him although she did manage to keep a smile etched on her face.

Bart seemed briefly startled and then he regarded her askance. "Talked to your father yet?"

She didn't quite understand what he was referring to. "About what?"

"Ah. Okay. You talk to him. Then we'll see."

With that curious suggestion, he swaggered away, clearly confident that matters would turn in his favor once Elizabeth got done speaking with her father about…something.

That enigmatic comment was enough to weigh on Elizabeth's mind for the rest of the day. No one else who encountered her during the day could have determined that she had something else on her mind, but it was most definitely there.

She had a good day, finishing selling all the eggs she had before the end of the afternoon. She headed home and attended to the chickens, feeding them, cleaning up after them. Once she had done everything she could, she retired to her small room and proceeded to read her copy of the Bible. It had been a gift given her by her mother on her sixth birthday and the pages had become severely dog-eared over the years. Books were not easy to come by, no matter how rich one was. And considering Elizabeth's parents were quite poor, the fact that her mother had acquired it for her was nothing short of monumental. She would always sniff it first, adoring the smell the musty pages continued to emanate even to this day. Then she proceeded to leaf through it, looking for some of her favorite passages. She was particularly enamored of anything having to do directly with the Virgin. What had that been like, to have the son of God growing in her belly? She wondered if Mary had known the end to which her son had come. If she had, would she have done whatever she could to prevent him from living a life that would get him crucified? Yes, he had a destiny and was fated to die for the sins of mankind, but would Mary have declared to hell with that notion? Would she have said, "He is my son and he is going to live a long and happy life instead of dying for some cause? What is the purpose of having the being that created free will as a father if one then has no real will over their own destiny?"

It seemed a reasonable question. She wondered if perhaps she should ask the priest about it this Sunday when she attended mass.

She lost herself in the Bible until her father came home. He was carrying the dead body of a rabbit in one meaty hand and he tossed it onto the table. "Dinner," he said.

Elizabeth nodded. She knew it was her job to skin the thing and cook it up for her father and her to eat, but Bart's odd words to her earlier had never been far from her mind. So instead of picking the rabbit up and tending to it, she turned on the small bench on which she was seated and faced her father. "You know Bartholomew? The farmer? He said I should speak to you about something, but he was rather vague about it."

"Ah," said Thomas. His hands were covered with sawdust; he had obviously had a busy day. He shoved them into a large pot of water near the fireplace and cleansed them. "I was going to speak to you about this after dinner, but if we are to discuss this now, then so be it." He dried his hands on his leggings and sat down on the other end of the bench, facing his daughter. He looked as if he believed he should be smiling at that point, but as near as Elizabeth could determine, he had forgotten how to make his facial muscles crease in that manner, and so he just sat there and stared at her. "Bartholomew has spoken to me. About you."

"About me in what sense?" A faint trill of danger was sounding in Elizabeth's head, although she didn't know exactly why she should be feeling a sense of jeopardy. It was just her chatting with her father about—

"He wants to take your hand in marriage."

There was no romance in the way he said it. Bartholomew could well have made an offer to buy the chickens and Thomas would have conveyed the proposed deal to his daughter with the same degree of passionless enthusiasm. To him, he was simply relating the specifics of a business deal rather than discussing the future of his daughter's life.

"What?" she said tonelessly.

"He wants you for his wife."

"He's...he's twice as old as I am. At least."

"Why would you want to marry a man your age?" said Thomas, clearly not understanding her protest. "A sixteen-year-old boy has nothing. Owns nothing, has no property to speak of. Here you have a man with land who wants to wed you. This is an excellent opportunity for you. And for me as well. He's offering a very respectable dowry."

"I'm not interested."

"Not interested?" He gaped at her. "I'm doing you a favor!"

"Do me less favors. I don't love him!"

"Love?" Thomas gaped at her, clearly having no idea what in the world she was going on about. "How is that relevant?"

"I should have a say in who I marry!"

His eyes widened in incredulity. "Since when? Since when do you have a say in any damned thing! You are my daughter! You do as I say! And if I say you'll marry Bartholomew, then that's what you will bloody well do!"

She wanted to give in. She wanted to do as she said. She wanted to lower her gaze and apologize profusely and agree that yes, of course, he was right and she had no business standing up to him. Her duty as daughter was quite clear, and her responsibility was to do what she was ordered to do.

Then she envisioned Bartholomew. Yes, he was more than twice her age. Yes, his breath had a foul stink to it and his eyes possessed a lifeless gaze that made her wonder if his soul was even intact. Yes, he...

But he...

But...

"No." She heard her own voice as if the words were being spoken by a stranger. As if something else, some other creature or entity had taken possession of her body and was speaking on her behalf, saying things she would not have dared to say. "No, I will not marry him. I don't care how much he's offering you. You need me here."

"To do what? Care for the chickens?" Thomas made a dismissive noise. "With the money he's paying me for the dowry, I can hire someone to come in and do it while I'm out. Hell, that'll cost me a fraction of what I have to spend raising you."

"If it's a matter of money, I'll get a job somehow..."

"Doing what! You've no skills!"

"I could teach," she said, and she held up the Bible. "I could teach the Bible. I know it backwards and forwards..."

Furiously he knocked the book out of her hand. It sailed across the room and thudded in the fire that was roaring in the fireplace.

Elizabeth let out a startled scream, leapt off the bench and bolted for the fireplace. Heedless of the danger to herself, she thrust her hand in and snatched the book out of the flames while it was still smoldering. She banged it quickly with her hand, snuffing the fire out, as she pivoted toward her father and cried out, "How could you do that?!"

He obviously did not have the slightest interest in arguing with her or explaining his actions. He rose to his feet, towering over her, and in a low, angry voice, said, "You will marry Bartholomew, or you will get nothing more from me. Do you understand? *Nothing!*"

"Fine!" she said heatedly.

"Fine!" he shouted back. He strode forward and she clutched the Bible to her bosom. He ignored it and instead grabbed at the shoulder of her dress.

"What are you doing?" she said.

"Take it off!"

"*What?*"

"I bought you this! It's mine, not yours! I gave it to you! Now I'm taking it back! Remove the dress! The undergarments, too! My money bought those! Strip naked or I'll do it for you!"

Elizabeth couldn't believe it. But she saw the look on her father's face, his determination to show her her place.

She knew that all she had to do was agree to marry Bartholomew. If she did that, all of this insanity would stop. *Just give him what he wants. Just—*

And for no reason that she could discern, she suddenly thought of Robyne Hood.

She hadn't seen Robyne herself. She had only heard rumors passed along from other villagers. About how Robyne had stood up to Richard the Lionheart himself; how she had defeated him in one to one combat. The word was that she was fighting for the rights of all women. That she was forming a band of Merry Maids and they were united in battling against the sheriff and his cursed father. Robyne supposedly advocated that women had a place in the world beyond whatever it was that men were willing to allocate to them.

Maybe the only way to support that fight was to join it.

Without a word she undid the fastenings on her garment and seconds later the dress was a pile of cloth at her feet. She divested herself of her undergarments as well and stood there in front of her father, naked and defiant. "Happy?" she said.

All the color vanished from his face. She hoped that he was feeling deep shame over this stunt. That he would see the error of his ways, instruct her to dress herself, go and tell Bartholomew that his offer, while appreciated, was rejected.

Instead his face twisted into an expression of fury as he grabbed her by the wrist and dragged her toward the door. "You want nothing! You get nothing! No clothing! No shelter! Good luck making your way in the world on your own!"

He slammed the door and she heard the thud of the bolt falling into place. The door was secured against her. She was locked out, naked.

Suddenly all thoughts of Robyne and equal rights for women vanished from her head and was replaced by shame and mortification.

Her impulse was to bang her fists on the door, to beg for her father to let her in, to succumb to whatever he desired. Because really, didn't he actually have her best interests at heart?

He stripped you naked and threw you out of the house because you wouldn't give in to his demands. And you want to reward him for that by bending under his weight?

She wanted to keep screaming, but the desire died in her throat. Instead, crouched next to the door, her arms crossed in front of her breasts, she glanced around. There was no one about to witness her shame. She had never been more thankful that her father's desire to keep to himself had caused him to build their small house on the outskirts of the town.

Elizabeth did the only thing she could think of to do.

She fled.

Stepping carefully since the ground was thick with projecting rocks and sharp branches, she ran away from the only home that she had ever known and vanished into the thickness of the woods. Sherwood Forest opened its branches to her and swallowed her and she vanished into the lengthening evening shadows.

CHAPTER XVIII

I do not see many naked women

SHE WONDERED IF ROBYNE WOULD FIND her, take pity on her. Provide her succor, clothing, food because her stomach was rumbling and empty.

Elizabeth stumbled through the forest, having no idea where she should go or what she should do. She had never had much patience for Sherwood. To her, it was the home of thieves and gypsies, of people who would just as soon do her harm as look at her. She had always believed that if you entered Sherwood with food, robbers would set upon you and take it. If you entered Sherwood with the flower of your maidenhood upon you, they would rob you of that, too. Elizabeth had no food, but her maidenhood was still intact and she was naked to boot. Any man who found her would ravage her without question. If he had company, they would take her as well. She could do nothing to stop it. She had no weapons, no fighting skills, no chance.

She sought a cave in which she could take refuge, but nothing presented itself. She prayed that Robyne would encounter her, but the princess of thieves likewise did not seem especially inclined to make her presence known.

"God, help me," she whispered. She clutched the Bible, the only object that her father had allowed her to keep in her possession, closely against her breasts.

God responded.

She heard a crack of thunder and dark clouds rolled in, and she felt the first pelts of water sprinkling down upon her. "Oh no," she murmured, "please, no."

There was another blast of thunder and lightning, almost at the same time, which was enough to tell her that not only was there a lightning storm, but she was right in the midst of it.

Elizabeth began to run, desperately seeking shelter, without having the slightest notion of where she was going. For a brief moment she considered returning home, begging her father to let her in, promising to do whatever it was he wanted. But she rejected it even as the downpour began. *At least my clothes aren't getting wet* she thought grimly and, to her shock, actually chuckled. She was astounded that she could find anything remotely humorous about her situation.

At least, she reasoned, robbers likely wouldn't be roaming about in the rain. They'd have no more interest in getting soaked than anyone else.

She had departed what passed for the road in Sherwood and was wandering helplessly, and suddenly she saw a building in the near distance. She squinted against the rain as it filled her eyes. She had no idea who resided within the unassuming structure. Perhaps it was the home of bandits who hied themselves there during bad weather. It was certainly no place for a naked, helpless teen to seek shelter, and yet she was beginning to shiver as the cold water pounded down upon her. If she stayed out, helpless before the weather's wrath much longer, she would very likely contract some sort of lung illness and likely die. That was certainly not how she imagined her life ending: dying naked, coughing her last bits of life out on the merciless floor of Sherwood Forest. Realizing she had no choice in the matter, she moved toward the house.

Her bare foot hit a branch and she stumbled forward, landing hard. She cried out in pain as she felt the skin on her left shin get torn up. Lying helpless on the dirt that was rapidly turning into mud, she clutched at her leg and examined the damage. Blood was swelling from it and she moaned at the sight. She didn't do well with blood, even her own.

Elizabeth staggered to her feet, biting her lower lip to prevent herself from crying out. Tears on her cheeks mixed with the rain as she staggered forward, limping fiercely. She almost fell against the door of the small structure and pounded her fist on the door. Then she braced herself, convinced that some brute would open the door, take one look at her, and ravage her. *Maybe he'll kill me. Send me to be with my mother. That wouldn't be such a horrible thing. And I won't have to live in the tortured thing that my body will be after he's had his way with it.*

The door swung open and her eyes widened in shock, as did the eyes of the man who had answered it.

It was a monk.

He was thin, almost emaciated, with a ring of thin, graying hair surrounding his otherwise bald head. He was wearing a brown cassock that was threadbare around the elbows. His face was grizzled. It wasn't a beard; he just obviously had ceased paying the slightest bit of attention to his personal appearance and he hadn't shaved in days.

"Good lord," he whispered, and put out his arms to Elizabeth. With a soft wail, she sank into them. "Child, who did this to you?"

"My...my father," she said in a soft voice.

"What? Why? No, never mind," he said quickly, changing gears. "The why doesn't matter. There is no excuse. Come. Come, my child. Come in to God's arms; you'll be safe here."

"I knew it," and she clutched the Bible even tighter to herself. "I knew he would protect me."

Suddenly the world went black. Her legs sagged under her and she began to fall. The monk prevented her from doing so, displaying surprising strength considering how unimpressive his physicality was. She started to say something but had no idea what it was and then she lapsed into unconsciousness.

―—« »—―

Elizabeth slowly opened her eyes and let out a gasp, and the abrupt exclamation of sound startled the young man who was sitting next to her bed...

Her bed?

She sat up and the thin sheet fell away from her. Reflexively she brought her arms up to cover her bosoms and then discovered that it wasn't necessary; she was wearing a gray hassock that wasn't dissimilar from what the monk had been wearing. She looked in question at the young man. He was simply dressed in a black tunic and leggings. He was a young man but wore seriousness that far exceeded his years as if it were a shroud. "Sorry about the hassock. We don't have much in the way of women's clothing here. We're a monastery, after all. Well," and he glanced around ruefully, "what passes for a monastery, I suppose."

"Are you a monk?"

"No. I'm the sexton. I take care of the place around here. Tend to the brother, help the prayerful. My name is Randolf."

"I'm Elizabeth."

"Elizabeth. And may I ask how you wound up naked and wet at our door?"

"It's, uh..." Her voice trailed off a moment. "It's a difficult story. Do you really have to know?"

"Have to? No. I just admit I'm curious. I do not see many naked women. Not in my line of work, anyway."

"That's enough, Randolf." A strong voice came from the doorway. The monk who had permitted her entrance into the monastery was standing there. He was smiling faintly. "It is her life and she is under no obligation to share it."

"No, but I am," she said after a moment's thought. "You took me in, no questions. You should know what's going on."

So she told them. She did it as straightforwardly and without exaggeration as she could. She made no effort to describe Bartholomew in negative terms or characterize her father as the insensitive brute that she believed him to be. She simply described what her father wanted her to do; her reaction; and his subsequent stripping of her and throwing her out of the house.

The monk and sexton listened without interruption. When she was done, she glanced over at the simple, small table that was next to the cot upon which she lay. Her Bible was perched on it. She reached over and took it, holding it lovingly as if it were a child.

The room fell into a hush when she stopped talking, and then the monk slowly shook his head. "Pardon my saying so, but your father is a monster."

"No, it's just that—"

"He is a monster," the monk repeated. "Only a monster would do such a thing to a child. Whatever his intentions were, however much he thought he was granting you a good life, that does not remotely excuse what he did to you. He should be ashamed of himself. You were right to flee him."

"I had no choice. He stripped me and threw me out."

"You did have a choice." He pulled over a short stool and sat upon it. "You could have gone back and done what he demanded. Instead you chose to stand up for yourself."

"Like Robyne of Sherwood would have," she said eagerly. "Have you seen her? Met her?"

The question seemed to catch the monk off guard. "I have... heard of her. Randolf saw her in the village when she battled Lionheart."

"She was lucky," Randolf said dismissively. "His highness was clearly ill. If the king had been at full strength, there would have been no way that she could have stood up to her."

Elizabeth was stunned to hear his words. She had heard very differently from the other villagers who had witnessed the duel. Most agreed that she had Lionheart at her mercy; that she could have dispatched him if she had been so inclined. The fact that Richard was still breathing was due entirely to her refusal to dispose of him. "Others...have described it in a different manner," she said.

"People see what they want to see."

"Yes, that is true, Randolf," said the monk, and his voice was mildly scolding. He looked as if he wanted to say more, but then changed his mind and shifted his attention back to Elizabeth. "So what do you see yourself doing now, my child? Do you have any other relatives with whom you can reside? Any place else in the world to which you can go?"

Slowly she shook her head. "My father was the only person in the world that I had to take care of me, and the home from which he evicted me was the only one I knew. I am willing to work, to earn a wage. To do whatever it is necessary to do to make a living for myself. But I've no idea what path to follow."

"Do you have any skills? Aside from your obvious love of the Bible," and he nodded toward the volume that she was clutching.

She had been wondering that very thing herself not all that long ago. At the time, she hadn't come up with an answer. And then, somewhat to her surprise, an answer popped into her head. "My mother became ill some years ago," she said slowly. "During that time, there were various herbs and medicines that she would make in order to provide her pain relief from her increasingly bad...and eventually fatal...condition. As she became weaker, she taught me how to make them. She said I was quite skilled at it. That I learned the techniques and formula very quickly. I developed something of an interest at it. I've not had much occasion to employ those skills since my mother's passing, but I remember it all very clearly."

"That's excellent to hear," said the monk readily. "That can be very useful. People around these parts oftentimes use me for medical aid. They do not trust the leech-lovers who present themselves as practitioners of the healing arts, and I cannot say I blame them. They find my various formulae far more useful for their common ailments, and I could very much use an assistant to aid me and learn from me."

"Now hold on, Brother," Randolf said immediately. He was on his feet and he was clearly not pleased with the direction the conversation had taken. "This is a young, unmarried girl. She cannot reside here. This is not a nunnery."

"And she is not a nun, so certainly that is a handy development," replied the monk. He raised an eyebrow skeptically. "Randolf, my dear sexton…are you implying that I cannot be trusted? That the girl's virtue is somehow threatened were she to extend her stay here?"

"How would it look?" said Randolf.

"To whom? To the villagers? The Sheriff? The king? The Pope? To Jesus?"

Randolf didn't have an answer; all he managed to do was stammer slightly.

The monk didn't wait for him to reply. "I am a monk, Randolf. I live here with you. On occasion the needy or the prayerful show up, seeking my help. They do not need to see young Elizabeth here, and even if they do, they will not ask for explanations. They will assume that she is exactly what she is: a young woman in need of aid whom I have chosen to help. Is there anything in that explanation that requires further discussion?"

"I suppose not," said Randolf, and he bowed slightly and stiffly. "I suppose I should attend to my duties."

"That is an excellent thought and I would do precisely that."

Randolf nodded to him once more and then turned to Elizabeth. "Welcome to our home. Enjoy your stay."

"Thank you." She watched as Randolf strode out of the room. She had the feeling that he wanted to cast a glance at her over his shoulder, but resisted the impulse to do so. Once he was gone, she turned uncertainly to the monk. "I do not think he likes me."

"You are different," he said with a slight shrug. "Randolf does not do well with change, which is why he is the ideal choice for sexton. He wants things to remain the same. It is his nature. But that is unrealistic. Things change and one must be prepared to adapt to those changes."

"I suppose so." She cocked her head and studied the monk. "What is your name?"

"I have left such things as names behind," said the monk. "Simply address me as Brother. I am satisfied with that, for it accurately describes my relationship to the rest of the world."

"You're everyone's brother?"

"The world could use one," said the monk. He patted her shoulder. "Trust me, my dear. You will be safe here. Everything will be attended to."

—« »—

Thomas sat there, staring blankly at the flickering flame in the fireplace, the main source of light and warmth in the room.

Why didn't she understand? Why didn't she comprehend that I was helping her? That I was setting her up for life? If she was married to a farmer, she would never have to worry about starvation. Does she have no idea what a genuine concern that is? She's sixteen summers old. There are girls who are already the mothers of two or three by that age. What in the name of God is she waiting for? I had her life all laid out for her and she would rather go off naked on her own than submit to being married...

But...what about love...?

He snorted derisively. *Love. What sort of mad aspect is that to have? Women don't get married because of love. They get married because it's a smart business move. Does she think her mother loved me? It's not about love. It's about building a family, making connections, surviving. Unless she's planning to go off and become a nun, she's going to need a man to take care of her. How can she not realize that? How can she put me into this situation?*

What's she going to do? Where's she going to go?

She's probably run off into Sherwood. A helpless, naked girl in the middle of the forest, alone, unarmed, unprotected. She's probably been raped and murdered by now.

In the very inner reaches of his being, guilt began to surface. He was the one who had stripped her, thrown her out. If she was in danger, it was because he had thrown her into it.

But what choice had he had? Really?

For what seemed the hundredth time, he stood up to head for the door and then sat down again. He had already crossed to it a while earlier, thrown it open and expected to find Elizabeth hunched there, begging to be let in. When he hadn't, he had stepped out and walked the circumference of the house, stunned when he didn't find her. Then he had gone back inside and spent the intervening time debating whether to go out into the woods and seek her out. Up, down, up, down, so he had gone, unable to decide. At this point he was no closer, and when he heard a knock at the door, he sighed in relief.

She was back. She had seen the error of her ways and returned to beg forgiveness.

For a moment he was tempted to play it coy. To stand at the door but not open it; instead act confused that someone was there and play a round of "Who's there?" Make her stand out there and shiver for a few minutes.

But he couldn't do it. He was so relieved that she was back that he went straight to the door and threw it open.

He blinked in surprise and confusion. It wasn't Elizabeth. It was some young man who seemed familiar somehow...

"Mr. Carpenter. Randolf," said the young man. "I'm a sexton at a monastery nearby. You built some shelving for us."

"Oh, right, yes. Yes. Is there a problem with them?"

"No problem."

"Well, if you want to hire me for another job, could you perhaps return tomorrow? I'm not in the best of moods right now to—"

"Because your daughter ran off, yes?"

The question brought Thomas to a halt. He stood there, staring. "How did you know that?"

"Let me come in," he said, "and I'll be more than happy to tell you."

CHAPTER XIX

Let's go get her

BARTHOLOMEW WAS GETTING IMPATIENT. AND WHENEVER he got impatient, he would hie himself over to the pub and avail himself liberally of the drinks that the innkeeper, Ivan, was willing to provide.

Ivan was a mainstay of Nottingham, as was his pub. He had won it in a card game some years earlier and was absolutely obsessive about keeping his regular customers happy. He was a burly, jovial man who seemed endlessly amused at the world and the challenges it presented his customers who did not hesitate to unload on him with their litany of problems. Ivan had been the first person that Bartholomew had told about his importuning Thomas to provide him the hand of his daughter, and Ivan had generously provided him a free drink as a means of congratulations. The fact that Bartholomew had nothing further to report on the proposal was extremely irritating to him. He had fully expected Thomas to deliver the girl to his doorstep, preferably with a priest in tow in order to join the two of them in wedded bliss. Bartholomew was not the most romantic of individuals and wasn't the slightest bit interested in making a big deal out of the union. He had made clear his intentions to Thomas and Thomas had seemed likewise sympathetic to the notion of keeping the ceremony simple.

So where the hell had he been? What was taking so damned long?

"Bart? Everything all right?" asked Ivan. He was standing behind the bar, wiping mugs clean, looking concerned.

Several other men glanced in his direction, and the attention did not sit well with Bart. He wasn't all that interested in admitting that Thomas was keeping him waiting. Bartholomew detested being made to wait.

He was about to respond when the door suddenly banged open, not because someone had shoved it hard, but because it had been kicked. Everyone in the pub jumped in startlement as Thomas strode into the pub, looking so angry that he appeared as if he could have bitten a metal bar in half. He didn't order any drink, didn't offer any greeting. He simply stormed across the pub and dropped into the nearest available chair.

Bartholomew approached him cautiously. "Thomas...what the hell—?"

"She won't marry you," growled Thomas, and then he allowed his fury to overcome him and he practically shouted, "My bloody daughter has turned down the marriage proposal of this good man!" and he pointed at Bartholomew.

Bart's face flushed slightly in embarrassment, but the clear rage radiating from Thomas was enough to ease it considerably. He dropped into a chair opposite Thomas and said, "What happened?"

Already, though, even as he asked, the answer flashed into his mind: *He killed her. The bastard killed her.* He knew that Thomas had a bit of a temper, and if his daughter stood up to him, stated desires that were contrary to what he wanted, Bartholomew could easily see him beating the poor girl to death. It wasn't as if he was a murderer or any such thing. But a temper could be an overwhelming trait to possess and it could easily take him down a road that would prove terminal for the helpless girl.

Thomas's eyes shifted; it was as if he had something he wanted to say, but was thinking better of it. Instead he growled, "She ran off."

"Ran off?" *Well, of course he'd say that. He's probably buried her body and when she can't be found, he'll just claim that she's set out for London or someplace like that. The poor girl's body is going to be rotting in an unmarked grave somewhere...*

"Yes. Run off into Sherwood. And she's taken up residence in a monastery there."

That pronouncement caught Bartholomew completely off guard. "Wait...what?" he said in confusion. "The monastery...?"

"Yeah. The monk who lives there took pity on her and took her in. He said she can stay there for as long as she wants."

"Well...that's not right!" said Bartholomew.

This aroused agreements from the other men in the pub. "How dare he?" "Interfere with a father and his daughter?" "Disobedient brat!" The fact that their opinions were supplemented by the amount of alcohol that they had already ingested certainly did not help the situation.

Thomas visibly took heart at the expressions of outrage and support that he was receiving from the others. "Damned right!" he said. "But what am I supposed to do about it?"

Bartholomew took a long drag on his ale and then slammed the metal mug down upon the table. "I'll tell you what you're supposed to do about it. We go and bloody get her, that's what we do!"

Thomas stared with open incredulity at him. "You're serious? You are serious? You are willing to do that?"

"Some monk sticks his nose into our business? What right does he have?" said Bartholomew. He finished his ale and tossed the mug aside. It slid off the table and Ivan snagged it before it hit the floor. "I'll tell you what's right. None, that's what. And we're going to take care of it right now. Thomas, do you know where this monastery is?"

"Absolutely. I did work there."

"Who wants to come with us and get Thomas's daughter out of the hands of this monk?" Bartholomew called out.

Half a dozen hands shot up. Bartholomew grinned widely; it was exactly the response he had hoped for.

He turned to Thomas and his grin transformed into a most unpleasant sneer.

"Let's go get her," he said.

CHAPTER XX

Mary?

"HE'S GOING TO COME AFTER ME."

The monk blinked in confusion, looking up from the medication that he was endeavoring to put together. He put the vials aside and stared at Elizabeth? "'He' being your father?"

"Yes," said Elizabeth. Initially she had felt uncomfortable wearing monk's robes, but she had obviously become comfortable in it. She had seated herself on a stool, her hands folded on her lap. "He sees me as his property. Yes, he threw me out of the house. But I suspect that he thought I would just sit outside until he let me back in. He's not going to be thrilled when he discovers I fled."

"He's not going to know to where you fled."

"He'll figure it out."

"My child," said the monk gently, and he rested a hand on her shoulder. "God is protecting you."

"Jesu was His son and he got crucified. I think we have to realize that having God protecting you isn't necessarily an assurance of anything good."

Despite the notion that what the girl had just said was borderline sacrilegious, the monk could not help but smile. "I imagine that there is some validation for that point of view. But for what it's worth, you are under my protection as well. And believe it or not, I can be formidable when the situation requires it."

"You?" She raised a doubting eyebrow and then laughed. "I'm

sorry. I shouldn't…I don't mean to insult you. Honestly. You've been so kind to me. But I just find it hard to imagine you somehow battling forces that come here to take me back."

"With any luck," said the monk, "you will never have to witness such a—"

That was when a loud knocking came from the door.

The monk's eyes narrowed in suspicion.

Elizabeth noticed the look in his eyes. "What's the matter?" she said. "You never get visitors here?"

"Not generally this late in the evening, and so soon after inclement weather. The roads tend to become somewhat boggy, as you well know. Plus they typically pull the bell chime. There was anger to this knock. It doesn't bode well."

"You can tell all that from a knock?"

He glanced at her and there was something unsaid in his face that nevertheless spoke volumes. "Trust me, my dear. I have had some experience in knowing when danger is present. Remain here."

There was a lengthy walking staff leaning against the far wall. It seemed quite thick and it was elaborately carved with various symbols and designs, none of which she recognized. The monk strode across the room and gripped it securely. She wondered what its purpose was, since the monk had never displayed any inability to walk. She had just assumed it to be some manner of display or souvenir, although she couldn't imagine of what.

"Wait in here," he said firmly. "No matter what you here, do not make yourself seen. Do you understand?"

Her head bobbed up and down. "All right. I'll wait here." But then, as he turned to leave, she reached out and rested a hand on his shoulder. "If it is my father, and he threatens you, you must call me and I will go with him. I do not want any harm to come to you, and I will not let you suffer in my stead."

"Do not worry, my child," said the monk. "Be concerned instead for your father. Believe it or not, I have been in a scrape or two in my life."

Elizabeth really did have trouble believing it. The monk seemed harmless. She wondered who in the world would possibly pick a fight with him that the monk would have gotten into any manner of "scrape" with him.

The monk, for his part, strode out of the study and went to the front door. He got there just as Randolf was approaching it and said briskly, "Stay back. I will attend to this." Randolf looked momentarily puzzled but then nodded and stepped back.

The knocking, meantime, was becoming louder and more insistent. The door was bolted and the monk made no endeavor to unlatch it. "Make sure the shutters are all closed and locked," he said to Randolf, who immediately nodded and headed out of the room. The door itself had a small viewing door, which the monk now opened. He instantly recognized the face on the other side. It was the carpenter who had installed shelving in the monastery. He hadn't connected it with Elizabeth's tale of her father, Thomas, since it was such a common name, but now he wondered if they were indeed the same. "Thomas," the monk recalled. "What can I do for you this evening?"

"Let me in," said Thomas, and now the monk was able to discern that Thomas was not alone. There were about half a dozen men behind him, and they were scowling and endeavoring to look as fierce as they could.

"It's somewhat late in the evening, Thomas. Can it wait until another day?"

"You have my daughter in there, monk. Let her out and we'll be on our way."

So now the monk knew his suspicion was correct. He hadn't made the connection when Elizabeth had referred to the father who had thrown her out of the home. He had failed to put two and two together and realize that he had met the man. He remembered him as being a reasonably decent sort who pretty much kept to himself. He did the job briskly and then moved on.

The monk cleared his throat. For a moment he considered lying, pretending that the girl wasn't there and he had no idea what Thomas was talking about. But he realized immediately that wouldn't work. First of all, he was a terrible liar. Thomas would know in a heartbeat that what he was saying was untrue. Next Thomas would demand to be given entrance so that he could affirm it for himself, and he would find the poor girl in no time. There seemed to be no positive alternative to the truth, and so that was what the monk settled on. "I'm afraid that is not possible, Thomas. She has sought sanctuary here and I have granted it."

"She is my daughter!"

"She is the daughter of the lord, and I am acting as His representative in this matter," said the monk stiffly. "If you have an argument with that, I suggest you consult your priest." His voice grew cold as he continued, "Perhaps you can avail him of the story of how you threw the poor child out of your house stark naked. I'm sure that will endear you to him most readily."

"You know nothing of children, monk! You do not get to sit in judgment on me!"

"That is true. But eventually Saint Peter will attend to that, so you may wish to brush up on your defense for your actions. I'm sure that will be quite the interesting encounter."

"Enough of this!" came the shout of another, and suddenly there was a loud slam against the door. Someone had endeavored to kick it open; fortunately the heavy bolt enabled the door to remain in place.

"You do not have permission to enter this premises!" the monk shouted.

They were clearly not waiting for it. The door shook again, and a third time. It was not designed to withstand this sort of battering. The monk knew that there was no way it was going to withstand the pounding, and he backed up several steps, raising the staff so that it was horizontal and ready.

With an explosion of noise the bolt snapped off and the door flew open. It was not Thomas who was standing there, but another man who looked both belligerent and drunk, but drunk in the way that made a man dangerous rather than simply amusing and harmless. He charged at the monk and the monk swung the staff down

and around, catching him behind his knees and tripping him up.
The attacker fell and slammed his chin on the hardwood floor, but
now there were more men following behind and the monk knew
he was in trouble.

Thomas pushed through and he shouted, "Bartholomew! Dispose of the monk! I'll find my daughter!"

The man whom he had called Bartholomew charged forward
and the monk readied himself. Then he saw that Bart was wielding a small scythe and he wasn't thrilled with the odds that were
presenting themselves.

That was when a sound that the monk would never forget cut
through the air, a noise like no other.

It was an arrow.

For an instant the monk's mind flashed back to another time,
another life.

The arrow thudded into Bartholomew's right shoulder and he
screamed and sank to the floor. The men who had been shouting
encouragement fell silent in shock, unable to believe what they had
just seen.

And suddenly Thomas was lifted off his feet. He let out a startled shriek and the monk saw, to his complete astonishment, that
there was a woman behind him. She was large, the bulkiest female
that the monk had ever beheld, and she was hauling him upward as
if he were nothing more than a damp dish rag. Then she slammed
him to the ground with such a reverberating thud that the monk
could feel the vibrations in his feet.

She had what appeared to be a massive axe strapped to her back
and she strode forward, placing her booted foot on Bartholomew's
throat, keeping him pinned to the floor.

From outside there was the sound of weapons being drawn, of a
fight under way. Swords clanged together and were knocked aside,
and now an armored, helmeted knight strode in. There was blood
on the edge of his sword and it was quite obviously not his. "Care
to tell us what's happening here?" said the knight.

At that moment Elizabeth emerged from the monk's study. "I

told you to remain hidden!" said the monk.

But she was paying him no mind. Instead she pointed at Thomas, who was lying moaning on the floor. "That's my father," said Elizabeth. "He stripped me naked and threw me out of the house because I wouldn't marry him," and she shifted her finger to the fallen Bartholomew.

"*He did what?!*" The knight clearly couldn't believe what he was hearing. He strode over to Thomas and said angrily, "Does she speak truly?"

"Not exactly," Thomas managed to get out.

"Then *what* exactly?"

"Well," and Thomas licked his suddenly dry lips, "yes, I did that, but I had good reason t—"

That was all the knight needed to hear. He stepped forward and kicked Thomas in the gut. Thomas grunted and the knight continued to kick him viciously. He snarled, "You call yourself a father? What father would do that? What man of any decency would do that!"

Thomas moaned and rolled over onto his side, trying to get away. The knight drove his sword point downward into the floor, stopping Thomas's roll before he could get any further away. Thomas's head snapped around and he looked up at the knight in terror. The knight raised his sword once more and the point glistened above Thomas's head.

"*Clarence! No!*"

The knight called Clarence froze, clearly ready to execute the man but not doing so because a female voice had ordered him to stop.

A green clad woman, her face masked, strode in. There were two more women right behind her: one with dark skin, and the other quite young and carrying a morningstar. The dark skinned woman was wielding a sword that also had blood on it, and there was blood on the Morningstar as well. Clearly they had been busy. But the moans that were floating through the air from the outside told the monk that at least some, if not all, of the men were still alive, although they weren't as in good shape as they had been a few minutes earlier.

The knight stepped back and the green clad woman said, "Want to tell me what's going on here?"

In a few words, the knight laid out for the woman what Elizabeth had just said. Her eyes narrowed and what the monk could see of her face darkened. She reached back to the quiver of arrows she had mounted on her back, nocked one into her bow and took aim at Thomas's chest. But then her gaze shifted to Elizabeth. "He lives or dies; it's up to you."

For a long moment, Elizabeth actually seemed to consider it. Then her gaze shifted to the monk and she looked at him questioningly.

"As the Lord has forgiven you, so you also must forgive," said the monk.

To his surprise, the broad shouldered, red-haired woman said, "Colossians. Don't remember the verse number off hand."

"Three thirteen," said the monk with a raised eyebrow. "Very good."

"My late husband was quite the Bible enthusiast."

Slowly the green clad woman withdrew her arrow. She glared down at Thomas and said, "Gather your men and go. We've damaged them somewhat, but they are still capable of movement. Take them and leave, and I swear, if you ever attempt to harm this girl—if you even track her down just to look at her—I will find you and no amount of pleas or forgiveness will spare your life. Do you understand?" His head bobbed up and down. "Say you understand."

"I understand."

"Good. Now get out of here."

Thomas managed to get to his feet as the red-haired woman stood there and just glowered at him. He hauled the moaning Bartholomew upright. "I'd wait until you get him home before removing that arrow," the helmeted knight advised him. "I assure you, you don't need it to start bleeding until you can get him bandaged."

"Thanks," Thomas was able to get out. They limped toward the front door and moments later they and their friends were vacating the area.

The green-clad woman then turned and for the first time looked directly into the monk's face.

He gasped, clearly unable to process what he was looking at.

She was saying something to him, something about being sure to keep an eye on him and then she shifted her attention to Elizabeth, asking if she wanted to accompany them. But the specifics of what she was saying faded into a distant buzz in the monk's ears because he had looked straight into her eyes and couldn't believe what he had seen.

It's not her. It can't be her. She's much too young and besides, she's dead, at least I've always assumed she's dead, and she was never much with a bow anyway, and how could it be her, it couldn't possibly be, but...oh my God...could it be...?

"Mary?" The word escaped his lips.

She had been addressing Elizabeth, but her attention snapped back to the monk. Her eyes widened in shock and she took a step forward, staring at him incredulously as if she was truly seeing him for the first time. She reached up as if her hand was moving on its own and she pulled down the cloth that was masking the lower half of her face. She revealed her chin, her mouth that was hanging open in astonishment, and slowly she reached out. Her hand stroked his cheek as if she was a blind woman touching a face to familiarize herself with it.

Until that point she had spoken in strident, commanding tones. But all of that was gone now as her next word was barely above a whisper

"*Tuck?*"

The monk began to sob and as tears rolled down his cheeks, he managed to say, "My God, you have your mother's eyes."

With a roar of joy, Robyne threw her arms around Friar Tuck and cried out ecstatically.

CHAPTER XXI

I take it ye know this fellow?

ROBYNE SIMPLY COULD NOT BELIEVE IT. She had been convinced that the Merry Men were all dead. She had witnessed her father's death herself. The heads of several of the Merry Men—John, Will Scarlett—had been displayed on the parapets of Nottingham Castle for weeks. She had never seen them herself, but she had heard about them. About how the skin had slowly rotted away while crows picked at the eyes and other delicate bits of matter. She had never heard anything about her mother, whom she assumed had slipped away and died somewhere privately. Her body was doubtless lying in an unmarked grave somewhere. But no word had ever reached her ears about poor Friar Tuck.

Yet now here he was, far slimmer than she had ever recalled him being. His hair was long gone, his face no longer round and cherubic but instead gaunt and lean. And his eyes, God, they looked so tired as if he had seen far more than he had ever wanted to see. More than any man should have to see.

But there he was, real and alive and standing in front of her as if welcoming her back from some lengthy vacation.

She embraced him fiercely. If her father had risen from the dead and come forward to greet her, she could not have been more enthusiastic.

Standing several feet away, Innis Rae made no attempt to hide her confusion. "I take it ye know this fellow?"

Robyne realized that there were tears of happiness running down her cheeks. Quickly she wiped them away before any of her followers could see them and turned to face them. "This is Tuck. He was a member of my father's original band."

"Friar Tuck!" Clarence said as he stuck forward a gloved hand and shook Tuck's. "This is an honor, sir. I have, of course, heard of you. I am Sir Clarence."

"You can remove your helmet, Sir Clarence. You are among friends here," said Tuck.

Robyne rested a hand on Tuck's forearm. "He'd rather not," she said gently. "He's a leper."

"Really," said Tuck. "You've no need to be ashamed of your condition here, my son. I've ministered to your kind in colonies. I have no fear of you."

"Oh," said Clarence uncertainly. "Very well." He reached up and removed his helmet.

"That's better," said Tuck. He glanced around. "And who are these others?"

"This is Innis Rae. And Khalida, and Alys. They are my—"

"Merry Maids?" said Tuck.

Robyne rolled her eyes, but Innis Rae said immediately, "That's exactly right."

"And this is Elizabeth," said Tuck, gesturing to the young woman standing a short distance away. "Please, come in, my children. Let me serve you bread and ale. It is the very least I can do. Randolf!" his voice carried through the monastery.

Moments later the young man whom Tuck had summoned ambled forward, staring suspiciously at Robyne and her crew. "This is Randolf, my sexton," said Tuck. "I would be lost without him."

That hardly struck Robyne as a ringing endorsement. There was something about the sexton that rubbed Robyne the wrong way. She had no idea what it might be. He had said and done nothing to trigger her suspicions, and yet she didn't exactly trust him.

Ease up, for God's sake. If Tuck trusts him, then there is no reason you should not as well. Tuck's word should be sufficient.

"Greetings," said Robyne, and she extended her hand. Randolf shook it willingly and smiled graciously at her. He certainly had a nice smile. "I am Robyne."

"Since when are you Robyne?" asked Tuck.

"Since I undertook this," and she waved her arm in a general fashion. "My father's work."

Tuck seemed about to respond immediately but then he held his tongue. "Come," he said, gesturing for her to follow him. She and the others did so and moments later they were seated in what appeared to be a galley of some sort where food was prepared. Randolf had poured wine carefully into goblets and Tuck raised one in a toast. "To you parents," he said, and Robyne and the others matched the gesture and drank.

"First things first," said Tuck, placing his goblet carefully on the table. "Where have you been all these years?"

"I was raised by a woman called the Magistar."

"Theresa?" said Tuck in surprise.

Robyne rolled her eyes at that. "Does *everyone* know her real name but me?"

"Theresa and I go way back," said Tuck. "Indeed, before we went our separate ways, she was with me when I worked at the colonies," and he nodded toward Clarence, "that endeavored to help your kind, sir."

"Very considerate, Friar."

Tuck shifted his attention back to Robyne. "So tell me everything."

She did. She laid out the entirety of her history in broad strokes and, aside from a few places for quick questions, Tuck didn't interrupt her. Instead he listened intently to her story, his face so impassive that she couldn't discern what he was thinking.

Finally, when she concluded, long moments of silence passed. She wanted to ask him what was going through his mind but restrained herself, certain that he would tell her once he had put the words together.

Then he looked down sadly and shook his head. "Mary, Mary,"

he sighed heavily as if chastising a child.

"Robyne," she corrected him politely but firmly. "I'm Robyne now."

"Your father was Robin," said Tuck. "You are…". He hesitated, glancing around at the rest of the Merry Maids who were sitting or standing there, watching intently.

"You can say what you will in front of them," Robyne told him. "I have no secrets from them."

"All right. You are pretending to be Robin. Pretending that you are your father. As if this is all some manner of vast game."

"A game!" she said incredulously. "You think this is a game to me? We are helping people, Tuck! We are saving lives in the same way that you and father did!"

"You think your father did it voluntarily?" said Tuck. He rose now and began to pace. "He did it out of necessity! He did it because he had nothing to lose!"

"Nothing to lose? His name, his property…?"

"That was already taken," Tuck said. "Didn't you know that? He made the mistake of openly criticizing Richard, and because he did so, his lands were forfeit and he was supposed to be arrested. Your father fled and took up residence in the forest because he had nowhere else to go! All his friends shunned him. He had no money, no property. All he maintained were his wits and his fighting abilities. But he didn't seek out people to aid them. He was simply a thief, robbing passersby in the woods in order to survive."

"He was a hero," Robyne said, her anger starting to rise.

"He was transformed into one by the bards telling of his many great adventures, the vast majority of which I assure you were fabricated or exaggerated. Make no mistake, my child: he was a good man. He had a great heart and cared for the welfare of the people. Indeed, in many ways he became that which they believed him to be because he became so enamored of the tales that it gave him something to live up to. But there was no great plan, Mary. He had no great scheme to challenge Richard or defeat the Sheriff. He was just trying to survive. And I can assure you, he wanted a better life for his children, for you and Basil. His son is likely long dead, but you survive. You could live a decent life, away from all this," and he gestured around himself as if to take in the entirety of Nottingham. "There is nothing holding you here. You could relocate to London, say, and start over. Live free of war and battle and risking your life in a way that your father would never have wanted."

"You don't understand, Tuck. I need to do this."

"Why?"

"Because my father died because of me. I told you—"

'Your father died because the Sheriff killed him, not you," Tuck said firmly. "You are carrying this guilt that isn't yours. Trust me when I say—"

"Why should I trust you?" Robyne demanded.

That statement drew gasps from several of her band, but she ignored it. "I mean it. Why should I? Why are you even alive? The others died. Why didn't you?"

"I should have," said Tuck.

⸻   «   »   ⸻

Tuck stares at the manacles around his wrists, shaking his head, his spirit hopelessly crushed. He sits there on the straw-covered floor, wondering how long it will be until they take him and execute him. Until he joins the rest of the Merry Men in the kingdom of heaven...

Or will he indeed wind up in heaven? He was a thief, after all. He broke king's law, defied authorities, stole money, committed so many sins. Yes, granted, he is a Friar, but that does not exempt him. If anything it may well condemn him further because he should have to live up to a higher standard. It is entirely possible that he may be condemned to the flames below. This thought has never occurred to him before, but now that the end of his life is impending, he cannot help but dwell on it...

There is a clicking of the lock upon his door and it swings open, sparse light filtering in from the torches that line the walls outside. The Sheriff strides in, taking a few steps and then standing there as if he is waiting for a coach or something to come along and pick him up. He gazes at Tuck for a few seconds and then says, "You killed none of my men when you were captured."

Tuck simply shrugs. He is not being told anything he does not know.

"In point of fact," the Sheriff continues, "I do not recall any actual deaths being laid at your door. Why is that?"

"I seem to recall there was a commandment about that. The sixth one, as I remember."

"There was one against stealing as well," the Sheriff reminds him. Tuck shrugs and says nothing further.

The Sheriff continues to study him. "May I ask how a churchman winds up in the service of an outlaw?"

"I am in the service of the Lord. He sends me where He will."

"Well, you will be pleased to know that Robin is doubtlessly conversing with the Lord right now. I'm sure your name will feature prominently in the conversation. And he will have plenty of company, I can assure you of that."

Tuck has been unsure until this moment what the fate of his friends has been. But as he sits there and listens to the Sheriff boast of his friends' fates, he knows immediately what the man is saying. The Merry Men are dead. Robin is dead.

With a roar of fury, Tuck lunges to his feet and charges the Sheriff. It is a pointless undertaking because the chains that manacle him to the wall draw him up short. They yank back his arm and he howls. He has never been so angry in his life, and he does not care if the Sheriff sees it.

The Sheriff studies his rage as indifferently as if he is watching two male wolves battling over a mate. Although he is the cause of Tuck's anger, he does not particularly care about it. Finally the wrath subsides and Tuck sinks to the ground, his passion spent. The Sheriff says nothing for several seconds and then asks, "And what are you going to do about it?"

"Do?"

"If I turned you loose and gave you a sword, would you attack me? Endeavor to avenge their deaths?"

"What good would that do? Vengeance serves no purpose. It is not

part of God's plan. He did not avenge himself against Cain when he slew Abel."

"True. So true." He sighed. "You are useless as a warrior, do you know that? Because you are not willing to slay your opponent."

"Death is not the way."

"Perhaps not yours and not the Lord's, but it's our way. And until such time as you accept that, you are always going to be somewhat useless."

Tuck does not respond. There is nothing else for him to say.

The Sheriff then takes a few steps back and gestures to someone that Tuck can't see. Moments later the jailer strides into view and stands there, waiting for instructions. "Free him," says the Sheriff, pointing at Tuck.

The jailer allows surprise to appear briefly on his face, but then shrugs, moves toward Tuck with his key and unlatches the manacle. Tuck cannot quite believe it. Slowly he rises, shaking his hands to restore circulation to his wrists. "Why?" he says.

"Because you are not a threat. Granted, you are a formidable fighter if armed with a staff, but that is all. You could not use it in a fatal undertaking. You could, of course, return to life as a thief, yet I somehow doubt that you are going to do that. Not without serving beside Robin Hood. Instead, I expect you to retire somewhere and concentrate on doing God's work." He smiles, which is a most disconcerting thing to see. "Believe it or not, Friar, I am a good Christian, or at least consider myself as such. I believe in Jesu as much as you do. Perhaps I do not serve all the commandments as zealously as I should, but I do what I must in the service of the king. A good Christian, yes, but a good Englishman am I as well, and one must learn to balance the two. In finding that balance, I am allowing you to live. Go on about your business and serve God as best you can. Go in peace, Friar."

"Go to Hell, Sheriff."

The Sheriff shrugs. "That will not be up to me. My concerns are more based on the mortal plane. I leave those such as you to determine my eventual fate. Lead him out of here," he says to the jailer and walks away, not bothering to so much as glance behind himself.

"So he let you live," said Robyne. She made no attempt to hide her disbelief.

"He did not see me as worth killing, I guess."

"He had some other reason," said Innis Rae immediately. "Henry does nothing to benefit others. He cares only about himself. So why ever he decided to let ye live, it was to serve his own purposes."

"It has been well over a decade and I have not heard from him in all this time. I cannot imagine what those purposes might be."

"You'll find out," said Innis Rae. She didn't have the slightest idea what they could be, but clearly she didn't trust the Sheriff to have simply been generous. That made sense to Robyne, though. Innis Rae had witnessed him killing her husband. And unlike the death of Robin Hood, it had not been in the midst of a combat situation, a mutually agreed upon duel to the death. Instead Sir Henry had been a guest who had ignored the rules of hospitality, snuck a weapon into his host's domicile and slain him without warning. So it made sense that Innis Rae would not have the slightest tendency to credit Henry with any motivation that was not self-serving. No, Robyne could not blame her in the least.

"Well, I certainly hope you're wrong," said Tuck. "But that is really irrelevant to my main point."

"Which is?"

He sighed once more, clearly not thrilled about the prospect of discussing the matter so openly with her, but finally he brought himself to do it. "Your father would not have wanted this for you, Mary—"

"Robyne," she corrected him once more.

"Fine, Robyne. After you and your brother were born, he spoke to me oftentimes of the world he wanted to build for you. One in which you could live free of the menace of those in authority. Where you didn't have to fight for respect, for food, for life. He wanted better for you than he himself had. I suppose that's the case for every parent, really, but moreso for him. He would never have wanted you to follow in his footsteps."

"Unfortunately," said Robyne, "he didn't have the opportunity to see what sort of life I would have. And Basil didn't get to have any life at all. So you'll pardon me if I improvise to the best of my ability."

He reacted to the rising heat in her voice. "You don't have to be angry with me, Robyne..."

"I'm not angry, Tuck. I'm disappointed. I thought that if anyone could readily understand why I'm doing what I'm doing, it would be you."

"It's because you're a woman," said Khalida. "He won't accept such activities from a female."

"That is not true," Tuck said, and now he was the one whose ire was clearly rising. "I have no issue with her gender. Her mother was as heroic as her father, easily a match for most men when it came to combat. Frankly, it's clear that that is who she takes after."

"I'm flattered," said Robyne tonelessly.

"I know you feel committed to what you're doing. All of you do..."

"You don't even know what I'm doing. I'm not embarking on the same road my father did. I fight for the rights of women."

"That's a laudable goal..."

"It's not just a goal, Tuck," she said urgently. "You don't understand what we've been doing. Do you have any idea how many women are abused in Nottingham and the surrounding areas? How many are treated like chattel? Abused by their husbands, even by their children in some instances? Treated like property instead of people? Worse than property; the average farmer takes better care of his cows than he does his wife."

"Certainly not all men are like that," said Tuck.

"Not all, but enough. And I'm helping them."

"How?"

"We have a hideout," said Innis Rae. "We're building it in the trees of Sherwood. The Sheriff and his men can never find it; it's obscured by the underlying branches. An' we have lookouts to tell us if anyone is in the area, so our women and children know to quiet down..."

"Women and children?" Tuck had trouble believing it. "You're helping children too?"

"What, do you think that if we free a woman from her ogre of a husband, we're going to leave the children behind so he can inflict punishment on them?" said Robyne. "Someone has to fight on behalf of families, Tuck. Certainly even my father would agree to that."

"I suppose he would," Tuck admitted. "But I don't think he'd want you risking your life every day of the week."

"Someone has to risk something or things will never change," said Innis Rae.

Tuck looked her up and down. "You're obviously her Little John," he said with a smile.

"Who?" said Innis Rae.

Tuck looked to Robyne in surprise. Robyne shrugged. "She's not from around here."

"So I gather. Where the blazes is Randolf with our food? *Randolf!*"

The sexton immediately appeared from the adjoining room with a helping of bread and slices of beef neatly piled up on the plate. Alys was the first one at it, devouring the pieces she took before anyone else had even taken a bite. "She's typically very hungry," Khalida said apologetically.

"No apologies necessary," Tuck said. "Believe it or not, there was once a time when I had enough appetite for several men."

Robyne smiled at the recollection.

"So how many women are residing there now?" said Tuck.

Innis Rae leaned forward to reply, but Robyne put a hand on her shoulder. "I'd rather not discuss our numbers, Tuck. In fact, we've really already said too much."

"My dear girl!" Tuck said in surprise. "Are you implying that you don't trust me?"

For a long moment she sat there, and then said softly, "I want to. But I've been spending fifteen years living in fear and suspicion. Terrified every day that the Sheriff was going to show up at my home, looking for the daughter of Robin Hood. That breeds a permanent sense of caution. And I certainly don't know him," and she indicated Randolf. "I've just met him. I can trust you as much as I wish, but why should I trust him? Frankly, if I were wise, I'd cut him down right now just in case he overheard something he should not have."

Randolf's eyes widened and he backed up in obvious panic. "I didn't hear anything! I swear!"

"She is joking, Randolf. Calmly, my son. She was only joking." He turned his attention back to her. "You *were* only joking, were you not?"

She shrugged.

"Randolf, go to," Tuck advised, and Randolf immediately scurried out of the room. He did it so quickly and clumsily that Innis Rae actually chuckled, which struck Robyne as odd considering Innis Rae rarely laughed at anything. "That was cruel, Robyne."

"No, just honest. For a moment I really did consider just putting an end to him."

"My God, child," whispered Tuck. "Your father wouldn't recognize what you've become…"

"Stop it!" She was on her feet and was right in Tuck's face. "Stop doing that! Stop telling me what my father would or would not done. What he would or would not have wanted from me. You don't know! You're only guessing! You knew me as a child; you've no clue, none, what it is that I have grown up into and what I've become. So stop it now or—"

"Or what?" He spoke very calmly, not coming close to losing his patience.

She hesitated, and then dropped back into her chair. She hung her head. Innis Rae patted her on the shoulder and Robyne reached up and stroked her hand. "I'm sorry," she said softly. "I should not have shouted at you."

"It's all right, child," said Tuck. He reached out and she took his hand, and he squeezed it quickly, affectionately. "These are stressful times. If venting your spleen at me helps you in any way, then indulge yourself by all means."

Robyne smiled. "I'm starting to recall why my father and mother loved you so much."

"Well, I am very lovable."

They chatted for a time longer, and then Tuck turned to Elizabeth. "And what of you, my dear? Are you going to accompany Robyne to her home for troubled young women?"

Elizabeth's mouth moved for a moment with no words emerging. Then she said to Tuck, "You said you were going to teach me about making medicines and such. Were you serious about that?"

"Of course I was, child. I've given my word, and my word is my bond. You, however, are not bound by it. I'm simply telling you that you can do whatever you wish."

She looked at Robyne and said, "Would you…be insulted if I said I wanted to stay here?"

"Certainly not," Robyne said immediately. "You should go wherever you wish to be, and much happiness to you."

"Thank you," she said, and then to Robyne's surprise she stood and curtsied. Robyne was going to tell her that wasn't necessary, but then she realized that she actually appreciated the little gesture of courtesy.

"And if your father does try to come back and harass you, don't worry. I'll know about it," Robyne assured her.

"How do you know?" asked Tuck.

Robyne was about to tell him, but then decided against it. Tuck was a good Christian, after all, and she had no idea how he might react to the discovery that an act of magic was involved. Even though it was a minor bit of magic, the Magistar was no sorcerer, and the powers of Satan were not remotely being invoked, it was still impossible to predict how Tuck might react. She was not the slightest bit interested in provoking him.

"I think it best for some things to remain private," she said. "You understand."

"I certainly do," Tuck said immediately. "Take your leave as you wish, Robyne. Be aware, though, that you are welcome as a guest here anytime."

"Thank you," she said.

Robyne stood and her band did as well. Clarence replaced his helmet atop his head. Robyne was used to that. He had no desire to cause alarm in others by letting them know that a leper was walking among them, even though it was highly unlikely that he could possibly transmit the disease to them. He was just sensitive to the needs of others. "Remain in touch with me, Tuck. It's good to see you."

"You as well, Robyne."

"See? That wasn't so hard to say."

"Harder than you know," said Tuck.

CHAPTER XXII

Arrest them all

RANDOLF LAY ON HIS COT, STARING up at the ceiling, counting.

It was what he typically did when he wanted time to pass. Often he did it just as a means of falling asleep, but that wasn't the case here. His mind was going a mile a minute; it wasn't coming close to let him drift to sleep.

He could not believe that the situation had finally presented itself. He had resigned himself to the eternal reality of his existence, and although it was not an especially gratifying one, he knew that it was necessary and he was carrying a sacred trust that had been thrust upon him. It was not one that he had asked for, but he had risen to what was required of him. Now, though, it had come to fruition, and he wasn't entirely sure how to feel about it.

You don't have to feel anything about it. You have to do your job. That is the only thing that is required of you.

He knew that he was right. He had a job to do and he was going to attend to it.

Believing that enough time had passed, he finally rose from the couch. There was no moonlight filtering through his window, which made sense since it was a new moon. His instinct was to tip toe, to try and be as silent as possible. But he warned himself not to do that. The last thing he wanted to do was sneak around so that, if Tuck happened to be awake and caught him out, he would certainly know that something was up. And he was reasonably sure that he wasn't going to be able to stand up to extended questioning from an irritated Friar.

He stood in the narrow corridor for a long moment, straining to hear what he was sure he would be able to detect. And in a short time, he did indeed hear what he was listening for: a gentle snoring. Tuck always snored, sometimes softly, sometimes loudly. In the old days, Randolf had found it so distracting, even disconcerting, that sleep had eluded him, sometimes for hours. Those days were long past. He had become so accustomed to it that now he actually had trouble falling asleep if Tuck happened to be sleeping on his side and consequently didn't snore. He also knew that Tuck slept deeply and more or less never woke up during the night, so Randolf would not be missed as he attended to his errands.

He left the building and went around to the small stall that stood adjacent. Standing there dozing was the monastery's trusty horse, Samson, who Randolf typically used when he needed to ride into Nottingham to acquire provisions. Gently he woke the horse, and the beast's eyes snapped open and focused on him in confusion. A young horse, Samson most definitely was not. But he was sturdy and reliable and Randolf had every conviction that the beast would take him where he needed to go.

Once Samson realized that Randolf genuinely wanted him awake, the horse grunted out a soft neigh. Randolf did not bother to saddle him. He always rode bareback, never seeing the need for a saddle. It wasn't as if he rode all that fast anyway, but he would certainly be able to reach his destination more quickly on horseback than on foot. He clambered onto Samson's back, snapped the reins, and headed out.

The ride took nearly an hour. Typically he could do it in half that time, but the general lack of light caused him to ride more slowly than he usually did. He certainly didn't need the horse tripping over some stray branch, falling, perhaps breaking its leg. On several occasions he passed stragglers, people who were heading somewhere on foot to accomplish something or other. He saw them look his way in momentary fear. He understood why; they were worried that he might be some sort of highwayman intending to steal from them. Naturally he galloped right past them, paying them no mind. He had matters of far greater import on his mind than molesting random individuals.

Eventually he drew within sight of his goal. Nottingham Castle stood before him, stretching up into the darkness. Torches illuminated it, making it impossible to miss even in the lightless sky. He rode toward the front gate and there were two armed guards at their station, casting a wary eye upon him. "I'm here to see Sir Henry," he said briskly.

"He's asleep," said the larger of the two guards.

"Awaken him."

The guards exchanged a look and shared a laugh. "Why in the world would we do that?" the smaller one said.

"Because I told you to."

"And who the bloody hell are you?"

"Canaan," said Randolf.

The mere speaking of the name incited an immediate reaction from the guards...at least from the larger one, who snapped to instantly. His companion looked confused as he saw the change in his mate's attitude. "Wait here," the larger guard said, and added to his associate, "Keep him here. Don't let him leave."

"Why in God's name would I leave?" said Randolf. It was a reasonable question. He had just arrived there, after all, and wanted to enter. So obviously he had no intention of turning around and departing.

The larger guard entered the vast castle. The smaller guard studied Randolf with open curiosity. "Never met anyone named 'Canaan' before."

"You still haven't. That's not my name. It's a code word, given to people who may end up possessing information that the Sheriff will find of interest."

"Ah. See, I'm new here, so I didn't know that."

"Obviously."

There seemed no reason for Randolf to continue speaking to

the oaf and so he decided that he would simply stop. The guard made a few lame attempts to keep the conversation going over the next few minutes, but Randolf simply sat there astride his horse and didn't bother to respond. Eventually the oaf got the idea and fell silent.

There was a stirring at the door then and the large guard stepped out with Sir Henry right behind him. "Randolf," said Sir Henry with a nod of his head.

"Sir Henry."

"Come in," he said. He turned to the shorter guard. "Stable his animal for him."

"Yes, sir," said the guard and he walked forward. Randolf dismounted and handed him the reins and then followed Sir Henry into the castle's interior.

"Remain silent until we have privacy," he said, and Randolf did as instructed. They walked up a flight of stairs and into a large room. Henry swung the door shut behind him and then turned to face Randolf. "It's been quite a while, Randolf."

"Yes, indeed, it has," he agreed readily.

"So I assume you have news of some sor—"

There was a knock at the door. Henry rolled his eyes in irritation, not having the slightest idea who it was, and he called, "Come back later."

"I'd rather not," came a familiar voice.

Henry had just been sitting, but immediately he sprang from his chair and went to the door. He paused before he opened it, turned to Randolf and said, "Remain calm."

Randolf had no idea why he was supposed to remain calm until the door swung open and he saw none other than Richard Lionheart standing in the corridor. Immediately Randolf dropped to his knees. "Your majesty," he breathed.

"Proper obeisance," Richard said approvingly. "Nice to see from time to time. On your feet, on your feet," and he gestured for Randolf to rise. Randolf obediently did so, but he kept his gaze lowered. Richard strolled into the room, his hands draped behind his back as if he was surveying the contents of a zoo. "I was having difficulty sleeping, so I thought I would walk the halls of the castle. See if anything was going on. I don't know you, do I?"

"No, your majesty," said Randolf. "I'm—"

"I didn't ask you," Richard reminded him and turned his inquiring gaze to Henry with a cocked eyebrow, clearly desiring to be filled in.

Henry immediately did so. "Randolf is a spy for us, your majesty. He has had one job over the years: to keep an eye on Friar Tuck."

"Tuck? Of Robin's men?"

"Yes, your majesty."

"He's still alive?"

Henry nodded. "I was loathe to kill a man of God if it wasn't necessary, and I felt he did not pose a threat. Furthermore, I considered him to be an appropriate lure."

"A lure for what?"

Henry gestured for Richard to sit, and the king did so. *Amazing,* thought Randolf. *He makes any chair he sits in look like a throne.*

"We were reasonably sure we wiped out all the commanders and senior members of Robin's band," said Henry, "but we could not be sure, beyond a doubt, that there were not lesser officers who might have survived. I reasoned that if we let Tuck live, then sooner or later they would find their way to him and attempt to reorganize and carry Robin's quest onward. Randolf was dispatched to serve as his sexton as the friar withdrew from the world and instead became a monk. Although truth to tell, he was rather poor at it. A monk is supposed to be withdrawn from the world, but he could not help but continue to serve any who needed him."

"And he's been with him all this time?" said Richard. "And has anyone shown up?"

Randolf shook his head. "He keeps mostly to himself. He even ceased using his own name; he ask that others simply address him as 'brother.' No one speaks to him of Robin or likely by this point know that he was ever even associated with him. Yet I've stayed on because that was my job."

"And you've done it well," said Henry. "And now that you're here, I assume that someone finally did show up?"

"None of Robin's men, no. But his successor."

Richard had been slouched in the chair but now he sat bolt upright as if he had just been struck by lightning. "The girl?" he demanded. "The swordswoman?"

Randolf bobbed his head. "The very same. And her minions as well."

"They came to recruit him?"

"No. They had no idea that he was there. The girl had even assumed that the man she knew as Friar Tuck was long dead. No, they came to help a girl who had sought refuge from us."

"Why?"

Randolf was about to tell him, and he froze.

He did not know Richard personally, but he knew of him. He knew the stories: that Richard was unpredictable. Seemingly indifferent to human needs. Casually homicidal. If he told Richard about Elizabeth's fleeing of her father, and that Robyne had taken her side, Richard would undoubtedly take action against her just because he knew it would upset Robyne. He was just that capricious. At the very least, he would likely demand that the girl return to her father and agree to do as she was bidden. If she refused to do that, why, that would be that. Disobeying her father was one thing. Disobeying the king was requesting a death sentence, and Richard would likely execute it himself.

He had no idea why the thought chilled him. She was just some random peasant girl, after all. He owed her no loyalty. He had no reason to do something as risky as lie to the king on her behalf.

And yet...

If he told the truth, told her story, he was sentencing her either to life as an unhappy bride or to death. There was no middle ground.

All of that went through his mind in a second, and then he shrugged. "I've no idea. Some cranky peasant girl who wasn't happy with her life. Do not know the reasons, nor do I care especially."

"No reason that you should," said Henry, much to Randolf's

relief. "We have matters of far greater immediacy to concern our-selves with. Did she reveal anything useful?"

"Very much so. Apparently Robyne was raised from childhood by a woman named Theresa, also known as Magistar. I've no idea where—"

Richard was immediately on his feet, his eyes wide with shock. His face went slightly pale. The move was so abrupt that it startled Randolf and he jumped back slightly in concern. "Are you quite certain?" said Richard. "Magistar? Theresa?"

"Yes, she was quite certain about it," said Randolf.

"Perhaps she was lying to confuse you..."

"I was not in the room, your majesty. I was in the adjoining chamber, listening in, hoping I could discern exactly this sort of information. I hope my actions have been satisfactory, your majesty."

Richard's expression went away. His mind had clearly vacated his body for a moment, apparently to consider weighty matters of great importance. Then it returned to the matter at hand. "We must act immediately," he said.

"Suggestions, your majesty?" said Henry.

Richard stared at him as if he were an idiot. "It's obvious. Go to the Magistar's lair and arrest her, arrest Robyne. Arrest them all."

"Robyne may well not be there," said Randolf.

That puzzled Richard. "Then where would she be?"

"Apparently they are constructing some manner of tree top for-tress. It may well be impossible to find, at least as she described it."

"Very well," said Richard. "Then we will not indulge her by seeking it out. Instead we will compel her to come to us. We will capture the Magistar and that will lure her to us."

"How can we capture her?" asked Randolf. "We've no idea where she resides."

"You may have no idea," Richard said. "But I know exactly where she is."

BOOK FOUR

Richard and Theresa

INTERLUDE

I've never done that before

Richard cannot believe it. Cannot believe it.

Is this how it ends? A life in which I am the warrior king of England and it is now ending simply because I decided to be stupid and indulge myself?

My mother warned me. She goddamned warned me. A king does not go out hunting by himself. No wise man does, but a king most definitely does not. Something bad will happen to you. Oh, but you knew better, didn't you, Richard. You knew so much more than that worthless hag. And now you are paying for it.

Richard staggers, his hand clamped over the bleeding, endeavoring to slow it down somehow. It is only a surface wound, he tells himself. Something that you can survive. It should be no effort for you at all. The king of England is not going to die like some no one in the forest. You have a country to rule, crusades to lead. This cannot be happening. It cannot *be happening.*

You're seventeen years old. You can't die at age seventeen. That's insane. You're going to live to be an old man, forty, even fifty years old. You cannot give up the ghost now. You haven't accomplished anything. Not a damned thing.

You should have brought a sword. Why in the world did you not bring a sword?

Because he had had confidence in his bow and arrow, that was why. He knew himself to be quite a formidable archer. What is the point of hunting with a bow and arrow if you have to bring a blade with you because you don't truly believe in your marksmanship?

And where in the hell had that wolf come from anyway? To the best of Richard's knowledge, there were no packs of wolves anywhere in the forest. So how in the hell had that thing come leaping out of the woods at him, with no warning whatsoever?

It didn't have the madness, that was certain. There was no frothing at the mouth. It just must have been extremely hungry, and it had seen the lone hunter as a potential meal.

Richard should already be dead. If the damned wolf had kept its mouth shut, if it hadn't growled as it came up behind him, it would have caught Richard completely off guard. It could be blissfully devouring his corpse right now. Instead it had made sufficient noise to warn Richard. Unfortunately it had not done so in enough time for Richard to nock an arrow. He had spun when he heard the creature behind him, had yanked an arrow out of his quiver, but before he could place it into the bow and aim it the beast had been upon him.

The king had cried out as the beast bore him to the ground, snarling, clawing at him. Its claws had torn up his chest, its teeth had hovered mere inches above his throat, snapping furiously. It had taken all of Richard's determined strength to keep the creature's teeth at bay with one hand while his other desperate hand had reached out for the item he had dropped. Finally, after what seemed an interminable amount of time, his questing fingers had closed around the shaft of the arrow. He had swung it around in a perfect arc and driven it deeply into the wolf's throat. It let out an alarmed shriek and tumbled back off Richard. Lionheart sat up and yanked the arrow clear of the wolf. Blood had sprayed out and the beast had tumbled around, its life's blood seeping out from it and cloaking the forest floor in arterial red. Richard didn't hesitate but instead drove the arrow straight into the wolf's head with as much force as he could muster. It went straight into the beast's brain, and that was all for Richard's assailant. The wolf's eyes rolled up and it flopped to one side. A death rattle emerged from what was left of the creature's throat and that was it.

That should have been it.

Except obviously it is not. The wolf's claws had run deep, wounding Richard quite badly. If he is unable to find a way to stop bleeding, he is not going to make it back to the castle.

What in God's name is he doing in Nottingham anyway? Yes, granted, the hunting in Sherwood is most excellent. But he was the Duke of Normandy, of Aquitaine, of Gascony. Why was he wasting his time in this backwoods area? He should be back in France, not dallying around here. He liked France and honestly despised England. Miserable place. Lousy weather. The people were officious and annoying.

And now you're going to die here. Idiot.

He stumbles forward, feeling his legs beginning to buckle. In his mind he continues forward with grim determination, refusing to let the wolf have the last laugh. In reality, however, his body is giving way to his weakness. He takes two steps forward, then a third, and then the strength vanishes from him entirely and he crumbles to the ground. So weak, so damnably weak. Weakness is for lesser men *his brain shouts at him, but his body literally fails to rise to the occasion.*

So this is it. This is how he dies.

He lies there, breathing heavily, disgusted at himself. This is the warrior king? This is the man known not as Richard I, but Richard Lionheart? Doubtless some passing peasant will discover his body, loot it for valuables, and leave him there to rot. The best that he can hope for is to be dumped in an unmarked grave somewhere. Thus will end the short and unremarkable reign of the heart of the lion.

"*Good lord, what have we here?*"

It is a female voice that startles him. He is so detached from his surroundings that he did not hear the advent of this new person before it was too late. He squints, looking up in the dim light. He has no idea what time it is. He had been hunting during daylight hours, but now long shadows are beginning to stretch. He looks up and she is standing there, a cloaked woman with a hood. "*What happened to you?*" *she asks.*

"*Wolf,*" *he manages to say.*

"*Can you stand?*"

He shakes his head.

To his surprise, her voice becomes stern. "Well, I'm afraid you're going to have to, because all my medicines are back at my home, and I can hardly carry you there. If you wish to survive, then you are going to have to draw the strength from somewhere and get to your feet. Either that or I will simply stand here and watch you die. It is entirely your choice."

"Do you know who I am?" he says incredulously.

"No. Should I?"

"I am your king!"

"You're God?" she says with one eyebrow arched.

He has no idea how to respond to that, and to his surprise, he laughs slightly. Hell of a reaction to have. "To some," he says, and then he puts aside any further thoughts of repartee. Instead he shoves his arms down as if doing a push up and slowly, laboriously, begins to stand.

The woman steps forward, reaches down for his arm, and hauls him upward. She is strong for a woman and within seconds has helped to draw him erect. He leans against a tree, steadying himself, his breath coming in ragged gasps. "Did it," he says.

"Indeed you did. Very good. Now we need you to start walking. Do not worry, it isn't far."

He leans against her, feeling weak in requiring a woman to bear his weight, but he tells himself he has no choice. He needs her. It's just that simple.

They do not speak as she guides him through the woods. There is no point in doing so; it requires all his strength and concentration just to stay on his feet. Several times the world begins to darken around him, yet somehow she seems to be aware when such weakness threatens to overwhelm him and she manages to stir him to walk once more.

Before long he sees the low outline of a building. He sees the large cross that hangs from the front door. "Is this a convent? Are you a nun?" he asks.

"Yes to the first, no to the second."

He does not want to go in there. It is a place for women, not for a man such as him. Yet he realizes that he has no choice. He, the king, has no choice. That is a very unusual position for him to be in. He could of course issue her an order not to take him in there. And then, for all he knows, she will just allow him to slide to the forest floor and die there within reach of possible salvation. So Richard wisely keeps his mouth shut and allows her to lead him into the building.

There are some nuns in there, and one of them says, "Theresa! What is—" and then gasps when she sees him. "Your majesty!" she says.

"Not feeling quite so majestic at the moment," he says dourly. That much is certainly true. He has never felt less royal.

"Really," says the woman he now knows is named Theresa. "So you really are the king. I had no idea you were ever in England."

"Rarely," Richard admits.

Theresa says nothing more but instead focuses on helping him further into the convent. She brings him to a small room and lays him out on the cushion that is the main decoration. He has never felt happier to lie down.

Briskly she brings forward a pair of scissors and cuts through his tunic, exposing his chest. She purses her lips as she studies the gashes and then brings forward some cloth to stop the bleeding. The blood had defied Richard's ministrations but seems to respond to Theresa's, slowing and then stopping over a period of several minutes. "Stay here," she says, which strikes Richard as ridiculous since obviously he's not going anywhere. She is gone for several minutes and when she returns she is mixing liquid of some sort in a small bowl. Sitting next to him, she gently pours it upon his wounds. Richard sets his jaw against burning pain that threatens to overwhelm him, but he will be damned if he shows any further frailty in front of this woman. He is the damned king of England, and he will be strong no matter what the circumstances.

As if she is reading his mind, Theresa says, "I know that it hurts. You can acknowledge pain in front of me. I will not think the less of you."

"So you say."

"Yes. So I say."

At which point, despite all his desire to the contrary, Richard allows a gasp of pain to escape through his lips. Oddly, it makes him feel better.

His entire body relaxes and suddenly darkness threatens to overwhelm him. From the gathering shadows her voice floats to him soothingly. "Your body wishes to rest. Let it do as it will. You are safe here. I will protect you"

The very notion is an affront to Richard. A woman protecting him? Outlandish! He wants to tell her so. He wants to let her know that he has no need of her protection. That he is the damned king of England. Protect him? The gall! The unmitigated—

"Thank you." He hears the words coming from his mouth and scarcely recognizes his own voice. He never thanks anyone for anything, for he is the king and he is entitled to everything and thus owes no one any thanks at all, ever. Yet there he is thanking her. Thanking. Her.

"You are most welcome," she says graciously.

And then sleep overwhelms him.

"Tomorrow. I think you will be ready to leave tomorrow."

Richard has lost track of how long he has been laid up in the convent. The nuns have, for the most part, steered clear of him, and that is fine as far as he's concerned. He doesn't have much patience for women under even the best of circumstances, and certainly not pious ones. Doubtlessly they sit in judgment upon him, holding him to a standard set by Jesus Christ. How is any man, much less a king who must make decisions that affect the lives of millions of people, supposed to stand up to that?

But Theresa seems very different. She is genuinely helpful, affectionate, caring. He is like no woman that he has ever encountered. She respects the fact that he is king, but it does not overwhelm her. She treats him like a man, no different from any other. One who is in need, and she services those needs without hesitation.

She is a fine woman.

A very fine woman.

Honestly, women are generally of only minimal interest to Richard, but this one is very atypical.

Most atypical.

She's well read, she's educated, she's witty, she's very attractive.

Damnation, she IS attractive, isn't she.

She is seated next to him and is startled when she abruptly reaches up, brings her lips down to his, and kisses her passionately. She is clearly not expecting it. Her reflex is to draw back, but then the intensity of the kiss draws her in. Obviously she has little to no experience in these matters. That does not seem to matter, though, as after a momentary hesitation she returns the kiss.

Reality then blurs for Richard as he throws himself into the moment. His body, fully healthy, comes through, and the rest happens as nature designed it to.

Sometime later they are lying on the cot, squeezed together since it was not really designed for two people. She is staring into space. Richard regards her for a time. Finally: "Nothing to say?"

"I've never done that before," *she whispers.*

"And your first time was with a king. I'm afraid it is downhill from here."

"I did not think I would ever do it. It was not something that interested me."

"Yet you certainly warmed to the idea most quickly. You may wish to consider expanding your horizons."

"And become what? Your consort?"

Richard is prepared to laugh at that, but then realizes she is serious. And for a moment, he does consider it. She would be valuable to have around. She is certainly familiar with the healing arts. Plus considering that it was her first time, she wasn't bad at all. She would undoubtedly improve over time. "Is that of interest to you?"

She stares at him for a moment and then laughs. "I thank you, Richard, but no. I am satisfied with my life here. I am doing good work. Indeed, if I were not here, England would be minus its king right now."

"That is very true." *Then he squeezes her hand and says,* "I owe you a great debt, Theresa. Someday I will repay that debt. Trust me."

"I do," *she says.*

"Never forget."

"I never will."

CHAPTER XXIII

I shot you, didn't I?

"THAT MONK IS FRIAR TUCK?" THE Magistar couldn't keep the surprise out of her voice. She had known the monk for some years, had had occasional interactions with him. But the notion that this polite, quiet elderly man had battled side by side with Robin Hood…it was a lot for her to wrap herself around.

"He is indeed," said Robyne. Clarence was with her; the rest of her band had returned to their treetop forest home. Clarence was quietly sipping tea while Robyne was holding a cup of mead in her hand. "He seems happy enough, as surprising as that sounds."

"It doesn't sound surprising at all. He accomplished a good deal in his life, and now he is content to allow it to trail off to its reasonable conclusion."

Robyne shook her head.

"You disagree?" asked the Magistar.

"Of course I disagree! Sir Henry, my father's murderer, still holds sway. The Sheriff and his followers continue to oppress the people. The work isn't done! Why does he feel that he is able to step away from it?"

"Because he can," said the Magistar. "That is his option. It is him exercising the free will that the lord provided all of us. I think we have neither the right nor the business to question him, much less challenge him in that regard."

Robyne studied the Magistar with clear incredulity, then

turned to Clarence. "Do you believe this?"

"Of course I believe it," said the knight. "If I had the option, I'd retire from all this as well."

She couldn't believe it. "You would?"

"Robyne." His voice sounded very distant, as if he were speaking from very far away. "I've ridden on crusades. I've seen villages taken. Do you know what happens when they take a village? Khalida could tell you. They kill the strongest men, if they're lucky; otherwise they take them as slaves. The best-looking women are likewise made slaves, or unpaid whores. The rest are slaughtered. I have seen the ground running with blood more times than I can count. The first time I did, I was horrified. Eventually it chipped away so much at my soul that I enabled myself to feel absolutely nothing. I am tired of feeling nothing, Robyne; that is part of the reason that I joined with you. To try and make up for the many occasions where I witnessed brutality and did nothing to stop it." He pointed at his face. "That's why I never curse the luck that did this to me. I see it as my punishment. I deserve this."

"Don't be absurd, Clarence," Robyne said. "You don't deserve what happened to you. You deserve to..."

"To live peacefully, growing old in my marriage?" He shrugged. "That is not my fate, and I am content with that. But if that were my fate, would you condemn me for that?"

"Of course not, if for no other reason than that you would be a stranger to me."

"So why would you condemn a friend, but not a stranger?"

Her mouth moved a moment with no sound coming out, and then she frowned before allowing the frown to transform into a smile. "Now you're just saying things to annoy me."

"That was my intent. I'm pleased to see that I have succeeded."

"Fine," she said, throwing up her hands in exasperation. "I rescind my disapproval. Satisfied, Magistar?"

"For the time being," said the Magistar. "Will you two stay for supper?"

"I'd best get back to my women," said Robyne.

"If it's all the same," said Clarence, "I wouldn't mind staying. The, uh…I think my presence makes the women uncomfortable."

"I've explained to them that your mere presence doesn't expose them to any risk," Robyne reminded him.

"So you have, and I very much appreciate that. But you're endeavoring to overcome a lifetime of fear that has been driven into them, and that is not easily done. The looks they give me, the way they encourage their children to shy away…" He shrugged. "I just think it easier if I steer clear of them for one evening, just to allow everyone to sleep a little more soundly."

"Your place remains in the cellar," said the Magistar. During the time when Clarence had slept there regularly, she had set up a private place for him in the convent's cellar. It was warm and dry down there, nor did he need concern himself with his unsightly presence catching the notice of any unexpected visitors. Best of all, the entrance was hidden beneath a trap door, guaranteeing his security.

"That sounds excellent," said Clarence.

Robyne said her farewells at that point and departed. The Magistar chatted with Clarence for a time and made them a perfectly serviceable supper. They spoke about random things. They did not discuss Robyne, not once, as if coming to some mutual undiscussed agreement that they were not going to do so. The Magistar was actually pleased that she didn't have to concern herself thinking about Robyne and what she was up to. The girl had consumed so much of the Magistar's time over the years that if she had been the Magistar's own child, she could not have been more preoccupied with her.

Finally she couldn't help herself. "Do you think she's doing the right thing?" she asked Clarence.

He put down the mug of ale he had just emptied and licked his lips. "Robyne, you mean? I think she's doing what she feels is right."

"I just worry about how it's all going to end," she said. "The problem is that when you focus so much of your attention upon the enemy, you become the enemy."

"What's that supposed to mean?"

"It means that you become accustomed to thinking like your enemy in order to our plan them. If you do that for too long, your own personality can wind up being subsumed and you become that which you despise."

"That won't happen with Robyne," said Clarence, but there was already a hint of uncertainty in his voice. The Magistar heard it, even though she knew that Clarence would never admit to it.

She placed her hand atop his gloved one. "So you say. But I've been watching it slowly happening. She was ready to kill Richard. The only thing that stopped her was me. He was helpless. She was going to kill a helpless enemy."

"In her defense, she thought you were dead."

"And slaying Richard would have brought me back to life?"

"Obviously not. But—"

"No. There's no 'but' after that statement. You admit that her slaying Richard would have been pointless. I mean, I'm not a fool, Clarence. I understand the stakes of what Robyne is engaged in. Sometimes people are going to die at her hands; that's just a given. But when someone is helpless…when they pose no threat…then she must not forget the principle of mercy. For if she does, she forgets who she is."

"Do you even know who she is?" asked Clarence.

The Magistar sat back in her chair and looked inward. "You should have seen her when she first came to me," said the Magistar. "So helpless, she was. Grieving for her father. Blaming herself for his death."

"She still does. She has carried that guilt within her for fifteen years. I'm reasonably sure she's never going to let it go."

"And that guilty transforms itself into rage as she dispatches her enemies without hesitation. Perhaps," said the Magistar, "if she ever forgives herself, that won't happen anymore. But the chances are she never will, and so she will continue on the path of her enemies until she will become just like them."

"I will endeavor to make sure that doesn't happen. Trust me on that, Theresa."

"Magistar," she corrected. "I haven't been Theresa in a very long time."

"Sorry."

"No apologies necessary. I suppose it's more a state of mind than anything."

They chatted a while longer, and then the Magistar stretched her arms and yawned. "It's been quite a long day," she said.

"Most of them seem to be," he observed.

"True. Good evening to you then, Sir Clarence.

She rose then and walked to a carpet that lay a short distance away. She rolled it back and hauled up the trap door. "There you go," she said. "Your bed just as you left it."

"Much thanks, my lady." He bowed slightly and moments later had retreated down into the cellar. She replaced the trap door and put the carpet back upon it. *Can't be too careful,* she thought.

She stayed awake for a while longer, then retreated to her small room. She dropped to her knees at the side of her bed and whispered, "Dear lord: please watch after Mary. Guide her down the road to righteousness. Guide her in your commandments. When her time comes, please welcome her into your arms in respect of not what she has done, but what her intentions were. Thank you."

Then she decided that, before retiring to sleep, she should take one more fast pass at her chart table and see if there was anywhere that Robyne might be needed.

If that was necessary, she had the means at hand to inform her. She maintained a small coop in the back where she bred rock pigeons to be employed specifically to transmit messages. Ever since Robyne had mostly relocated herself to her tree top hideaway, the messenger pigeons were extremely useful in conveying news to her. She was still easy enough to reach during the daytime when she continued to work in the public square, but the evening was more problematic. Not for the birds, though, who were able to find her flawlessly. She assumed that that would be the case if she was needed now.

She removed the amulet that she wore around her neck and

held it over the map. The charm immediately pointed directly to the left.

The Magistar stared more closely at where it was indicating and she didn't understand. It was pointed straight at the convent itself. *Mary is needed here? I don't…why? Why is she needed h—?*

That was when the front door was smashed in. No knock. No warning. Just a splintering of wood and the sounds of heavy feet stamping across the floor.

Her impulse was immediately to run and hide, but she dismissed the notion as quickly as it occurred to her. If someone had the temerity to disrupt her evening, they were going to answer to her directly.

Suddenly a towering man, dressed in black leathers with half of his face obscured, strode in and stared at her. "Sheriff!" he called. "Got someone!"

"Is it Robyne, Drogo?" came a reply.

"If it is, she's wearing quite a cunning disguise."

In walked the Sheriff of Nottingham. "Fan out," he ordered more men who were coming in behind him. "Check the area. See if she's hiding anywhere…" His voice trailed off as the soldiers obeyed him and he stared at the Magistar. His eyes widened. "Wait a minute. I recognize you. I shot you, didn't I? Yes! You blocked my shot of Robyne!"

"So you're the one who almost killed me. Very considerate of you."

"Sit down."

"I think I'll stand, if it's all the same to—"

"*Sit down!*" he thundered.

She paused a moment, then drew her chair over. She placed it squarely on top of the carpet that was covering the trap door and sat down, her hands folded in her lap. She remained right where she was as the soldiers made their way through the convent, searching for something she knew they would not find. Long minutes later, the one called Drogo returned to the Sheriff and shook his head. The Sheriff then turned to the Magistar. "Where is she?" he demanded.

"Where is who?" she asked innocently.

"Robyne of Sherwood. The woman who you were willing to sacrifice yourself in order to save."

"Oh, is that who that was? All I saw was a woman brave enough to battle Richard the Lionheart. I believed her worth saving, especially from a cowardly attack by a bowman in the shadows."

He brought his hand up to slap her viciously across the cheek, but he hesitated and then lowered his hand. He couldn't bring himself to do it. She noticed the abortive effort and smiled. "A gentleman, masquerading as a brute. This will not end well for you, I fear."

"Your fears are not my concern," he said testily.

"What do we do now?" asked Drogo.

The Sheriff considered it a moment. "I will take her back to the castle," he said after thinking about it. "The rest of you will remain here. Remain in hiding inside. Sooner or later, Robyne will return here and then we'll have her."

"You will be waiting here for a good long time," said the Magistar. "I have no connection to her. She won't come here."

"You'll pardon me if I don't take your word for it."

"No, I don't think I will pardon you. You burst into my home, you make all sorts of accusations. Your behavior is most unpardonable and I—"

"Wait." He was staring down at the carpet and there was clearly suspicion growing in his eyes. "Stand up."

"Why should I—"

The Sheriff didn't wait for her to finish the sentence. Instead he crossed over to her and yanked her arm so she was pulled clear of the chair, which toppled over in response to her violent exit. He pulled up the carpet and a smile split his face. "Where does this trap door lead?"

"To the wine cellar," she said.

He turned to Drogo. "Go down there. Find out if anyone is hiding."

Drogo gestured for two men to follow him. He threw open the

trap door, sword in his hand, and charged down the stairs, the other two men right behind him. The Magistar braced herself for what she knew would follow: the sound of broadswords clanging together.

Instead long silence followed and then Drogo's voice floated up. "Nothing here, sir."

"Are you certain?"

"Positive, yes. There is an empty cot but no one hiding. We've made a thorough search and really, it's not especially large. I assure you it's unoccupied."

The Magistar managed an indifferent shrug of her shoulders. "See?" she said.

"Yes, I see. I see very well," said the Sheriff. "What I see is a woman who excels at lying. You may be alone at the moment, but you are most definitely connected to Robyne Hood. I know her type all too well. She will endeavor to rescue you from the hands of King Richard, and when that happens, it will be the last thing she ever does."

"Funny. I've heard it said that she claims she will kill your father if *that* is the last thing she does," said the Magistar. "It will be interesting to see who's right."

The Sheriff was clearly not interested in trading remarks with her. "Bind her," said the Sheriff.

Drogo approached her with a length of rope and the Magistar actually snickered at that. "Think I'm going to fight you? That I'm a danger to pound you to death with my bare hands?"

"I think I'm not going to take any chances, if that's all right with you, and even if it isn't."

She nodded indifferently and placed her hands behind her back. Drogo lashed them tightly and she winced against the pressure, but she made no sound. She'd be damned if she provided them any outward sign of her weakness.

Yet that was not her greatest concern.

Where the hell had Clarence disappeared to?

⸻ «— —» ⸻

Clarence hid in the shadows outside the convent, watching as the Magistar was led out of the building. For a moment he mentally fought over what he should do.

He could, of course, go to the rescue. He knew that he was strong enough to overcome the Sheriff. But the Sheriff had a number of men with him. There was every possibility that the king might wind up with two hostages instead of one. Plus Drogo would doubtlessly recognize him from that time when he had aided Robyne and Innis Rae. That would unquestionably tie the Magistar into Robyne and prove that the Sheriff was right to take her prisoner.

At least he had managed to get out of the cellar through the alternate entrance that led directly to the open air. Fortunately the long shadows of the building had shielded it from any casual inspection of the building's exterior. If it had been daylight, they easily would have spotted it when they patrolled the area, but the darkness served Clarence's needs.

But now what?

He stood and watched helplessly as the Magistar was led outside and helped up onto the back of a horse. The Sheriff then climbed on behind her, took the reins in his hands and snapped them authoritatively. The horse promptly galloped forward and moments later was lost from view.

Clarence was alone.

He needed to alert Robyne, to tell her what had happened. The Magistar was in the hands of the Sheriff and, even worse, King Richard, and Richard was unpredictable. He could take one look at her and slay her for the charge of harboring an enemy of the king. There would be no trial, no proof required of the charge. The king would state it, pronounce her guilty, and that would be the end of her.

Except then she would be useless in Richard's genuine goal of catching Robyne herself. She might well ride into danger to save the life of the Magistar; she'd be far less interested in rescuing her corpse. So the odds were that the Magistar had some time. Her fate wouldn't be as rapid as he was originally concerned.

Nevertheless, time was not on his side.

That was when the obvious solution suddenly flashed into his mind.

He made his way around to the back area of the convent and there were the rock pigeons cooing softly, as if greeting him and inquiring how they could be of service. There were also several rolls of parchment, a quill pen and a stoppered bottle of ink off to the side. The Magistar thought of everything, apparently. Quickly he scribbled a note, attached it to the leg of one of the pigeons as he extracted it from its case, and tossed the bird into the air. It beat its wings furiously and rose, setting off for its destination.

Clarence immediately became concerned. There was no guarantee the pigeon would be able to accomplish its mission. A passing hawk or eagle or even an owl might intercept it to make a meal of it. But he realized he had no choice. He had to remain there and pray that Robyne would show up.

Because if she didn't, he wasn't sure what he would do next.

—« »—

The Magistar could not recall if she had ever seen Nottingham Castle up close. It was certainly a most impressive domicile. She could not imagine how many people resided within or what they did with all the room. Certainly hundreds of people could live there. It seemed a bit…showy for her tastes.

The Sheriff led her in without saying a word to her. She expected that she would be brought to a dungeon, but she wasn't. Instead he brought her to a room that was sparsely furnished but was otherwise accommodating. He gestured for her to seat herself in a single large chair that was situated over by a window and then exited the room. The Magistar glanced out the window and immediately dismissed any notion of trying to escape out of it. She was several stories high and there was only ground below her rather than a moat. So she had no choice but to stay put and wait to see what happened next.

As it happened, she didn't have to wait long. There was noise at the door and then a new arrival walked in. He was an older man, but for some reason he seemed dangerous to her. She didn't flash any sense of fear; she didn't want to give him the satisfaction. Instead she simply sat there with her fingers interlace upon her lap.

"I am Sir Henry," he said as he swung the door shut behind him. "And you are Theresa, are you not?"

"I prefer Magistar," she said.

"Whereas I prefer to speak to people by their true names."

"Because you believe it gives you power over them, I assume."

He shrugged. "My dear woman, I already have all the power I need. So I really don't require more." He stood before her, his hands draped behind his back. "The Sheriff informs me that you deny the charge that you are associated with Robyne of Sherwood. I know this is a lie and you know it's a lie, so let us have enough respect for each other to speak truthfully. Did you adopt her the day that I slew her father or did any time pass?"

Her eyes widened. "So you are the former sheriff, are you."

"I am indeed. I was the one who slayed the little girl's father as she looked on, and then cut off his head for good measure. Tell me," and he cocked an eyebrow as he studied her, "how does that make you feel?"

She said nothing; simply glared at him.

He brought his face close to hers and repeated, "I said how does that make—?"

He didn't manage to get the words out because her fingernails raked across his left cheek. Streams of blood welled up and Sir Henry jumped back, letting out a startled yelp.

Immediately the door flew open and the Sheriff strode in. "What happened?" he said and then saw the blood on Sir Henry's cheek. He spun and faced the Magistar angrily. "You bitch!" he snarled and extracted a dagger from his belt. The Magistar didn't look away or even blink in fear. She was ready to die.

But Henry placed a hand in the way of the Sheriff's intended assault. "No, son, it's all right. It didn't hurt."

"You cried out. And it's bleeding." The Sheriff produced a handkerchief and began to dab at the bleeding in order to stop it.

"She startled me, that's all. She didn't strike me as the violent sort. It's all fine, son. On your way."

The Sheriff hesitated, but then nodded after firing off a final angry glare at the Magistar. She ignored him.

Sir Henry continued to hold the cloth against his face until he was satisfied that the bleeding had ceased. Then he tucked the handkerchief in his pocket and regarded her. "You basically just admitted your complicity," he said. "That was done with the anger of a woman who has lived with a girl that was mentally scarred by what she witnessed. Now answer my question without causing me to bleed, if you'd be so kind. Did you take her in on that day? Or did she wander about on her own for a time?"

"Why do you care?"

"Because I'm not without sympathy."

"You killed her father!"

"As he was trying to do to me," he reminded her. "It was a duel to the death, my dear woman."

"I am not your dear woman."

"No, but you are hers. Once again, answer my ques—"

And suddenly her exasperation outweighed her desire to be coy. He knew. Somehow he knew and he was never going to shut up about it until she admitted that of which he was already aware.

"Yes," she said. "It was that same day. A few hours afterward."

"So you ad—"

"Yes, yes, I admit it, you fool. I took her in because you're the murdering bastard who took advantage of her father's momentary distraction to slay him right in front of her."

"Of course I took advantage! You say that as if it's a sin or crime. He was bleeding Robin Hood. He gave me an opportunity to live and I seized it. I wanted to live! Is that such a crime? For God's sake, you should be thanking me."

"Thanking you?" Her eyes widened in incredulity. "For what?"

"Because I didn't kill her! She tried to kill me. She picked up her father's bow and arrow and tried to fire it. Fortunately, she was a child and her endeavor failed, but she tried to murder me when my back was turned. Did she ever tell you that?"

She lowered her gaze. "No."

"I could have slain her right then. Gutted her like a pig. Cut her throat, disemboweled her, stabbed her in the heart. She was helpless. Do you know why I didn't? *Because she was helpless.* I'm such a murdering bastard that I took pity on a helpless girl. I had just taken her father from her. I couldn't bring myself to take her life as well. You know who would have slain her? Richard. Without a second thought, without a moment's hesitation. He would have gutted her and then checked her gizzards to see if she'd swallowed any treasure. That's your king. Had it been up to him, there would have been no girl for you to raise to become an outlaw scourge."

"I didn't raise her to become that," the Magistar replied. "I raised her to become a good person. But the blood of her father runs through her veins and, apparently, she is unable to resist the urge to follow in his footsteps. And I would be careful were I you, because sooner or later those footsteps are going to tread right over you. Sooner or later, she is going to avenge her father's death."

"She is certainly welcome to try," said Sir Henry. "And I can assure you, I will be waiting for her. So if she gets the opportunity, I recommend she give it her best try, because I can assure you that if she gets one chance…she won't get a second."

He turned and headed for the door.

"And what's going to happen to me?" she said.

He glanced at her. "Nothing good," he said and walked out.

—« »—

A noise in the forest alerted Clarence immediately.

He could not recall a time in his life when he had ever felt so relieved. He had been going out of his mind with boredom. Furthermore, time was not on his side. As the night wore on, the eventual rise of the sun was inevitable. Once that happened he would no longer have the shadows to hide in and even a casual inspection of the building's exterior would reveal him. He'd have no choice but to take refuge in the forest and hide there for who-knew-how long. He was most definitely not thrilled with the options that were being presented to him.

That was when he heard the approach of footsteps from nearby. His hand went to his sword's hilt immediately.

"Calmly," a familiar whisper floated to him.

Relief flooded over him as Robyne, Innis Rae, Khalida, and Alys materialized from the darkness. He couldn't recall the last time he'd been so glad to see someone. "So the bird got through," he said.

"It did indeed. So what do we have?"

"Remember that fellow with half his face covered?"

"Very well," Innis Rae said immediately. "Drogo. The good right arm of the Sheriff. Good fighter. Wouldn't mind taking him on again."

"You may well get your chance. He's in there along with about a dozen soldiers waiting for you to walk in."

"Because they know about the Magistar," said Robyne grimly. "I knew it."

"You don't think Tuck told him…" said Khalida.

"No. I think it was that sexton. Randolf. I felt something was wrong with him, but Tuck vouched for him. I should have known. Damned churchman having faith in people."

"Never trusted churchmen," said Alys.

"Yes, but you don't trust anyone," Khalida reminded her.

Alys thought about it and nodded. "That's fair," she said.

"All right, then," said Robyne as if the conversation hadn't happened. "They know she's connected with me. Her life here at the convent is effectively over. I say we use that to our advantage."

"How?" said Clarence.

"I have a plan," said Robyne with a grim smile. "And I can assure you that the men inside are not going to like it." She then turned and waved in a "come here" manner toward the woods, and a dozen

women emerged from it. Clarence recognized several of them immediately. And they were carrying planks of lumber, hammer and nails.

"They're all from the hideaway," he said.

"That's right," said Robyne.

"They're here to fight?"

"No, they're not fighters. They're here for something else."

———« »———

The door swung open once again and the Magistar prepared herself for the return of Sir Henry. She was a bit surprised when it was
not him; surprised and yet somehow not.

King Richard walked in, studying her calmly. "Theresa," he
said with a slight nod of his head.

"Your Majesty," she replied.

"I see we're being formal today," he said as he seated himself in
a chair opposite her. "No 'Richard' this time."

"I felt the circumstances didn't justify the familiarity."

"Your instincts are fairly on target." He smiled. The smile
did not touch his eyes. "So it appears we have a problem here. Sir
Henry tells me that you admit to raising Robyne of Sherwood to
young womanhood."

"He more or less seemed to be aware of it, so I honestly didn't
see the point in continuing to deny it."

"Reasonable indeed. But I have many more questions about her
that I would like you to answer."

"With all respect, Majesty, no," said the Magistar firmly. "I've
spoken about her all I am going to. Anything else I could tell you
would violate confidences she has shared with me over the years. I
am neither permitted to, nor inclined to, discuss her any further."

"I see. Hmm. That could present a problem," said Richard.
"Fortunately enough, I have the answer. *Dolf!*" The last word was a
name that he called in a louder voice.

The door swung open and a large, barrel chested man strode in.
He was bald, with a thick drooping mustache, and his eyes did not

appear to be alive. It was the Magistar's experience that one could always see the soul in a person's eyes. These were vacant. She would have thought him dead if he hadn't been standing there.

"This is Dolf," he said somewhat unnecessarily. "Dolf, this is Theresa. She knows all about Robyne and I would like her to tell me all she knows. I want to know if anyone taught her to fight. I want to know all about her associates. I want to know where they are currently residing. I want every bit of knowledge in your head, Theresa."

"Again, with all respect...I cannot do that."

"That is a shame. Dolf."

He didn't shout the name this time. He didn't have to. Dolf took three steps forward so that he was standing directly in front of the Magistar and his right hand swung.

The Magistar had never been physically struck in her life and so was not prepared for it. The moment's warning her brain gave her presented her no time to ready herself and so she was caught completely off guard as his hand cracked across her face. It did so with such force that she was literally knocked out of her chair. Reflexively she put a hand to her cheek, felt the sharp stinging and the blood rushing to it. The room was spinning around her. She took in a deep breath and let it out slowly to try and compose herself.

"Get her up," said Richard.

Dolf reached down, grabbed her arm and hauled her back up into the chair. He did it so easily that she felt as if she weighed nothing.

"Have you rethought your answer?" Richard asked her.

She coughed deeply and spat up some blood. Apparently the blow had caused her to bite her tongue. It felt sore as hell and she waited for the bleeding to stop. Then, slowly, she shook her head.

"Dolf? Less gently this time."

When the next blow came, it was not a slap. His fingers were curled into a fist and when he struck her this time, she once again tumbled off the chair. Blackness threatened to overwhelm her but she fought her way back to consciousness. She felt something in her mouth and spit it out. A tooth skipped across the floor.

"This is going to become increasingly painful, Theresa," Richard warned her. "Believe it or not, it's difficult for me as well."

"If it's all the same to you, I don't believe it." It was getting hard for her to speak. Her lips were swelling up. So was her left eye; in a few minutes she wouldn't be able to see out of it. "I think you enjoy this?"

"*Enjoy* this?" Richard sounded incredulous. "You think I enjoy standing here watching a man beat a helpless woman?"

"I think you enjoy exerting power. This is you showing off that you are the king and can do whatever you wish, with no fear of recrimination. But God is watching you, Richard. He sees what you're doing, and whatever else you have going for you, you are not immortal. Some day you will be called to account for your actions. You will be judged, and I don't think you're going to like what that judgment will be."

"My dear woman, are you mad?" He actually laughed at her warning. "I am royalty. I am guaranteed a seat at God's side. He will welcome me. And if you behave yourself right now, I promise you that I will rescue you from the bowels of hell that your actions will certainly doom you to."

"How do you figure that?" she asked with genuine curiosity.

"Isn't it obvious?" He spoke slowly, carefully, as if explaining something to a child. "You've allied yourself with Robyne of Sherwood. That alone guarantees you a one-way trip to perdition. Don't you understand, Theresa? I'm trying to save you."

And the Magistar laughed. She couldn't help it; it exploded from her chest like a Chinese firecracker.

Richard's eyes hardened. The smile that he had plastered on his face disappeared. "Dolf," he said calmly. "Teach her the errors of her ways."

Dolf went to work.

CHAPTER XXIV

Get ready for a fight!

DROGO WAS GETTING IMPATIENT WITH WAITING. Still, as time wore on, he knew that it was on his side. It was obvious where Robyne was: She was operating under the still of night, doubtlessly robbing from helpless passersby so that she could give their wares to the poor. That was her entire reason for being, wasn't it? Rob from the rich, give to the poor.

"Idiot," he growled to the fire that was burning in the fireplace, providing warmth to the room.

"Who?" asked Calvin, one of his men. They were scattered about in this room and others, all having taken up stations to await Robyne's inevitable return.

"Robyne. This entire business of robbing from the rich and giving to the poor. What is the point of that?"

"Not sure it has a point beyond being what it is. Trying to enrich one group of people at the expense of the other."

"People who worked hard to achieve all that they have!" Drogo countered. "Why is she depriving hard working people so that she can provide free riches to people who do next to nothing to achieve it?"

"Seems to me most of those who are rich wound up inheriting their family's money," Calvin pointed out. "Just sitting around waiting for someone to die doesn't really seem to be doing all that much."

Drogo scowled. "Whose side are you on?" he said.

"It's not a matter of sides, if you must know, but frankly I kind of admire her," said Calvin. "I was there when she fought Richard. Were you?"

"No," said Drogo.

"I couldn't believe it. The man is the most formidable gladiator in the land and at first, he was beating her handily. But then she rallied, drew inner strength, and she kept coming at him until she had him helpless. *She* had the king of England helpless. I think that was bloody remarkable."

"I'm so happy for you." Drogo made no attempt to keep the sarcasm from his voice.

"All I'm saying is that she is a force to be reckoned with. And that maybe consideration should be given to—"

That was when something bright came flying through the open window. Drogo's head snapped around and his jaw dropped.

It was an arrow, and the head was burning viciously.

It thudded squarely into the middle of the room, striking the carpet which promptly went up in flame.

Drogo lunged to his feet and then a second arrow, and third and fourth hurtled through the window. Within seconds the room was filled with smoke. Drogo did the only thing he could think of: He staggered toward the window and reached out. There were heavy wooden shutters hanging on the outside, and he swung them shut to prevent more arrows from being fired in.

"Someone's firing flaming arrows at us!" came the alarmed shout from another room.

"The shutters! Close all the shutters!" he shouted.

As they did so, he looked around desperately to find a source of water that he could splash on the flames, but nothing presented itself. The fire was increasing in ferocity, and that was when he heard some sort of banging at the shutters.

That was when he realized.

Quickly he banged into the shutters, but they didn't budge. He recognized the pounding sound immediately. Someone was driving nails into the wood. They were blocking the windows.

He had completely screwed up. His instinct had been to hole up within the building, reasoning it would afford protection. But he'd been wrong. The fire was burning with a life of its own and the exits were being blocked.

"Out the front door!" he shouted.

Calvin was just ahead of him, running as quickly as he could. The door was sitting there and Drogo realized that, like the shutters, it opened outward as well. If they had blocked the door as well, Drogo and his men were dead.

Calvin grabbed the door and pushed it open. Drogo let out a sigh of relief and then shouted once more, "The front door! Out the front door! Get ready for a fight!"

That much was obvious. They were clearly being ambushed by Robyne and her band. The moment they emerged from the building, they would be assailed by a volley of arrows, maybe burning, maybe not. Either way, their chances of survival were not good. But Drogo was not going to go down quietly, that was for sure.

He emerged from the building into the early morning air and a fist swung in from the right and clocked him in the head. It hit him so powerfully that he was knocked off his feet and fell off to the side.

Drogo looked up and saw someone he recognized immediately. It was Innis Rae. Robyne was next to her. Calvin was off to the side, being held immobilized by more women.

"You got him?" Robyne asked Innis Rae.

"Aye. I got 'im."

Robyne then gestured to the other women and they charged forward with boards, hammers and nails. Within seconds they were hammering them across the door, sealing it.

Drogo scrambled to his feet and lunged toward the door, but Innis Rae blocked his path. She wasn't holding her weapon; it was strapped across her back. Obviously she wasn't prepared to kill him. That was going to be a decision to her detriment.

He swung a massive fist at her and she ducked it, returning with a series of blows to Drogo's gut. He doubled over, gasping as the wind was knocked out of him, but then he charged forward, slamming into her. Innis Rae and Drogo tumbled to the ground.

A dark-skinned woman with a sword started toward them, but Innis Rae shouted, "Nay! Th' bastard's mine!" She pounded repeatedly on the side of his head. The world spun around him but he managed to focus himself and maintain his consciousness. He brought his fists around and down, trying to punch Innis Rae in the face. He didn't succeed. She brought her arms up in front of herself, blocking all his attempts to land a blow.

Then she twisted her hips and drew her knee up abruptly. It struck him in the groin, hitting her target cleanly. Drogo gasped, the world swimming around him.

There was a sizable rock immediately to Innis Rae's right. She grabbed it, swung it around, and slammed Drogo in the head. A huge gash appeared and blood started to flow. Drogo tried to roll off her but she clamped her left hand on his right arm, immobilizing him, and she continued to pummel his head. Drogo tried to fight back but discovered that his body was no longer attending to his mental commands. Then his eyes rolled up and he was out.

—« »—

Robyne stood there, watching the convent burn. Her feelings were mixed. It had been her home for so long, but on the other hand, its sacrifice was necessary.

"Let them out!"

It was the soldier who had preceded Drogo from the convent. He was being held immobilized by Khalida and Alys, and his eyes were wide with horror. "They're dying in there! Let them out!"

"So that they can attack us? I don't think so," said Robyne.

She heard their screams of agony and knew it wouldn't go on for much longer. The smoke within would collapse their lungs and that would be that.

"*You bitch!*" howled the soldier. "To think I was sympathetic to you!"

Robyne turned and looked at him. "What's your name, soldier?"

"Calvin."

"I don't need your sympathy, Calvin," she said. "I've lived my life seeing what your sympathy results in. Now I'm going to play it my way. And you are going to help."

He scowled. "Help how?"

"You're going to be my messenger," she said. "We are going to go to Nottingham Castle and you will take my message to the Sheriff." She pointed to the unconscious body on the ground. "You're going to inform him that he is going to let the Magistar go. Because if he does not, then he'll be able to welcome back the corpse of his right-hand man. Do you understand?"

Calvin nodded, his face going pale.

Robyne turned to the women who had pounded planks of wood over the shutters and doors. "Return to the hideaway," she said. "We've no further need of you here. Your jobs are done."

The women glanced in satisfaction at the raging fire of the convent. The screams from within had ceased. Now all that remained was for the flames to incinerate the remains of the men inside.

They moved off back into the darkness of the woods, and then Robyne pointed at the unconscious Drogo. "Tie him up. Make sure his hands are secured. I've no interest in another battle with him."

"I can take him again," Innis Rae said confidently. She wiped away a trickle of blood that was seeping from a cut on her lip.

"That shouldn't be necessary," said Robyne. "But I appreciate the confidence. Round up the horses and let's go."

—⚔ ⚔—

As the horses made their way along the road, Robyne noticed that Clarence seemed to be holding back. That alone wasn't all that unusual; thanks to his physical condition and his concern that it might prompt negative reactions from others, Clarence tended to keep to himself more often than not. In this instance, though, Robyne was concerned that something else was bothering and so allowed her horse to drop back until she was alongside him. "How now?" she said as he regarded her. "Is there a problem?"

He seemed to be deciding whether he should speak his mind and finally elected to do so. "I do not like this plan," he said.

"Whyfore? Do you perceive a problem? Because I don't. We are dealing with them in the only manner they will understand…"

"That, right there. That indeed is the problem. The Magistar and I were speaking of this just last evening. You are trying to emulate your enemies, and that will not end well because they have far more experience being them than you do."

"You are being ridiculous, Clarence. They threaten us. They comprehend threats. So they will know when we threaten them right back that we are serious."

"Something clandestine would be far more preferable," he said. "Adopt disguises. Sneak into the castle, find the Magistar, free her in that manner…"

"That is exactly what they are expecting us to do!" Robyne said. "You think they will not be prepared for that? That they will not be watching carefully for any new faces who happen to show up in the castle? We will be walking right into their trap. They are not prepared for us to use their exact same tactics. That man," and she indicated Drogo's unconscious body that was draped over the back of Innis Rae's horse, "works closely with the Sheriff. The Sheriff will not let him die. He will be willing to bargain."

"And if he's not? If he defies you to kill him?"

"He won't," Robyne said confidently. "I know I'm right. You have to trust me, Clarence. Do you? Trust me?"

"I trust that you believe you know what you're doing," said Clarence. "But the fact of the matter is that I have been a warrior for far longer than you, Robyne. I know what men are capable of. I know the sacrifices they can make. You are going up against men who are accustomed to winning and they are not going to be inclined to graciously admit defeat. You must realize that."

"I do," said Robyne. "But the fact of the matter is that I've been ahead of them this entire time. Thanks to your warning, I disposed of a dozen or so of their soldiers and I've captured one of their most important men. I am teaching them that they dare not underestimate me."

"I know you are," he said but then added, "I just hope they do not endeavor to provide you the same lesson. The Magistar is worried about you, Robyne. She is worried that you are going to lose your soul."

"I leave such ephemeral concerns to Friar Tuck, Clarence. My concern is getting the Magistar to safety. And I'm going to do that, whether you have confidence in me or not."

The truth was that he did not. But he said nothing.

Later he would regret his silence.

CHAPTER XXV

I'm letting you go

RICHARD SAT CALMLY IN HIS CHAIR, chewing on a piece of bread, watching the Magistar lying on the floor and trying to breathe. She was managing, but not without effort. It was entirely possible that Dolf had broken one or more of her ribs and that would certainly result in some respiratory problems. "Are you all right, Theresa?" he asked calmly.

She lay there on the floor, doing everything she could to continue breathing. One eye was swollen completely shut; the other was open, but narrowly. Her graying hair was hanging in front of her face, obscuring her battered features. She licked her swollen lips, exposing a gap in her mouth where now several teeth were missing. Her hand trembling, she brought it up to her face and wiped away blood that was smeared all over her mouth. "Fine," she said, speaking in a tired rasp. "Never better." She coughed raggedly and spit out a glob of red mucous.

"I don't like doing this to you. Truly. I know you don't believe it, but I really derive no pleasure from this."

"You're still insisting that? Because it's getting progressively harder to believe you."

He got up from his chair and crossed the room toward her. Dolf stepped back, clearing the path for him. Richard crouched near her. "You're doing this to yourself," he said. "If you just answered my questions, I could tell Dolf to stop."

"If I answer all your questions, then you'll kill me," she said, her voice rattling. "You'll have no reason to keep me alive."

"That's not true. We once meant something to each other. We could again."

"Ohhh, I very much doubt that," she said with a short laugh. It was short because it caused pain to lance across her chest. "I don't even think I was all that to you the first time. You may remember me affectionately, but I think it was because you were trying to prove that you were capable of behaving as a man does."

"What is that supposed to mean?" said Richard uncertainly.

"I think," she said with a smile, "that you weren't certain you could actually have sex."

Richard gaped at her and then roared with laughter. He laughed so hard that tears ran down his face. "Are you serious, Theresa?" he asked when he finally managed to control himself. "Why do you think I'd be concerned that I couldn't have sex?"

"Because I don't think women are attractive to you."

That was when his face darkened as he fully understood what she was implying. "Tread very carefully, woman, in what you are accusing your king of."

"I accuse you of nothing, your Majesty."

"You claim…"

"I claim nothing. I suspect things, but suspicions are not assertions. Rumors are not information. Suppositions are not facts. I cannot help how I feel, Majesty, but need I remind you that I am merely a woman and so what I say should not be taken all that seriously."

He was standing now, rocking back and forth on his heels, clearly uncertain how to respond to any of that. "You," he said finally, "are not making this easy, Theresa."

"My apologies, Majesty. Making your life easy is of the utmost importance to me."

At that moment the door burst open. Sir Henry and Basil were standing there, and there was much concern on Basil's face. However it was Henry who spoke: "There has been a development, Majesty."

"Development? What sort of development?"

"Come with me, my lord, and we'll tell you."

"Dolf, keep her comfortable," he said, nodding toward the Magistar, and then he followed Henry and Basil out of the room.

"Can I get you something to drink?" Dolf said politely.

She gaped at him. "You're serious?"

"No reason I can't be polite," he said with a shrug.

She pulled herself upright. "You've been beating the hell out of me! Isn't it a little late to be polite?!"

He shrugged a second time. "It's my job. Can't help my job. So...something to drink?"

The Magistar sighed. "A mug of ale would be wonderful."

"Coming right up," he said.

———— ⚔ ————

Calvin dropped to one knee when Richard entered Henry's study. The king, however, had no patience for it, and gestured for him to get to his feet. "Tell the king what you told me," Henry instructed him.

"Robyne Hood is out in the forest, and she's captured Drogo," Calvin said quickly.

"Who?"

"My second in command," said Basil. "And a good friend. He saved my life years ag—"

"I don't care," Richard interrupted him. "So she's captured Drogo. I understand that. I assume she wants something."

"She wants the woman you captured. The Magistar. She says if you let her go, the she will release Drogo."

"And if we don't?"

"Then she'll kill him."

"I don't understand," said Richard, pacing the room. "If this Drogo is such a formidable fighter, how did Robyne defeat him?"

Basil was tempted to point out that she had managed to defeat Richard as well, but sensed—correctly—that pointing that fact out could be counterproductive to his continued health, a suspicion that was quite accurate. But it was Calvin who answered the question. "She had this large Scotswoman and she beat him."

Sir Henry moaned. "Innis Rae. I should have known."

"Who is Innis Rae?" said Richard.

"The widow of the late Sir Lewis," said Henry. "The noble who was speaking poorly of you that I executed."

"He was married to a warrior woman? What is the world coming to?" sighed Richard in exasperation.

"Your majesty," said Basil, "I have a suggestion. Let us accommodate her. She will free Drogo and then he can provide us with information that we can use to defeat her. A sense of her numbers, who her officers are, where they are hidden. He could be a trove of facts for us. So she escapes us now; we will have her in the end."

Richard stroked his chin thoughtfully. "You raise a valid point," he said after considering it. "You," and he shifted his attention back to Calvin. "She's in the forest, you say? The one that rings the castle?"

"Yes, Majesty."

"Very well. I'll attend to it."

Without another word he walked out of the room, leaving the three men behind, looking at each other. Then Henry said, "Basil, go down to the front gate. Bring some men with you. Make sure that Drogo is still alive. I'm not interested in negotiating just to reclaim a corpse."

"Good idea, father," said Basil, and he left the room. Henry remained alone in his study.

He did not like the way this was shaping up. And he was convinced that he was never going to see Drogo alive again.

———— ⚔ ————

Drogo was leaning against a tree, grunting furiously. Robyne knew why he was doing so: he was putting all of his strength in an attempt to breaking the bonds that tied his hands. He was welcome to do so all he wanted. She knew he'd fail; he was hog-tied far too well.

Innis Rae sidled over to her. "What if they decide to let him die?"

"Then it means they've already killed her, and there's no reason to keep him alive."

"Yuir sure?"

"Of course I'm sure. What, are you going to start challenging me, too?"

"Too?" The words obviously confused Innis Rae. "What are ye talking about? Who—?"

"Ohh, Clarence said the Magistar was worried about me. That I'm becoming indifferent to human life."

"Are ye?"

"I'm doing what I have to do, Innis. It's no more complicated than that." She turned away from Innis Rae and shifted her attention back to Nottingham Castle. The torches had been extinguished as the sun had risen on the horizon. But there were dark clouds rolling in which Robyne didn't like. Looked like another storm was going to be inflicting itself upon Nottingham. Bad enough that she had to hide in the woods. The prospect of getting rained on while she did so wasn't especially appealing to her.

Innis Rae, meantime, made her way over to Sir Clarence. He studied the approaching woman with a raised, questioning eyebrow. "Keep yuir opinions t'yuirself, if it's all the same to ye," she told him pointedly.

"You're going to have to be more specific."

"About Robyne killing."

"Ah. I was just telling her what the Magistar said."

"Well, stop it. She's got enough on her mind without ye adding to it."

"As you wish," said Clarence. "But...what if she asks me my opinion?"

"Say that ye have none."

He seemed amused but nodded. "Very well. I'm not sure how convincing I'll be, but I'll do my best."

"Robyne of Sherwood!"

The loud male voice floated across the divide between the castle and the forest. Robyne stepped forward, remaining within the shelter of the trees but watching the speaker carefully. Even from this distance, she recognized him immediately. It was the Sheriff of Nottingham, the man who had tried to slay her from hiding. God, how she hated him. She didn't even know his real name, nor did she care. She just knew that she wanted to dispose of him at the first opportunity; almost as much as she wanted to dispatch his hated father.

"*Robyne of Sherwood,*" the Sheriff continued, "*before we agree to any exchange, we want proof that Drogo is still alive! Bring him forward!*"

"So their archers can target you," said Khalida. "I don't think so."

Robyne strode over to the tree against which Drogo was leaning and hauled him around in front of her. "They'll have to shoot through him to get to me."

"They will," Innis Rae said immediately. "Without hesitation."

To their surprise, Drogo said, "I should hope so. Your death is far more important than my life. If they put an arrow through my chest in order to dispose of you, I'd be the first to understand."

"I'm thrilled for you," said Robyne.

Then Clarence stepped forward. "This isn't an issue. My armor will resist their arrows, plus I have this." He swung a large shield into view. "I'll walk in front, you follow behind me with him. You'll be protected against any frontal assault."

Robyne nodded. "That makes sense."

"It does," agreed Innis Rae, and the rest of the womens' heads bobbed up and down in concurrence.

So it was that a minute later Robyne made her way into the open, bringing Drogo with her. Clarence led the way, keeping his shield elevated in case any arrows flew their way.

They made their way about fifty feet into the open and then Robyne said, "That's far enough." She was running calculations through her brain. She was sure they were still reasonably far enough from the castle that only a sharpshooter would be able to target her. And Clarence's intersessions between any direct assault and her was appreciated. For a man, he could be remarkably useful.

"*Here he is!*" Robyne shouted. "*Now your turn. Let the Magistar go or I swear, he dies!*"

⸺« »⸺

Richard moved out onto the balcony, pushing the Magistar in front of him. They had a decent view of the forest and Robyne was clearly visible. Richard gazed down upon her.

"Believe it or not," Richard said softly to the Magistar, "I still remember my vow to you from many years ago. That I owed you a debt and would someday repay you."

"Nice to know that you do," said the Magistar. "It's a shame that you haven't lived up to it."

"Of course I have," Richard countered. "Do you have any idea what I could have done to you? Of the torture devices that are available to me? The rack, the iron maiden. I could have just had you executed in a brutal fashion. Who would have stopped me, after all? I could have had you drawn and quartered. Beheaded. Hung. Disemboweled. Hell, I could simply have stabbed you in the stomach and let you bleed to death over several days. All this I could have done to you. But I chose not to. You don't appreciate that, and obviously neither does your protégé." He pointed toward Robyne hundreds of feet below. "She underestimates me, just as you do. She threatens to kill a man unless I let you go. That was her demand: Let you go. Unfortunately, she made two mistakes. She assumed that I cared about the life of a single man. And second..."

And suddenly Richard lifted her off her feet. He was surprisingly strong. He raised her to the edge of the balcony and just like that, her feet were dangling above open air.

"She should have chosen her words more carefully," said Richard. "I'm letting you go."

And he did.

⊢—« »—⊣

Robyne screamed.

Her plan had been so perfect. Drogo was important to the Sheriff; certainly he would bargain for his release. In adopting their tactics, she had backed them against the wall.

She thought that right up until she saw the Magistar being thrown off a balcony by Richard the Lionheart.

Robyne's shriek shattered the morning air.

The Magistar, for her part, did not scream. She did not utter so much as a single sound as she plummeted from the balcony and struck the ground. Robyne heard the echo of it as she stood there.

She shoved Drogo to the side and started toward the castle. "*No!*" shouted Clarence and brought his shield up just as an arrow slammed into it and then fell away. He grabbed Drogo from behind. "You can't help her, Robyne! All you can do is get yourself killed. She wouldn't want that. *She wouldn't want that!*"

The truth of his words managed to penetrate her brain. Clarence backed up, holding Drogo firmly from behind, and Robyne sprinted toward the welcoming woods as her mind spun. *She's dead, she's dead, those bastards, she's dead...*

They vanished into the shadows of the forest and just as they did, the skies cracked open and rain began to pour.

⊢—« »—⊣

Basil stared in horror at the unmoving body of the Magistar. Richard had just killed Drogo. Certainly Robyne would slay him in retaliation. How the hell could he have done that?

He pivoted and sped back into the castle. He got to the steps and started to sprint up them, but encountered Henry halfway up. "Where do you think you're going?" asked Sir Henry.

"Did you see what he did? *Did you see*?!"

"Yes, I saw."

"I've got to—" and he endeavored to push past Henry.

Henry slammed the startled Basil against the wall. "Got to what? Confront him? Scold him?"

"Make him understand—!"

"Understand what? He's the bloody king! Do you think that you're going to convince him that what he did was wrong? All you'll manage to do is convince him to kill you. Unless you're intending to commit regicide. Is that your plan? Because regicide or suicide are your only two options if you confront him. So which is it?"

Basil sagged against the wall then as if he were a balloon deflating. Henry released his hold on him. "Well?"

Basil shoved him away but headed down the stairs, in the opposite direction from the upper rooms where Richard was. Henry stood there and watched him leave and then breathed a sigh of relief. The truth was that he had been fully prepared for Basil to fight his way past him, go upstairs, and challenge the king to a combat to the death. Henry had little doubt that the king would have dispatched him, but honestly, if Basil had done the deed and killed the king, then England would never know what had happened to its monarch. Sherwood Forest was quite expansive, and hiding a dead body in its stately confines wouldn't be that much of a challenge. He was sure that Lord Collins would agree to it. Hell, he'd probably volunteer to help dig the grave.

CHAPTER XXVI

Go

ROBYNE SAT UPON A LOG, STARING out at nothing. The rain clouds had drifted in, obscuring the sun. The thick branches and leaves that surrounded them provided them some degree of shelter from the precipitation, but Robyne wasn't even noticing it. The rest of her gang was grouped loosely around her, waiting for her to instruct them, but no orders were forthcoming.

Finally Innis Rae stepped forward, holding her halberd firmly. Drogo was lying on the ground, hands still secured. He glanced up at her with what was clearly firm conviction that he was about to die. "Can ah dispatch him, Robyne?" she asked. "It won't bring muh husband back, but it'll be a first step for vengeance. They killed the Magistar. Pushed her to her death right before our eyes. There's only one way t'respond."

Robyne turned and looked at her, seeming to focus on her for the first time. Then she shook her head. Innis Rae was clearly disappointed, but she understood Robyne's preference. The Magistar had just been taken from her. Obviously if there was going to be vengeance, Robyne was entitled to avail herself of it first and foremost.

She rose then and extracted her dagger from its sheathe. She walked over to Drogo, clearly ready to plunge the blade deep. For a moment Innis Rae wondered if Robyne would inflict upon him a death that was popular among some more uncivilized tribes in

Scotland: extract his heart and devour it. Innis Rae had no taste for such a thing, but she certainly couldn't blame Robyne if she chose to indulge in the brutal tradition.

Robyne stood over him and surprisingly, her knife hand was trembling. That surprised Innis Rae. She had seen Robyne keep her cool in countless situations, so she was surprised to see that she appeared disconcerted in this moment. She told herself it was understandable. After what Robyne had just witnessed, she doubtless felt responsible for the Magistar's death. She had underestimated just how blood thirsty and callous her opponents were. But she had learned the error of her ways and now she obviously knew that for the future, bargaining was something that they would never understand. Death was the only option. They all had to be killed. That was just the long and short of it.

Then she crouched and cut through Drogo's bonds.

The women looking on gasped.

Innis Rae immediately was sure she understood. Robyne wasn't just going to slay him. She was going to give him the opportunity to fight for his life. That made sense. It would appeal to her—

"Go," she said.

Drogo stared up at her in utter shock as he got to his feet. "What?"

"I said go. Get out of here. Tell them I could have killed you. You've seen me kill others, including all the soldiers who accompanied you. You know that I'm capable of it. Tell them I spared you... because the killing has to stop."

He studied her as if seeing her for the first time. Then, slowly, he reached into his belt and withdrew something small. In the small bit of light that was visible, it twinkled. Robyne recognized it instantly. It was the Magistar's pendant.

"I took this from her," said Drogo. "I liked it. I was going to give it to somebody. But I think you should have it." He held it out to her and Robyne took it without a word. Drogo stood there a moment, as if sure that Robyne was going to bury an arrow in his back the moment he turned around.

"*Go!*' she said emphatically.

He required no further urging, but instead ran into the woods.

For a long moment silence hung over them like a shroud, and then Innis Rae lost it.

"*Are ye out of yuir mind!?*" she howled. "They killed the Magistar! You lay out conditions and they spat in yuir face, and your response was to let him go?!"

"Killing him would have served no purpose."

"Neither is letting him go! And ah'm not gonna let ye make that mistake!" She turned, ready to pursue Drogo into the woods.

The creak of Robyne's bow froze her in her tracks.

Slowly she turned in incredulity as she found herself staring at an arrow that was pointed directly at her.

"Don't," Robyne warned her.

Innis Rae spat at her. The spit sailed through the air and struck Robyne in the face. She did nothing to wipe it away; she simply stood there and let it run down her cheek. The arrow didn't move so much as a millimeter.

"Ye've lost yuir mind."

"You said that."

"Ye saw them kill the Magistar and ye will do nothing?"

Khalida stepped forward. "My mother threw herself to her death because of our master. I beat him to death. I enjoyed it. How can you let Drogo go——?"

"He didn't kill her. Richard did."

"And you let him go!" Khalida pointed out angrily. "You had him at your mercy in single combat. If you had disposed of him then, the Magistar would still be alive! You're as responsible for her death as you were for your father's!"

Robyne turned, faced Khalida and fired the arrow.

It thudded into the tree just to Khalida's right, missing her by scarcely any distance at all.

For a long moment nothing was said, and then Robyne said, "I'm going back to the fortress. Join me there or don't. It's up to you." Then she turned and walked off into the woods.

"T'hell with her," said Innis Rae. "Ah'm leaving. Any of you joining me?"

The rest of the women started to follow her and then Clarence said, "Cowards."

That froze them in their tracks. Innis Rae glowered at him. "Ah beg yuir pardon."

"Beg all you want; you won't get it. I'm disgusted with all of you."

"You're disgusted with us?" said Khalida. "Robyne just failed to follow through on a threat…"

"There was no point in doing so," said Clarence. "You follow through on a threat if it's going to get you something. Killing Drogo would have gotten you nothing except another body and enmity from the Sheriff."

"We already have his enmity."

"Because he knows nothing else!" said Clarence. "He knows what he was taught. Robyne is trying to teach him something different. She's trying to teach him mercy. That it exists. That people can live together because of it. Damnation, you all owe her your lives, and this is how you plan to repay her? By walking away from her because she decides to let an enemy live?"

"His people killed the Magistar," said Innis Rae.

"And do you think the Magistar would have wanted him dead because of it?" said Clarence. "She was worried Robyne was going to lose her soul. Become obsessed with killing. She stood here and in the face of the Magistar's death, she decided to take the action that she knew the Magistar would have approved of, and you condemn her for it! I thought you were her friends!"

"We are."

And Alys, who had been silent the entire time, said softly, "Then maybe we should act like it."

All eyes turned to her.

"He's right," said Alys. "Robyne isn't like us. She's better than us. And she's trying to make us better as well. We can either follow her on that quest, or we can abandon her. I'm going to follow her, if for no other reason than I pray she'll bring me to my son. And if I can be an improved mother when that happens, so much the better. What about the rest of you?"

Immediately they shifted their attention to Innis Rae. "What're ye starin' at me fer?" she demanded.

"You've known her the longest. What do you think we should do?" said Khalida.

Innis Rae stood silent.

"She let you go?"

Drogo stood there, facing the astounded Lord Collins, and nodded. Basil and Henry stood behind him in the study, and Richard was standing nearby.

Richard could have expressed astonishment. Instead, to Basil's surprise, he laughed. He laughed so loudly that he couldn't maintain his footing and sank into a chair. "What a typical woman," he finally managed to find his voice. "Unable to carry through on a threat. She doesn't have the nerve to kill. We can use that."

"With respect, Majesty, she has the nerve to kill, all right," said Drogo. "She's killed many of my men. She did so efficiently and ruthlessly. There is no doubt in my mind that she is capable of doing so again in the future."

"Then why are you still alive?" said Richard.

"She said the killing needs to end."

"Did she give a reason why it needs to end?" asked Lord Collins.

Drogo exchanged a confused glance with Basil. "I didn't think it...I'm not sure—"

"The answer is obvious," said Richard. "She is terrified that, having seen her mentor die, she is going to be next. She let you live because she seeks my mercy, my forgiveness."

"So what do we do, Majesty?" said Collins.

"We let her think that her plan has a possibility of success. We play to her female mindset. And when she fully believes that she is going to negotiate some peaceful resolution, that is when we bring the hammer down upon her."

He smiled then in self-satisfaction and left the room.

The remaining men stood there for a time, and then Basil said to his father, "There is something about her, father. Something that makes her very different from previous thieves...even from the previous Robin Hood. Perhaps we should be reconsidering how we—"

"Stop right there," said Henry sternly. "Do not finish that sentence, Basil. I would sorely hate to have to arrest you for treason."

"You would do that to your son?" asked an astonished Basil.

Henry studied him for a moment, then strokes his face gently. "Let's not find out," he said, and left Basil and Drogo to themselves.

—«　»—

Robyne moved through the woods, knowing where she was going, and yet unsure of what she was going to say when she got there. They'd want to know where the rest of the band was.

How was she going to explain it to them? They depended on her to be their leader. She provided them hope for a better future.

She had pulled them out of their miserable homes, their miserable lives, promising them something better. And now she had lost the confidence of the warrior women who formed the core of her army.

She stopped walking and sank down onto a fallen branch. The rain was lightening up, but there was still drizzle falling. Her hood was drawn up to provide her a bit of shelter. She had pulled down the cloth she customarily wore over the lower half of her face.

She sat there, not knowing for how long.

When she looked up, the Magistar was standing there.

Of course she was.

"Are you dead?" asked Robyne, not remotely surprised to see her.

"Afraid so," said the Magistar. "I can survive a lot, but a fall hundreds of feet goes beyond even my ability to survive."

"I let Drogo go."

The Magistar rested her hand on Robyne's shoulder. It had no weight. "Good," she said.

"The others don't understand."

"They'll come around."

"I'm not sure I understand either," Robyne admitted. "This isn't easy."

"Nothing of importance ever is. You'll understand, Mary. You'll grow as a person and you're going to accomplish great things. You're going to change the world."

"Or die alone and forgotten."

"No," and she shook her head. "That's not your fate."

"How do you know?"

She smiled. "When has a dead person ever lied to you?"

Robyne chuckled at that, and when she looked back at the Magistar, she was gone. There was no evidence that she had been anywhere save in Robyne's imagination.

She sat there for a time and then, deciding there was nothing else for it, she headed back to the lair.

Innis Rae was standing there on the ground, her arms folded, her face stern. She and Robyne stood there for a time, studying each other.

"Why'd ye take so long?" Innis Rae finally demanded. "We were gettin' worried."

"You were."

Innis Rae pointed upward. "Alys is making some damned French dish. I think she's using snails."

"Snails?" Robyne made a face. "She expects us to eat snails?"

"Go argue with the French," said Innis Rae. She then stepped forward, quickly embraced Robyne, and together they made their way up to their friends.

And after they had eaten, Robyne went over to a large expanse of bare floor. Pulling out her knife, she began to carve something into it. Innis Rae stood nearby and stared at it questioningly. "What are ye doin'?"

"Carving a new map," she said. She held up the pendant. "We're going to need one if this is going to guide us to where we're needed next."

"Then ye'd better keep at it," said Innis Rae. "Because who knows what trick Richard has up his sleeve next."

EPILOGUE

KING RICHARD THE LIONHEART TROTTED DOWN the long flight of stairs in his castle, nodding in absent acknowledgment of the guards as he passed them. He did not often visit the dungeons, and so it was always memorable to the guards when they had the opportunity to see their noble majesty close up. He understood that it was thrilling for them and didn't begrudge them their excitement.

He walked down a long line of cells, keys jingling at his side. When he reached the one he was seeking, he slid the key into the lock and clicked it free. The door swung open under protest, its hinges creaking loudly.

Richard stepped into the dank cell. There was a single figure seated on the floor in the darkness.

"It might interest you to know that Nottingham has a new Robin Hood running around," he said. "She could be somewhat problematic for me in the future." Slowly the seated woman swiveled her gaze toward him. "I will say one thing for her, though," and he smiled. "She has your eyes."

Marion stared at him and then wadded up spittle and spat at him. The spit sailed a foot and then splattered to the floor, coming nowhere near Lionheart.

Richard laughed as he stepped out and closed the door once more, shuttering Marion into the darkness again.

⟻ ·« »· ⟼

ABOUT THE AUTHOR

PETER DAVID IS THE AUTHOR OF more than one hundred books, almost all of them published. He has written such fantasies as *Howling Mad* and *Knight Life* as well as an assortment of bestselling *Star Trek*® novels including *Imzadi* and the popular New Frontier series (which he co-created with John Ordover). He also co-created the TV series *Space Cases* with Bill Mumy, and has written for *Babylon 5* and *Crusade*. His comic-book career spans more than a decade and includes an award-winning run on *The Incredible Hulk*. *Sir Apropos of Nothing* is his longest single work, mostly due to the use of the word "the." He lives in New York with his wife, Kathleen, and his four daughters, Shana, Gwen, Ariel and Caroline.

WELCOME TO CAMELOT!

You thought you knew about King Arthur and his knights? Guess again!

Learn here, for the first time, the down-and-dirty royal secrets that plagued Camelot as told by someone who was actually there, and adapted by acclaimed *New York Times* bestseller Peter David. Full of sensationalism, startling secrets and astounding revelations, *The Camelot Papers* is to the realm of Arthur what the *Pentagon Papers* is to the military: something that all those concerned would rather you didn't see. What are you waiting for?

THE HIDDEN EARTH CHRONICLES

On the Damned World, it's every man for himself. Only it's not just man-kind who inhabits this crumbling, desolate world. Twelve very different species, creatures out of Earth's mythology that live on the land, in the sea, and underground, vie for survival in a hostile land. Humanity is nearly extinct. But now the Twelve Races have discovered that their own fortunes are inextricably linked with the remnants of the human race.

As a result, a young slave girl named Jepp may hold the key to the future of the world. But can she and her new companions survive long enough to save everyone . . . or will they damn the world instead?

CRAZY 8 PRESS
www.crazy8press.com

There's a lot at stake here!

Meet Vince Hammond. He has a secret that, if his mother finds out, she will absolutely kill him.

No, he's not dating a girl she'd hate. No, he's not gay.

He's a vampire. And Mom is a vampire hunter. And all of his friends are vampire hunters. And his fiancee is a vampire hunter, and so are his future in-laws.

Need an antidote to every other vampire novel out there? Then you're going to want to be *Pulling Up Stakes*. After putting a silver bullet in werewolves in his classic *Howling Mad*, *New York Times* Bestseller Peter David now sinks his teeth into vampire lore, with bloody good results.

CRAZY 8 PRESS
www.crazy8press.com

It's 2012. Maxtla Colhua is an Investigator for the Empire–an Aztec Empire that successfully repelled Hernan Cortes in 1603 and now stretches from one end of what we call the Americas to the other. But now it is the Last Sun, and someone has decided to punctuate it with a series of grisly murders reminiscent of the pagan sacrifices of ancient times. Can Maxtla find the killer before his city is ripped apart?

CRAZY 8 PRESS
www.crazy8press.com